deadline

OTHER BOOKS AND AUDIO BOOKS
BY CLAIR M. POULSON:

I'll Find You

Relentless

Lost and Found

Conflict of Interest

Runaway

Coverup

Mirror Image

Blind Side

Evidence

Don't Cry Wolf

Dead Wrong

deadline

a novel

CLAIR M. POULSON

Covenant Communications, Inc.

Cover image and design copyrighted 2010 by Covenant Communications, Inc.

Published by Covenant Communications, Inc.
American Fork, Utah

Printed in the USA
First Printing: April 2010

15 14 13 12 11 10   10 9 8 7 6 5 4 3

ISBN-13 978-1-59811-976-3

To the good people of Duchesne who have played
such an important part in my life

CHAPTER 1

DALLAS DIXON TOOK A DEEP breath as he entered the small office and stood awkwardly, unsure whether he should sit down. Andy Norton, the managing editor of the *Chronicle,* continued furiously writing on the legal pad at his desk a moment longer, his bushy brows furrowed in concentration, before looking up and giving Dallas a curt nod, indicating the seat in front of him. He then promptly returned to writing. Dallas forced a smile and sat down. He'd been more than a little surprised when he'd been told to report to Andy's office two hours after arriving at work that morning after a quiet weekend. In the time he'd worked at the *Chronicle,* he hadn't received such a summons before and could think of no reason he would be receiving one now.

It had been just over five months since Dallas had been hired at the *Chronicle.* He'd been ecstatic to find a job only one week after graduating from the University of Texas at El Paso with a degree in journalism, and he'd worked hard to prove himself in the past months, volunteering to take the assignments no one else wanted and still producing articles that were both well written and carefully researched. He'd done everything possible to ensure that his work was above reproach, and he'd gotten the feeling his boss had been pleased with his newest employee. Andy had always smiled at him when they crossed paths, and he often had a word of praise about a recent article Dallas had written. *Andy isn't smiling now.*

The silence in the office was growing unbearable. Dallas glanced at the clock and fiddled with the collar of his pale green shirt. Andy still hadn't spoken; the burly man simply continued writing on the pad of paper in front of him, pressing the pen into the paper so hard that Dallas wondered that he hadn't torn the page.

After what seemed like an eternity, the pen stopped and the editor looked up, pointing the pen toward Dallas and making little jabbing motions. His usually sparkling gray eyes were cold and hard, and his large hands were shaking slightly.

Finally, looking away from Dallas, he muttered, "Young man, you're a fool." Dallas's look of confusion only seemed to amplify his irritation; he shook his head and growled, "And there's no place at my paper for fools."

Dallas sat back, stunned. He'd anticipated a reprimand about office dress code (he'd worn blue jeans the week before out of desperation when the washer in his apartment had died), or maybe a talk about source citations—but not this. Finding himself at a loss, he simply waited for his boss to go on. But Andy looked down at his desk again, lowered the threatening pen, and once more began to stab at the legal pad as though it too had offended him.

After a moment, Andy looked back up. "Why are you still here?" he asked angrily.

"Sir, I'm sorry for whatever—"

"When someone is fired, it's standard protocol for them to clean out their desk and leave—not stand there yammering!" Andy shouted, his double chin quivering and his eyes shooting daggers.

"I don't understand. What did I do wrong?" Dallas asked, his clear blue eyes, which had previously been wide with confusion, now narrowing as a sense of indignation grew inside him.

"Go, Dallas, before I lose my temper."

Dallas's frown deepened. *I thought you already had,* he thought bitterly. Shaking his head, he got to his feet and approached the door, certain now that talking this out with Andy was a lost cause. Suddenly, he stopped and turned back. Andy was busy destroying his legal pad again. "I think you at least owe me an explanation," he said evenly.

"I don't owe you anything," Andy Norton said, glowering and reaching up to adjust his striped tie, one that didn't need adjusting. "You haven't even been here for six months yet—that's the magic number. Until then, all new hires are at-will employees."

"So there isn't even a reason?" Dallas asked, feeling his anger spike.

"I didn't say that," Andy said flatly. He stared at Dallas for a moment, then said, "Be out of the building by noon. Stop by my secretary's desk and pick up your paycheck before you go. I'll see that it's ready."

Reeling, Dallas once more approached the door, glancing at his watch as he did so. It was eleven thirty. He shook his head in disbelief and stepped out into the hallway.

The usually bustling newsroom was uncharacteristically quiet as Dallas shut the door behind him. Gordon Townsend, Andy's assistant managing editor, passed him and opened the door Dallas had just closed. Curious eyes peered from every cubicle as he walked quickly toward his own, his face burning with shame and anger.

He turned into his cubicle and almost collided with Elliott Painter—a reporter on the crime beat—sitting in front of Dallas's computer. Dallas nearly turned back around when he saw the smug look plastered across Elliott's sharp, dark features. *Exactly what I need right now,* he thought in exasperation. Elliott, an experienced reporter, prided himself on being a favorite of the management and was the only reporter Dallas hadn't gotten along with very well in the months he'd been at the *Chronicle*.

His frustration spiked when he looked at the computer screen and realized that Elliott had been reading the article Dallas had been finishing for the next day's edition. "What are you doing?" he demanded angrily.

"Hey, from the look on your face when you left Andy's office, I could tell you wouldn't need this computer anymore, and someone needs to finish this piece," Elliott said, false sincerity oozing from his voice. He casually ran a hand through his thick black hair and then shrugged. "I thought I'd help out." However, at Dallas's glare he slowly got up and stepped away from the computer.

Dallas's anger gave way slightly to surprise. "You already know?"

Elliott gave him a peculiar look, then his grin widened and he shrugged again. "Maybe if you'd spent more time focused on your articles than flirting, you'd have seen it coming as easily as I did."

Dallas gritted his teeth at the accusation. He knew as well as Elliott did that he was not a flirt. Romance, if he had any in his life, would never be placed above his work responsibilities. However, he was sure he knew what Elliott was referring to—the reason that his animosity toward Dallas had been more pronounced lately.

He gave Elliott a hard look then turned away. "For the thousandth time, I didn't know you were interested in Heather, Elliott. I asked her to go to lunch with me, and she said yes. It was one date, if it can even be called a date." He sighed, not wanting to get into this again—especially since it was now almost 11:40. "Anyway, it's just a job," he said, shaking his head as he bent to open a drawer. "I'll get another one."

Elliott snorted. "You'll never work as a reporter again after you've been fired here. You might as well go back to driving trucks."

Dallas didn't know how Elliott knew he'd driven a big rig for a while in the interim between his discharge from the Army and his education at UTEP, but it didn't matter. He bit back an angry response and sat down at his computer. With a few keystrokes he had deleted the article he'd been working on.

"Hey, what do you think you're doing?" Elliott demanded and took a few steps toward the computer as if to save the article.

"I won't be needing that story anymore," Dallas said as he reached toward a drawer.

"You can't do that." Elliott's face flushed a deep red beneath his dark complexion.

"I just did," Dallas declared with satisfaction. "And what's more, I will empty my trash bin as well so you can't recover anything I've deleted."

"You really are an idiot," Elliott said, taking a step back and seeming to regain his composure. "But you got what you deserved. That'll teach you to check your facts a little more closely before you submit an article."

Without waiting for a response, Elliott chuckled and walked away. Dallas could hear him proclaiming as he walked by the other cubicles, "I got that one right. The hotshot got himself fired."

Dallas watched him walk away, perplexed by his last comment. He was beginning to wonder if Elliott knew more than he was saying about the reason Dallas had been fired—or if he had somehow been part of that reason. For a moment Dallas debated going after him or going back to Andy's office and refusing to leave again without an explanation. However, as he turned toward the managing editor's office, Elliott made a second pass by his cubicle, one eyebrow raised as if daring Dallas to go back to Andy's office. Exasperated, he opened his briefcase and began to shove his personal belongings inside.

Then he gathered up some papers in his in-box that he hadn't had a chance to sort through and shoved them into his briefcase as well. He wasn't leaving anything for Elliott to go through, either on his desk or in his computer. That done, he looked at his watch. He still had ten minutes before he was supposed to be out of the building.

He sat back and thought for a minute about Elliott calling him a flirt. That really irked him. Dallas hadn't dated since Gina Lawson had abruptly broken off their engagement eighteen months earlier. Gina hadn't even hinted at why she'd changed her mind. She'd just given him back her engagement ring, her pretty blue eyes full of tears, and said, "You won't hear from me again," and walked away from him. His heart had been shattered. Dallas had seen Gina just one time after that, and she'd been with Evan Stafford, a guy that Dallas never did like. He guessed that she'd left him for Evan. At any rate, the hurt had been deep and he'd reacted by avoiding dating and steering clear of women as much as he could, afraid of being hurt again. So to call him a flirt was totally absurd.

He was attracted to Heather Scott, though. And she had finally broken through the shell he'd grown around him, giving him the courage to ask her out to lunch that one time. And he admitted that he had talked to her in the office more than any of the other reporters since that lunch date. *But did that make him a flirt?*

He turned as that familiar female voice behind him said, "I'm sorry, Dallas."

He looked up and caught his breath as he always did lately when he saw her. Heather Scott stood to the side of his cubicle, her dark brown eyes filled with concern. Dallas was struck, as he had been the first time he'd seen her, by how beautiful she was. The deep red button-up blouse she wore complemented her long dark hair perfectly and brought out the blush in her cheeks. Tall and slender, there was something about her that did things to him no woman since Gina had been able to do.

"Thanks . . . who knew Monday could get this bad, huh?" he tried to joke.

"Anything I can do?" she asked with a sympathetic smile.

Dallas shook his head. "I'd just like to know what I did wrong." He looked up at her. "It was so weird—Andy acted like I'd committed a capital crime, but he wouldn't give me a single concrete reason why I was being fired. All he said was that I was still a *new employee* and could be *terminated at will*," Dallas said, the anger returning. "Then Elliott made some cryptic reference to my fact-checking. I have no idea what that's about."

Heather rolled her pretty brown eyes. "Don't worry about what Elliott says. He can be a real jerk sometimes. You're an excellent reporter—Elliott just saw an opportunity to get under your skin and took it. Unfortunately, Andy definitely doesn't see that side of him. Neither does Gordon. I've heard both of them say he's 'the brightest reporter this paper has ever had'—and I've had to bite my tongue each time."

Dallas smiled faintly and shook his head. "I always thought Andy was pretty levelheaded—except for liking Elliott so much."

Heather nodded thoughtfully. "He usually is. In the two years I've been here, I've only seen him upset a handful of times, but when he does get angry, people take cover." She paused a moment. "As for not giving you a reason . . . I don't know. What was the last story you worked on?"

"It wasn't my usual, but it wasn't any big deal either. It was a piece about some car thefts—Gordon gave me the assignment. It seemed like a dead-end story at first, but I dug around a bit, and I think it came together pretty well by the end—and all of it was completely accurate. It actually turned out to be kind of fun. I hope someday I can work the crime beat. I'd really enjoy that," he added as he glanced down at his watch. "We'll have to figure this out later, though. Andy told me in no uncertain terms that I need to be out of here by noon."

As he glanced back up, he was surprised to see that Heather suddenly looked uncomfortable. Her face had reddened, and her dark eyes were looking away.

"What's wrong?" He studied her face as she continued to avoid his gaze. "I did do something, didn't I?"

She slowly nodded her head. "Your article was about a guy named Tito Maggio, right?"

"Yeah. What about him?"

She finally looked up. "I'm sorry, Dallas. I would have said something if I'd known then what I know now."

"What are you talking about?" Dallas asked.

"That article—I'm surprised Andy didn't catch it before the paper was printed."

"It came out in yesterday's Sunday edition—Andy never comes in on Sundays so he probably didn't see it before the paper was distributed," Dallas said, puzzled. "But why would he have wanted to keep it from going to press? It turned out to be a really interesting story."

Heather shook her head sadly. "Elliott told me while you were in Andy's office that Tito Maggio is Andy's nephew." She paused. "I don't think anyone knew that before the article came out—except Elliott and probably Gordon. I certainly didn't."

At that moment, Gordon Townsend's voice boomed through the room. "Dixon, it's past noon. You're supposed to be gone."

"Call me later," Heather said quickly. "I'll tell you what I know." Then she slipped away.

Dallas picked up his briefcase, still shocked by what Heather had just told him. Tito Maggio had been one of the main players in the group of young thugs who had been arrested. And although he'd honestly had no idea that Maggio was Andy's nephew, Dallas knew that it wouldn't have made much of a difference if he had known. His ethics as a reporter bound him to report the facts—nothing more, nothing less—no matter whose nephew was involved. *Still,* he thought, shaking his head and glaring in the direction of Elliott's cubicle, *it would have been nice to have a heads-up, so I didn't refer to the guy as a rising star in the world of delinquents.*

When he stopped at the front desk to pick up his final paycheck, Andy's secretary seemed unable to meet his gaze as she handed the check to him. "Have a nice day, Dallas," she said, glancing to the side.

A nice day—fat chance, Dallas was thinking as he followed her gaze and saw Elliott and Gordon standing outside of Gordon's office. When Dallas caught Gordon's eye, the assistant editor shook his head. Then, after receiving one last smirk from Elliott, he walked quickly by the two men and out the door to an uncertain future.

CHAPTER 2

HEATHER SAT DOWN AT HER computer and sighed, replaying the recent dismal turn of events. Although she and Dallas had only been out to lunch one time, it had been the best first date of any kind that she'd been on in a long time. With his boy-next-door good looks, conservative manner, and easy smile, she'd been attracted to him from the start. But he had seemed to be in a shell, and she didn't know if she could ever break through it. But then she'd begun to hope that they might be able to develop a friendship when she'd learned he'd served a mission in Germany. There weren't a lot of members of the Church in El Paso, and none that she knew of at the paper. She was excited when she learned that Dallas shared her beliefs. After that, they talked about the Church frequently, and she'd been excited when he'd invited her to lunch. Their friendship had grown a lot since then.

"Dinner tonight?"

Startled from her train of thought, Heather looked up and groaned inwardly. Elliott Painter stood above her desk for the second time that day. But this time instead of sharing gossip, he had a hopeful look on his face.

"Thanks, but I have plans," she said curtly and turned back to her computer. Her plans included going home and seeing what she could stir up from her sparsely stocked pantry, but it was far more enticing than going anywhere with Elliott Painter. The man had taken it upon himself to fill the role of office Casanova, and he could not seem to understand Heather's repeated refusals to go out with him. They had nothing in common.

"Then I'll take a rain check," he offered. Then he added, "You know, you're a great reporter, but I'd be happy to give you a few tips that would really improve your writing."

He'd never tried that approach before. Trying not to appear annoyed, she smiled politely and said, "I'll have to think about it."

"You do that," he said, grinning. "But don't think too long. I'm here to help. Hey, and don't worry about Dixon." His smile turned to a sneer. "He messed up bad and got exactly what he had coming."

"All he did was report the facts. How was he supposed to know that Andy's nephew was involved?" She lowered her voice. "And I think it's pretty crummy that he got fired because of that."

Heather stood before Elliott could respond and turned to walk away. But before she had taken a step, Elliott quickly moved in front of her, crowding uncomfortably close.

"Don't waste your sympathy on this guy, Heather," he said.

Deciding she'd had enough of Elliott for one day, she tried to push past him. "I'm sorry, but I have an article to finish."

Elliott leaned closer, his face barely inches from hers, all signs of a smile gone. "I'd steer clear of Dallas if I were you. He's trouble."

And you're a snake, she thought to herself as he finally turned and walked away. *I think I'll stick with trouble.*

* * *

Andy Norton picked up the phone, fingers shaking. He was more upset than he'd ever been in his life, and his anger only grew as he waited for Frankie Maggio, his brother-in-law, to come to the phone. He'd never cared for the man his sister married, and now he had to admit to himself that he despised him.

"Hey, Andy, did you get the job done?" Frankie asked without so much as a hello.

"Yes," Andy muttered. "We're even now, Frankie," he added, trying to maintain control of his voice. "I've done more than enough."

"I don't think so, Andy," Frankie retorted, and Andy could hear the smile in his voice. "This was only a little favor, like the others were little favors. The dirt I've got on you is worth way more than the firing of one snot-nosed reporter."

"Dallas Dixon was one of the brightest reporters this paper has ever seen!" Andy thundered, despite his determination to remain calm. "Thanks to you, he's out of the business."

"My, my, aren't we testy?" Frankie said with a chuckle. "That'll teach him to write about my boy, now won't it? He shouldn't be telling lies about fine young men like Tito."

"Look, Frankie. You and I both know that Tito is out of control. You might get him out of jail, but it's only a matter of time before he'll get himself back in," Andy said.

"Your reporter is a liar, and you're the criminal," Frankie said darkly. "So let's not point fingers. Oh, and one more thing, Andy—I haven't got him out of jail yet. I thought you'd like to help me with that."

"I've done more than enough already," Andy said again, feeling his throat close and his breath shorten. "Please, this can't go on."

"Andy, Andy . . . Think about your dear sister. How would she feel if she knew what I know about her big brother—her successful, doting big brother? And what would your wife say? I think Kate would leave you, don't you? And what would the employees at your precious paper think?"

Andy clenched the edge of his desk so tightly he was losing circulation in his fingers. "Frankie, we both know it was an accident."

"Bail on Tito is set at fifty grand. I want him out tonight. And Andy—I don't want my son's name appearing in your paper again."

The phone went dead. Andy slammed the receiver down with a bang and dropped his head into his hands. It had been several years now that Frankie had been holding the horrible skeleton in Andy's closet over his head. *It has to end,* he thought desperately.

He had to get out of the office so he could think. But before he could leave for the day, he needed to speak with Heather Scott. Last week he'd grudgingly promised Elliott he'd take care of the matter by today. There was already enough friction between him and his lead crime reporter, and he didn't want to make it worse. He sat at the desk a moment longer then pulled himself together and buzzed his secretary.

* * *

Heather had finally gotten back into the groove of the article she was typing when she was summoned to Andy Norton's office. Her stomach knotted as she considered what had happened to Dallas only hours earlier. Was she about to get fired too?

She paused at Andy's door, gave her long hair a toss, then squared her shoulders and entered the editor's plush office, prepared to do battle. However, she was caught off guard when, instead of frowning, he greeted her with a smile.

She was unsettled to see Gordon Townsend sitting beside Andy's desk. His presence seemed to indicate that something was indeed wrong. However, he too smiled warmly at her, and she reluctantly smiled back. She didn't know Gordon well, although he'd come to the paper around the same time she had. Just a few months after he'd started working at the *Chronicle,* Gordon had received a promotion to assistant managing editor when the previous assistant resigned. Although Gordon clearly had a lot of experience to back up the move, more than a few eyebrows had been raised, since he was still a new hire, and a number of reporters felt they deserved the promotion. However, it seemed that most of the ruffled feathers had been smoothed over by now, and he'd been a decent boss.

"Miss Scott," Andy began as he nodded for her to sit, "I'll cut to the chase. I want you to know that we appreciate the work you've been doing here at the *Chronicle.* Gordon and I feel that you are ready for a more challenging assignment. How would you feel about a change?"

Heather was momentarily flustered; she'd come in prepared to defend her job, but this seemed to be going in an entirely different direction. She recovered quickly, though, and warily said, "Um . . . sure. If you think I'm ready for something more challenging, I'd be honored."

"We do," he said. "We'd like to pull you off society stories and put you on the crime beat. Can you handle that?"

"Yes, sir," she said, mixed emotions filling her chest. This would definitely be a step up, and she was excited by the promotion, but she also felt a twinge of guilt. She knew Dallas would have loved this very assignment. He'd probably done such a thorough job on the seemingly dead-end car thefts story in hopes that it might one day land him a position like this. Ironically, it had spelled the end of his work at the *Chronicle.*

"Very well, Miss Scott, you'll begin immediately. Finish up what you're working on and report to Elliott Painter. He's still our lead crime correspondent, of course."

Elliott. She hadn't thought about his role on the crime beat.

Her momentary rush of pride at the promotion withered considerably. "Yes, sir. Thank you."

Andy smiled with satisfaction then rose to his feet behind his immense mahogany desk and extended a hand. "Congratulations."

She shook it and then turned to Gordon. He too smiled and shook her hand, but the expression in his eyes was solemn. He glanced at Andy, who said, "Heather, we know you were friends with Dallas and that you're probably a bit upset by what happened today. But you need to know that Dallas got in over his head and made some serious mistakes. We're working to clean up the mess he made, and we'd greatly appreciate it if a young man by the name of Tito Maggio comes up in your new assignment, you let one of us deal with the matter. Is that clear?"

"Ah, yes, sir," she said, suddenly feeling uneasy. Gordon let go of her hand and she turned toward the door. As she stepped out, Andy called out, "Pay attention to what Elliott tells you. He's a great reporter. You can learn a lot from him."

In Creepy Flirting 101, she thought, shaking her head in disgust as the door closed behind her. She strongly suspected that her assignment to the crime beat had been Elliott's suggestion. And she was certain it hadn't been because he felt she was the most qualified for the job. He was clearly making his move. *But it's not going to work,* she vowed.

Mercifully, she didn't end up crossing paths with Elliott until she was leaving for a late lunch. He stood between her and the door to the hallway when she stepped out of her cubicle, his hands hooked casually through the belt loops of his slacks.

"Hi, partner," he said with a grin.

Heather nodded, mumbling something about needing to get going, and breezed past him. Despite the less-than-favorable circumstances that had likely led to her assignment on the crime beat—and the questionable company that came along with it—she knew she was going to have to learn to work with Elliott somehow. *But it can wait,* she thought with a little smile.

* * *

When Tito strolled out of the cell block, he gave Andy an indignant look. "It's about time you posted bail." He rubbed his wrists. "Dad told me about your reporter and his nasty article. I had nothing to do with those stolen cars. I don't even know those other guys. I'd think you could keep your people under control. I don't need jerks like this Dixon character bad-mouthing me to the whole city."

"You're welcome," Andy said between gritted teeth.

"If you expected me to thank you, you should know better. It's your duty to my family, considering what we've done to help you out," he said, his eyes cold.

So Tito knows now. Things were going to have to come to a head soon. With a sinking feeling, Andy knew that it was time the people he loved—his wife and his sister—learned the truth. And he needed to tell them before Tito mouthed off.

"Where are you parked?" Tito asked, looking around. "I'll need a lift home."

"Fine," Andy said in a low voice. "Let's go."

"Fine," Tito mimicked then smiled. "How 'bout I drive? Wouldn't want to accidentally drive us back to the police department and let them in on a few family secrets."

His patience worn thin and his nerves already taut, Andy turned on his heel and grabbed Tito's collar. "Look, you little punk, I've had it up to here with your father holding this over my head all these years, and I'm not about to take it from my no-good nephew now too. So be a good boy, keep your nasty little mouth shut, get in the car, and let's go."

Tito glowered at his uncle, and Andy took a step back. The

vein in Tito's forehead bulged, and his eyes bugged out slightly. For a moment, he thought that Tito was going to snap, but the boy simply turned and walked to the car without saying another word.

* * *

When Andy arrived at his brother-in-law's house, Frankie was nowhere to be found, so he left Tito and drove to the body shop Frankie managed. Finding Frankie in his office drinking an unknown substance from a dirty paper cup, he walked in and shut the door.

Frankie smiled. "How's my boy looking?"

"It's over, Frankie. No more *favors.*"

Frankie's smile darkened. "We've been through this already, if I recall, Andy. You will do whatever I ask whenever I ask. For the rest of your life."

Andy leaned across Frankie's cluttered, dusty desk. "Not ever again. I'm going to tell Kate and then Martha what happened. I'm finally going to own up to what I've done. They might hate me for it, but I think Martha will also have some feelings about how you've blackmailed me all these years," he said.

"You wouldn't dare," Frankie said, his face beginning to turn purple. "It'll ruin both of us."

"Actually, I would dare. You've pushed me too far. Good-bye, Frankie," Andy said calmly then quickly stood and left the office, shutting the door firmly behind him. He'd made up his mind. He drove directly home. It was time to level with his wife and pray she could forgive him.

* * *

"You're home early," Kate said with a smile when he walked into the house late that afternoon. Then she looked at him carefully, her hazel eyes narrowing with concern. "Are you all right, dear? You look like you don't feel very well."

"I've been better," he said glumly.

"Bad day at the paper?" she guessed as she rose and kissed him lightly on the cheek.

"The worst I've ever had," he admitted.

She waited for him to go on, her face filled with concern. He paused a moment, almost unable to go through with it. Finally, he said, "I ruined a man's life today. I fired him. He'll probably never work as a reporter again after being fired from the *Chronicle*."

Kate didn't respond at first, but he watched the color drain from her pretty face. "There must have been some reason. What happened, Andy?"

He gestured to the sofa in the living room. "Sit down with me, and I'll explain everything. But please, just promise you'll hear me out before you leave?"

"Andy, you're scaring me." Her eyes were wide with apprehension.

He sighed and sat down. Reluctantly, she joined him on the couch and placed a tentative hand on his knee.

"Do you remember—about four or five years ago—when we went through that rough time?"

Kate stiffened. "Yes," she said quietly.

Andy swallowed hard, remembering the horror of it all as clearly as if it had just happened yesterday. "I came home at 2:00 AM, drunk as a skunk, with lipstick on my collar. You found me sitting in my chair in the den, staring out the window. I looked at you and told you I was sorry, that you deserved better. If I recall, you walked back out into the hallway, and we didn't speak much after that for a few weeks."

"That's right. It took me a long time to forgive you, Andy, but I did," she said forcefully. "And I told you that you had to quit drinking. Which you have. But what does all that have to do with your firing a reporter today?"

"Kate, I didn't have an affair."

She jerked her head up sharply. "Andy—"

He raised a finger. "Unfortunately, it's worse."

She sat in stunned silence, and he found himself unable to meet her eyes. He forced himself to continue. "I'd had a lousy day at the office. As I was finally leaving for the day, Frankie called, asking for a ride home—his car was having trouble and he was leaving it at the shop overnight. Somehow he convinced me to stop at a bar with him on the way home, and one drink led to two, and then three, and by the time I looked at a clock it was midnight.

"I knew you'd be upset I'd been gone so long and that I'd had so much to drink. I was in too much of a hurry to get home and way too drunk. When I came around the corner, just a few blocks from the bar, I couldn't stop fast enough . . ." He stopped, the horror filling his mind.

Kate inhaled sharply, staring at him.

"She was probably only nineteen, maybe twenty. There was no blood, just that bright red lipstick she was wearing. I tried to help her, Kate. I really did. But she was gone." His voice rose an octave, growing more desperate. "Why should her life and mine be over, I thought. It would have been the end of my career, the end of our marriage . . ."

When she said nothing, he finished dully. "Frankie was the only witness. And he's been holding it over my head ever since. Tito's in on it now, too. I guess Frankie told him. I can't hide it anymore. I'm going to tell Martha tomorrow. Then I'm turning myself in."

Kate slowly leaned into her husband on the sofa where they were seated and began to cry. For a minute or two he held her. Then he said, "I need to finish. Dallas Dixon wrote an article about an auto theft ring. Tito was part of it. His name was mentioned. Frankie said he'd tell you and Martha what I'd done if I didn't fire Dallas. He was one of my most promising reporters." Andy also began to cry.

* * *

To say the least, it had been a long day. After leaving the *Chronicle*'s offices, Dallas had returned to his apartment, unsure what to do with himself for the rest of the afternoon. He was anxious to call Heather, but it would have to wait until that evening, after she got off work. He sighed and sat down on the navy blue futon in his living room, mulling over his prospects for the future. Without a solid recommendation from his previous employer—not to mention a firing on his record—applying for work as a journalist anywhere else in this part of Texas would almost certainly be futile. He slumped back against the cushion, slapping a hand to his forehead. The future was not looking bright.

Dallas briefly considered taking a nap to clear his head, but with the morning's stresses, he knew it was a bad idea. Almost without fail, whenever he was stressed or worried about something, the nightmares would come—the aftermath of his serving in Iraq. He shuddered involuntarily and stood up, pacing the apartment. However, after another hour, frustrated and at a loss of what to do, he finally relented and lay down to a restless sleep.

CHAPTER 3

AFTER A LONG CONVERSATION WITH Kate, Andy dialed Gordon's number. Confessing to his wife had been the hardest thing he'd ever done, and he was now determined to go all the way in making things right, regardless of what it cost him in his personal and professional life.

"Andy?" Gordon asked, clearly surprised he was calling so late, when he came on the line.

"Look, Gordon, I'll cut to the chase. We made a mistake. I know you and I talked about it, but I can't live with myself knowing I've blackballed Dixon's career over this thing with my nephew. We need to offer him his job back."

The line was silent for a long moment. When Gordon spoke, Andy was surprised to hear anger in his voice.

"What's done is done, Andy. We made a decision. If we back down on something like this, whether we were wrong or not, we'll lose the respect of our employees—respect I've worked hard to gain, as you know. One guy's job isn't worth inspiring anarchy at the paper."

Andy clenched a fist. "I know you've been very supportive of me, Gordon, and I appreciate it. I'm sorry that you don't agree with me on this matter, but it isn't up for negotiation. We're giving him his job back," he said firmly.

The line went silent again, and Andy heard Gordon sigh. Finally, he said, "Let's have Dixon come by in the morning. I think it's a mistake, but in the end you're the boss."

* * *

Tito shoved another handful of Cheetos in his mouth and glanced at the clock. His father was working late, and his mother wouldn't be home for another half an hour either, since she cared for Tito's grandmother at her house every other night. He flipped off the music video he was watching, wiped his neon-orange fingers across his shirt, and pulled out his cell phone.

"Hey, I'm outta jail and nobody seems to care," he said sulkily when Luisa Maggio, his aunt, answered the phone. Whenever Tito was down on his luck, he could always count on his favorite aunt to cheer him up. Nobody seemed to appreciate him for who he was quite like she did. "Dad sent Andy to get me," he continued, feeling the heat rise in his cheeks. "All I did was ask for a ride home, and he started throwing the insults around. I shoulda taught him a lesson, shouldn't I, Luisa?"

"Tito, Tito. Don't be upset. I'll send someone for you right now," she promised. "Your uncle Andy is a sorry excuse for a man. Someday he'll get what he has coming," she said confidently. She paused then said, "Why don't you stay here tonight? There's something you can help me with, and I'm sure you can use the cash."

"Sure, Luisa." Tito knew that whenever Luisa needed his help, she paid him quite generously. That was one of the reasons he stayed at her place quite often. The jobs weren't bad, and he'd never gotten caught when he was working for her. Luisa took care of the people who were loyal to her. He liked to think that he and Luisa were cut from the same mold.

The car that arrived ten minutes later was a black Cadillac Escalade. The driver, Marco Santini, wore a black suit and tie. Like Frankie and Luisa, he was Italian and had come to Texas from Chicago. Marco glanced back at Tito in the seat behind him, raising his dark eyebrows but not smiling. "Luisa said that I'm to deliver you to her place."

"Yeah," Tito responded. "I think she's got a little job for me."

"I hope so," Marco said with a bite to his voice, smoothing back his already slick black hair. "You can't handle anything big."

Tito scowled. "Just drive, Marco. That's your big job—being the chauffeur."

"Watch your mouth, kid. And take my advice. You'd better stay out of jail after this. If you don't, your aunt might not be so happy to have you around. Publicity is not something we need."

"Hey, it wasn't my fault," Tito said defensively. "One of the other guys slipped up and got me in trouble."

Marco rolled his eyes. "Small-time gangs are full of amateurs who are going to slip up. If you want to play with the grown-ups, you'd better wise up."

Tito started back with a retort, but Marco cut him off. "Just pay attention to what you're doing. Luisa's a good boss, and I don't need you causing her or anyone else any trouble."

Tito sulked the rest of the way. When he arrived, he walked in without knocking and found Luisa on the phone. She put her finger to her lips for him to be quiet then said, "Sorry, I haven't heard from him."

She listened for a few seconds then rolled her eyes in irritation. "Tell Martha to quit worrying about Tito. He's a big boy now. He can take care of himself," she said and then put the phone down.

"That Dad?" Tito asked, heading for the refrigerator.

"He'll be fine. I have a job for you, and I don't want Frankie—or your dear ma—getting on my case."

* * *

His sister Martha wasn't answering her phone. After trying her cell several times and pacing the house, Andy decided to go for a walk to clear his head. He paused outside the door to his and Kate's bedroom, raising his hand to knock, but then he decided to let her be for now.

He started down the walk, deep in thought, and then looked up in surprise. "What are you doing here?" he asked.

"There's a little problem. I've come to straighten it out. Don't worry, it'll only take a second."

* * *

The Baghdad night was stifling. Dallas drew in a deep breath and clutched his gun closer to his body as he surveyed the building, a known Al Qaeda hideout he and his squad had been assigned to clear. Looking around, he slowly stood and motioned for his men to approach the building. As he stepped into the first room with his rifle at his shoulder, a small noise to his right caused him to turn abruptly, bringing him face-to-face with another man. His dark eyes were filled with hatred and fixed on Dallas. The man was holding an automatic rifle. It was aimed at Dallas's chest.

As Dallas pulled the trigger, he heard the explosion and saw the body crash into the wall and slide to the floor. The man was dead, his rifle still clutched in his hands.

Dallas awoke with a jolt, his body clammy with cold sweat. He looked around him from the unfamiliar vantage point of the floor. *I must have fallen off the couch,* he thought, dazed and still reeling from the nightmare, one that came often, one that was based on reality. It was dark in the room, and he had no idea how long he'd slept. He stood up and walked over to the kitchen to check the clock. 9:45 PM. He picked up the telephone, feeling bad that he'd waited this long to call Heather. He hoped she hadn't gone to bed yet.

* * *

A loud knock on the door startled Heather to her feet. Dazed, she looked at her watch and realized it was almost ten. She'd been half reading and half dozing on the couch for a couple of hours, wondering why Dallas hadn't called and debating what she would say to him when he did.

She didn't think Dallas knew her address, but she couldn't imagine who else would be knocking on her door this late. He could have found her address easily enough.

Heather opened the door and choked back her surprise. Instead of Dallas, Elliott Painter leaned lazily against the doorframe, the porch light casting dark shadows across his handsome features. He grinned. "I thought you had plans tonight."

"I did—it's almost ten o'clock, Elliott," she replied. "I was actually just about to go to bed. I'm sorry you drove all the way over here, but I'll see you tomorrow." She moved to close the door.

"Not so fast," he interrupted her. "I'm afraid we've got work to do tonight. Are you ready to go, partner?"

Half wondering if this was just a veiled excuse for a date, she gave him a careful look. "I didn't realize we'd be working as partners. Andy just told me I'd be clearing my assignments with you."

He shrugged. "Maybe, but you need to learn a few of the ropes on the crime beat. I've been on this scene for a few years now, you know. So for now, think of me as your partner," he said decisively. "We'll go out tonight and I'll give you some pointers. Grab your stuff—we need to get moving. There's a big story that needs to be covered."

Heather had barely fastened her seat belt in Elliott's car when her cell phone began to vibrate. She pulled it from her purse and glanced at the display, groaning inwardly. *Perfect timing,* she thought, debating whether to answer. Glancing at Elliott, she pushed TALK. "Hey—I'm on my way to cover a story right now. Can I call you back?" she said quietly, careful to avoid saying Dallas's name.

"Sure. I'll be here."

She lost the rest of what Dallas was saying as Elliott said loudly, "I need to brief you on the situation before we get there, Heather. There's no time for social calls."

"Is that Elliott?" Dallas asked, sounding confused and a little hurt.

"Yes, but—" Heather sighed in frustration as Elliott gave her a pointed look and cleared his throat. "I'll explain later. I'm sorry, but I have to go."

"No problem. Sorry about my timing," Dallas said quietly. "Have a good night."

The line went dead, and Heather slowly closed her phone.

"Who was that?" Elliott asked.

"Just a friend," she replied casually. "Now, tell me what's going on that gets you out so late at night."

"There's been a high-profile murder," Elliott said. "The victim's name hasn't been released yet, but I talked to a couple of sources at the police department who say this is going to be a huge story."

A few minutes later, Heather felt her stomach tighten as she saw the flashing lights of dozens of police cars and other emergency vehicles blocking the street ahead. They were in an upscale neighborhood that Heather was unfamiliar with, and Elliott pulled the car to a stop at the curb a short distance back from the first wave of police vehicles.

A Channel 3 news truck parked behind them as Heather was getting out of the car. She and Elliott hurried toward the flashing lights, anxious to beat the TV reporters and cameramen to the scene of the crime. However, they weren't able to avoid the rush and were unable to learn anything in the next few moments except what they already knew—that there had been a murder.

Elliott squared his shoulders and flashed Heather what she could only assume was intended to be a confidence-inspiring smile. "Stick close to me. I'll show you how investigative reporting is done right." He then pushed his way through the growing crowd and right into the ranks of police officers who were stationed close together to keep the public back. Several of them seemed to recognize him, and one of them said, "Go ahead, Mr. Painter. Lieutenant Garcia said you'd be coming. He told us to let you through when you did, but he said only you; the lady will have to wait."

"It's okay. She's my new partner," he said matter-of-factly.

The police officer looked slightly unsure of himself, but he said, "Uh, okay, go ahead, then."

Heather shook her head as they walked past the officer and up the walk toward a large, sand-colored house with a red-tiled roof. *He's very confident; I'll give him that,* she thought with a small smile. The smile faded from her lips, however, when she looked ahead. There on the sidewalk, just a few steps from the front door, lay a figure covered with a black tarp. A group of officers from the crime lab milled about the victim, gathering evidence and shooting pictures. As Heather and Elliott drew closer, a plainclothes officer wearing a sports coat and slacks stopped them. His dark features were set in a serious expression.

"Hey, Rigo," Elliott said in a familiar tone.

"Hello, Elliott. Listen, I'm sorry about this."

Elliott looked slightly puzzled but nodded as the officer continued. "I told them to let you through when you got here, but I meant just you. Who's the lady?"

"This is Heather Scott. She's with the *Chronicle* too; we'll be working very closely together from here on out, so you'll be seeing a lot more of her," Elliott said. "Heather, meet Lieutenant Rodrigo Garcia. He's head of CAP—that's the Crimes Against Persons section of the El Paso Police Department. You can call him Rigo."

Rigo's expression remained grim as he glanced at Heather and said, "It's nice to meet you, Miss Scott. I'm sorry it had to be under the present circumstances."

"Yeah, you too," Heather said, glancing sideways at Elliott. Rigo certainly seemed sensitive for someone who was head of the CAP. And Elliott had been at a number of murder scenes before—it was part of working on the crime beat. Were there always apologies and condolences offered like this?

Elliott looked at her and shrugged. Then he turned back to Rigo. "What *present circumstances,* Rigo?"

The lieutenant looked surprised. "You mean we've been successful in keeping the name of the victim from the press?"

"You sure have," Elliott responded. "Believe me, I tried to find out."

His look of surprise faded back to a grave expression, and he nodded. "I wanted you to be the first to know, if possible."

"I appreciate it. Now, who's under that tarp that requires so much secrecy?" Elliott asked, craning his neck to see.

Heather found his flippant tone offensive, but apparently Rigo was used to Elliott, since his expression didn't change. "Why don't you two step over there with me?"

Heather's stomach knotted as Lieutenant Garcia asked the lab workers to step back. Then he reached down and lifted the tarp. As he did, Heather felt a wave of nausea overtake her, and the bile rose in her throat. There, lying on the cold pavement, his gaze fixed lifelessly in front of him, was Andy Norton.

She gasped. Elliott simply stared. Neither of them said a

word until the lieutenant said, "I'm sorry, folks. He was a good man."

"What happened to him, Rigo?" Elliott asked. Heather took a step back, floored by how steady he seemed while she struggled just to keep from throwing up.

"He was shot in the chest twice at point-blank range," Rigo said. After a few seconds he added, "He was facing his assailant. Indicates to me that it might have been someone he knew."

Elliott shook his head. "This is going to devastate the paper."

Rigo nodded. "I'm sorry to seem callous, but I'll need to ask you two some questions. The sooner we start putting the pieces together the sooner we solve this. Do either of you know anyone who might have wanted the editor dead?"

Heather began to shake her head when Elliott said, "I hate to have to say this, but Andy dealt with personnel problems at the paper this morning."

Heather's head jerked up, immediately seeing where Elliott was heading with this. *He can't possibly think that Dallas would . . .* She glanced down at the tarp once more and felt her stomach heave again.

Rigo took out a notepad, nodding for Elliott to continue.

Elliott glanced sideways at Heather. "There might not be a connection, but he did have to fire someone today," he said.

"Who did Mr. Norton fire, and what were the circumstances?" the lieutenant asked.

"A new reporter named Dallas Dixon." Elliott shrugged. "It was an internal decision. Dallas just wasn't cut out to be a reporter. He'd demonstrated poor judgment, and the managing editors had no choice but to let him go before he got the paper into legal trouble," Elliott said. "He'd only been with us for a few months, so he was still an at-will employee. Andy didn't have to give Dallas a reason for firing him, and he chose not to. Dallas was very angry."

Heather's own anger overcame her nausea. "Elliott, Dallas had nothing to do with this, and you know it. He was an excellent reporter and didn't deserve to be fired."

Rigo glanced back and forth between the two of them. "Nobody's being hauled off to jail yet. Why don't you tell me more about Dallas Dixon," he said, looking at Elliott. Heather silently fumed.

"I don't know him all that well," Elliott said. "But his basic information is in a file back at the office."

"You say he hadn't been at the paper long. Do you know what he was doing before he was hired?"

Heather jumped back into the conversation. "He was going to school at UTEP, studying journalism—graduated top of his class."

Elliott frowned at her. "Dallas was a trucker before that, and he also spent quite a bit of time in Iraq, in the Army."

Rigo nodded, writing the information down. Before he could ask more questions, Elliott turned to Heather and said, "I can handle things here—we could be missing out on key information with both of us tied up here. Go on in the house, and I'll meet up with you after I'm through here. I'll give Rigo your contact information in case he needs to ask you anything later."

When Rigo didn't object, Heather reluctantly nodded and walked toward the house, feeling dazed. Her boss had been murdered, and whether she cared to admit it or not, Dallas had a motive.

CHAPTER 4

AFTER HIS FAILED ATTEMPT AT talking to Heather, Dallas once again fell into a fitful sleep. However, at 4:30 that morning he awoke and found himself unable to fall back asleep.

He sighed, feeling restless and frustrated. Why had Heather and Elliott been out covering a story that late at night? Even as he asked himself the question, he suspected he knew the answer. Heather had been the reporter chosen for the crime beat spot it was rumored was coming up. Though he was happy for her, he had to admit that the salt in the wound stung. He was certain that Elliott had nudged the decision in Heather's direction more than a little, and though he knew Heather was definitely not interested in Elliott, a twinge of jealousy still stung him.

Resigned to the fact that he wasn't going to be getting any more sleep, he put on some sweatpants, a T-shirt, and his running shoes. Then he got in his truck and drove to his favorite spot outside the city, where endless country roads offered prime running grounds. Running was a release, and he suspected he would run a lot this morning before he found the release he was seeking.

He parked his Chevy pickup and spent a minute or two beside it warming up. He hadn't brought a flashlight as the bright, full moon overhead still offered plenty of light. As he set off, he let his thoughts unwind and travel where they would.

As they often did lately, his thoughts turned to Heather. As her warm brown eyes and dimpled smile flashed through his mind, he felt a pang of sadness. Whatever might have been with their relationship would probably never be—he might as well face that fact now. Her future was with the *Chronicle,* and his future was completely uncertain. It was probably time to forget her.

He then began to think about the events of the previous morning as he had done a thousand times since he'd been fired. He felt a great need to talk over what had happened with a friend, someone who might have some advice for his next move. However, most of the friends he'd made in the last few months were at the *Chronicle.* After he had been running for another half an hour, the name Michael Nugent popped into his head.

Michael had been a reporter with the Associated Press when Dallas first met him in Iraq. He'd been embedded there with Dallas's unit, and the two had become fast friends. In fact, it was Michael who had ultimately convinced Dallas to pursue a degree in journalism.

Dallas was pretty sure that Michael was working in San Antonio now—or at least he had been a couple of years ago. That had been the last time the two had spoken, Dallas realized with chagrin. He glanced at his watch—six o'clock in the morning. By Michael's standards this was late in the day. Hoping the number he had for him was still current, Dallas dialed.

"Son of a gun, it's good to hear from you, Dallas!" Michael exclaimed when Dallas greeted him on the phone.

"I hope I didn't wake you, but knowing you, I'm betting that's not the case," Dallas said with a smile as he slowed to a walk. The two proceeded to talk for some time, reminiscing about the time they had spent in Baghdad as if it had been yesterday.

As their reverie wound down, Michael chuckled and said, "It's sure good to hear from you, Dallas. Enough about the past, though. What's new? Where are you working now?"

"Well . . ." Dallas began, clearing his throat. "I actually followed your advice and got my degree in journalism. I've been working as a reporter for the *Chronicle* in El Paso for the past five months, ever since I graduated."

"Are you kidding? I didn't think you'd take my advice. I knew you'd make a good reporter, though—that's great news! That's a fine paper, too."

"The thing is," Dallas said slowly, a little embarrassed, "I *was* working as a reporter there. That's why I called . . . I could really use some more advice."

"Uh-oh. What happened?"

Dallas told him all about the previous day's unfortunate events. Michael said nothing until he had finished. "It sounds to me like this Elliott character had something to do with the well getting poisoned. I take it you haven't called this woman, Heather, back yet."

Dallas shook his head and kicked at a small rock. "I tried to call last night, but she was out on a story—with Elliott," he mumbled. "I'm anxious to hear what information she has for me, though."

Michael mused for a moment then said, "You know, if I were you I'd call that managing editor back, too, see if you can't get a little more information out of him. He might not like it, but what can he do to you that he hasn't already done?"

"Only make sure I don't get a job anywhere else," Dallas said miserably.

Michael gave a brief chuckle. "The world doesn't end in El Paso, my friend. You'll find another job, I'm sure of it. In the meantime, you might consider doing some freelance work. There's always a buyer for an interesting, well-written story. I could toss a few connections your way."

Dallas's spirits lifted slightly. "I hadn't thought about that. I could give it a try, at least until I figure out where I'm headed."

"You know, there's always San Antonio."

Dallas laughed. "That's true. I guess there's not much to keep me here anymore."

"Not even a woman?" Michael ribbed him.

He paused a moment then sighed. "No, not really," he said slowly.

"I could probably pull some strings," Michael offered. "I'm sure I could land you a job here. In fact, if you decided you were serious about moving to San Antonio in a hurry, I know of a position opening up pretty soon."

"Good to know; I'll think about it," Dallas agreed.

They talked for a few more minutes, then Michael said, "Hey, I've got to head out to work, but really, give San Antonio some thought, Dallas. I think you'd like it here."

Dallas pocketed his phone and resumed running, mulling over his conversation with Michael. Freelance writing had been a good idea, but he knew it might take some time before it began to bring in enough money to consider it a living. He also began to seriously consider Michael's offer to help him start over in San Antonio. With any luck it would be far enough from El Paso to be beyond the reach of the *Chronicle*'s black mark. Moving wouldn't be a problem since he hadn't accumulated much in the way of personal belongings. School had kept him tight on his finances, and his apartment had already been furnished when he moved in. He knew he could likely pack everything he owned in his truck.

Ten minutes later, Dallas made his decision. He was going to go to San Antonio.

* * *

Rigo, along with one of his detectives, Charlie Cornwall—or CC—rapped on the door to Dallas's apartment. When no one answered, they checked the parking space that matched the number of his apartment. "We'll come back in a few hours," Lieutenant Garcia told CC. "He must have gone somewhere early this morning. He might be job hunting."

"Or he's on the run already," CC responded, raising an eyebrow. "I have a feeling he's our man. And from what Painter told us, we might be up against a tough guy here."

Rigo nodded. "There's no question that Elliott thinks Dixon had something to do with this." He glanced at the closed apartment door. "For now let's head back to the station, do some digging there."

* * *

When Dallas returned from his run, he spent the next two hours packing up his belongings and loading them into his truck. When he finished, he looked around his apartment. There was nothing to keep him from leaving now except to let the manager of the apartment complex know he was leaving and that she could rent his place out. She wasn't in. He'd been renting on a month-to-month basis and had just paid the current month, so he simply slid a hastily written note beneath the door of the manager's apartment and headed for his truck.

* * *

After a sleepless night, Heather dragged herself out of bed. She had been unable to erase the images from the last twenty-four hours from her mind, and she debated calling in sick to work but knew she'd be better off busy.

When she arrived at the *Chronicle,* the building was eerily quiet. It was clear that the staff had been made aware of Andy's murder. As she walked to her cubicle, she looked over and saw

Andy's secretary discreetly wipe a tear that trailed down her cheek. As she glanced around at the rest of the employees, she saw expressions of fear, outrage, and sadness.

To make matters worse, an hour later Lieutenant Rodrigo Garcia and several detectives descended on the paper. All employees were subject to questioning. As each person was summoned into the conference room and came back out, the gossip began to spread, and it became abundantly clear that Dallas—and his rumored vendetta against Andy—was the top subject of conversation. Heather did her best to concentrate on her article, but more than a few glances drifted her way. Most people knew she and Dallas had developed a close friendship.

Elliott had spent the night at the paper after taking Heather home, writing the front-page article for the morning's edition of the paper. He'd become something of an office celebrity, and the other employees couldn't seem to get enough of hearing him tell the story of the previous night's events. Heather listened as he told person after person, his voice quivering with outrage, that Andy Norton had been his friend as well as his boss, and that whoever had done this would be brought to justice. When he learned from Rigo that Dallas had vacated his apartment sometime that morning, he and most of the rest of the staff seemed to instantly become convinced of Dallas's guilt. Heather was puzzled by Dallas's sudden move, but by no stretch was she convinced he had anything to do with Andy's murder. She gritted her teeth and put on headphones when she heard several people refer to Dallas as the alleged killer.

The paper's board of directors convened in an emergency meeting behind closed doors at ten o'clock that morning. When they emerged an hour later, they announced that in light of the recent tragedy, they had come to a decision. Rather than doing a search outside the current staff for a new managing editor, Gordon Townsend would be filling Andy's job, and Elliott would be replacing Gordon as assistant managing editor. They expected that things would move ahead with little interruption. More buzz circulated through the building, and Heather was almost grateful when Elliott assigned her to hit the streets to get public reaction to the murder of their boss.

* * *

As Luisa had promised, Tito Maggio had been plenty busy since arriving at her house. Currently, he was looking out the window of a bright blue Peterbilt tractor, which was pulling a trailer loaded with new Ford cars. At eight o'clock that morning, they had pulled out of a large warehouse near the Mexican border and had been headed east on Interstate 10 ever since. The trunks of the cars were filled with hundreds of kilos of high-quality cocaine. Tito felt pretty important.

Nick Abrams, the driver of the truck and an experienced drug trafficker as well, turned to Tito and grinned. Their job was easy enough—deliver the truck and its load to a warehouse in Chicago. The promised paycheck was a big one. Tito licked his lips in anticipation of the delicious, tax-free dollars.

* * *

Dallas awoke with a start and looked at the clock on his dash. He rubbed his eyes, amazed that it was already after eleven. He'd pulled over to rest after a few hours of driving when sleep had threatened to overcome him. That had been a couple of hours ago. He'd expected to catnap for half an hour and then get on his way, but he'd fallen into a deep—and thankfully dreamless—sleep.

He pulled onto the freeway behind a semi hauling a load of cars. The big rig was driving slightly below the speed limit, but when Dallas attempted to pass it, the truck sped up. Shrugging and not wanting to get into a road-rage battle, Dallas set his cruise control at the same speed as the truck and stayed a safe distance behind it. He was tempted to call Michael to let him know he was on his way, but he knew Michael would be at work for another several hours, and he didn't want to interrupt him, so to pass the time he turned on his radio. When the FM station fizzled out after about thirty miles, he switched to an AM station hoping to pick up the local news from El Paso before he was too far out of range to get that, too. He listened for several minutes before the news came on.

When the news resumed, Dallas half listened, focused mainly on the road, until he heard the name Andy Norton. Turning the radio up, Dallas paid more attention. With growing horror, he learned that the lead story was the murder of his former boss. He had been found dead on the sidewalk in front of his home at about 9:15 the night before. According to police, he'd been shot twice in the chest at point-blank range. Dallas gripped the steering wheel tightly, his knuckles turning red then white. Pulling to the side of the freeway, he put his head in his hands.

The reporter went on to say that Andy's body had been found when the son of the next-door neighbor had come home from his part-time job. Andy's wife hadn't heard the shots, presumably because she had been in her bedroom with the television turned on, and neighbors also hadn't heard anything. They too had had televisions or stereos going. At this point in the newscast, Lieutenant Rodrigo Garcia, head of the Crimes against Persons section of the El Paso Police Department, came on the radio. He stated that the police were looking for a person of interest in the case—a reporter by the name of Dallas Dixon.

Dallas's head jerked up so quickly that it slammed against the headrest. His stomach felt like it was twisting inside out as the lieutenant said, "Dixon cleaned out his apartment and left sometime during the night or early this morning. We have no idea what time. He has not been named as an official suspect, but he is a person of interest. Several sources indicate that the Iraqi war veteran and former Army Ranger was *very angry* when he left the *Chronicle* at noon yesterday."

Lieutenant Garcia went on to state that the police wanted to locate Dallas so they could talk to him about anything he might know that would shed light on the case. He then listed Dallas's stats: twenty-eight years old, short brown hair and light blue eyes, six foot one, and two hundred pounds.

Dallas began to tremble as he stared at his reflection in the rearview mirror. He felt like he was trapped in one of his nightmares as the officer described his vehicle as a four-year-old black Chevrolet Silverado pickup with an extended cab. The newscaster then came back on the radio and asked that anyone with information call the El Paso Police Department.

He broke into a cold sweat. Yesterday afternoon had marked the beginning of a downward spiral, and he didn't see how things could get worse. Not only had he lost his job, but now he was a murder suspect. His mind spun. The police had said *person of interest,* but he was certain that in the eyes of the police, he was a suspect. He thought quickly. Not only would they consider him to have a motive, since he had been fired that day, but they would soon discover that he didn't have any kind of solid alibi for his whereabouts the previous evening since he'd been alone in his apartment sleeping.

Dallas had faced snipers, roadside bombs, automatic gunfire, knife-wielding maniacs, and suicide bombers in Iraq, but never had his future looked so bleak as he sat with his head against the steering wheel of his truck alongside I-10, one hundred and fifty miles east of El Paso. His first thought was to turn his truck around, go back to El Paso, and attempt to clear his name. But a nagging feeling made him wonder if it would do any good. He'd have no way to clear his name from inside a jail cell, and so it seemed most logical to continue onward, pretending he hadn't heard a thing about Andy's murder.

He nodded, still shaking slightly, determined that later he would make a call from a pay phone to talk to the police and give them whatever information they needed. But for now, he wanted to put as much distance between him and El Paso as possible. He pulled onto the freeway and headed east.

* * *

Tito turned down the radio as the newscast ended, laughing and slapping the dashboard of the Peterbilt. "Well, that takes care of my no-good uncle and his idiot reporter. It couldn't be more perfect."

"As long as they can catch the reporter and pin your dear uncle's murder on him," Nick clarified.

"Oh, they'll catch him. The guy's obviously not too bright. And the police are going to be on him like vultures on roadkill. Uncle Andy fired him yesterday—what better motive could the cops want?" Tito asked, still chuckling. "Who else would want Uncle Andy out of the way?"

"How about Tito Maggio?" Nick asked evenly. "You were pretty worked up about those things he said yesterday. And it sounds like y'all had a little scene in front of the police department before he took you home."

The chuckle faded, and Tito turned on the truck driver in anger. "Don't you ever mention that again. Do you understand me?"

Nick shrugged and reached down into a bag of sunflower seeds. He popped several in his mouth. "Just pointing out the obvious. You know, what the cops might think about."

"Don't point it out again," Tito said angrily and faced the other way, lapsing into a brooding silence as they rolled onward.

* * *

Martha Maggio sat staring into her cold cup of coffee, unable to focus. Tears slid down her cheeks, splashing against the leather sofa. She had been notified in person by the police late the night before about Andy's murder and had been in a state of shock ever since. She had loved and admired her older brother deeply. Her sorrow was only intensified by the fact that her husband, Frankie, seemed relatively unfazed by the horrible news. She had never been able to understand why her husband disliked Andy so intensely, and even less so now. The friction between the two men had been a constant trial for her throughout her married life and only seemed to have gotten worse in recent years. When Martha had turned to Frankie after she had found out the news, he had held her, but then he'd simply made mention of the police theory that a reporter Andy had fired for incompetence was likely responsible.

Compounding her distress was the fact that their son, Tito, had been arrested a few days before—and not for the first time. Though Frankie scoffed at the notion, she found herself increasingly frightened that there might be some truth to the allegations the police were making against Tito. Martha had never been blind to the fact that Tito was headed down the wrong path and ran with a rough crowd, but the older he got the harder he was to control. She was worried that she hadn't seen him since his release from jail, but then it wasn't unlike Tito to simply disappear for a few days at a time, causing Martha endless worry. Frankie hadn't told her where he'd come up with the money to bail Tito out yet again, and she hadn't asked.

Around noon, Martha found the strength to get up and pour herself a fresh cup of coffee. Then she returned to the sitting room. After a few minutes, Frankie walked in and sat beside her on the sofa. "You heard from Tito yet?" he asked, nodding toward the cell phone on the table.

When she shook her head, he sighed loudly. "Can't even ask the last person who saw him where he might be. The police said that after Andy put up the bond for him, an officer saw them in the parking lot having a few words," he said bitterly. "I know you think Andy's always been this great guy, but I'm here to tell you that he isn't. I know he's dead, but that don't change the truth."

Fresh tears welled up in Martha's eyes. "At least he got him out of jail, Frankie. He didn't have to do that," she said, surprised in the midst of her grief that Frankie would ask Andy for such a favor. "I just don't understand why you've always disliked Andy so much. He was a good man!"

"A good man to have gone," Frankie muttered in a burst of anger. "People don't get murdered because they're nice to people."

Martha began to sob in earnest. "Frankie, that's a horrible thing to say. How can you be so callous?" She turned from him. "If that's how you're going to be, just go—let me be."

Frankie's face turned red. For a moment he sat fuming, and then he let loose. "You didn't know your big brother as well as you thought you did, Martha. Andy wasn't the good guy everyone thought he was. In fact, he was the worst kind of guy—a killer." At Martha's shocked expression, he nodded. "That's right. Andy deserved what he got—what goes around comes around, you know. A few years back, he was driving me home—he'd been drinking—and ran this girl down. I've kept his dirty secret all these years because I didn't want him to hurt you. I guess I shouldn't have. But he killed somebody and he got away with it. And on top of that, he's always treated me and my son like dirt. I hated the guy. And I don't know why you should feel any different."

"Get out!" Martha screamed, throwing her coffee cup at him with all the force she could muster. Frankie ducked, and the cup shattered against the wall, scattering coffee and glass over much of the room.

Frankie stood for a moment, his eyes blazing with anger. A moment later, Martha heard the door in the garage slam. She continued to sob into the sofa cushions as she heard his car start and then speed up the street.

Martha's tears soaked into the worn leather of the sofa, but after a few moments, her mind began to process what her husband had just told her. And even though she hated herself for it, she wondered if any of it could be true. It couldn't be, yet Frankie had seemed so sure of himself. Was that the reason his dislike of Andy had seemed to escalate in the past few years? Then a terrible thought entered her mind. *What if Frankie had somehow been responsible for what had happened to Andy?* A worse thought followed. *What if Tito had been involved?* Tito could be so hotheaded, and Martha was honest enough to admit to herself that it was possible that he might act out against Andy, especially given the hatred that his father harbored against him.

Never in her life had Martha been so miserable. She felt like she'd lost her husband, her brother, and her son in one violent act.

CHAPTER 5

HEATHER HAD SPENT THE PAST two hours on the street, trying to gauge public reaction to Andy's murder and dig up additional information, but she hadn't unearthed anything useful. The people she'd talked to all basically said the same thing—that they respected Andy Norton, were sorry he had been the victim of such a horrible crime, and couldn't imagine why someone would do such a thing. However, Dallas's name had come up several times as she pressed for more information. Suspicion and anger against Dallas Dixon seemed to be mounting in the community.

Elliott's article in the morning's edition had done nothing to divert suspicion. Although he had not directly said so, he had more or less accused Dallas of the crime.

It had been pure impulse that led Heather to give up on the street and look up the address of Andy's sister. She and her husband, Frankie Maggio, had been listed in the phone directory.

Heather approached the Maggios' residence and rang the bell. After waiting for several minutes, she was about to give up when the door opened a few inches and the face of a petite and attractive—but very red-eyed—woman in her mid-forties peered out at her.

"Martha?" Heather asked, offering a tentative smile. "My name is Heather Scott—I was hoping I could talk to you for a few minutes."

The woman nodded but didn't return the smile. She looked at Heather's notepad and professional attire and said, "I don't want to talk to anybody. I don't have a statement. Please, just go away."

"Please, Mrs. Maggio. I'm a reporter, yes, but I was also a friend of your brother's."

Martha hesitated, and Heather saw her expression soften slightly. "Something happened at the paper yesterday that I think you should know about," Heather said. "I'm hoping you can help me understand some things."

Martha still looked uncertain, but she slowly opened the door. "Okay, come in—but only for a minute," she said.

Once inside, Heather held out her hand and said, "I'm sorry for your loss, Martha. I had a great deal of respect for your brother, and it was an honor to work for him."

"Thank you," Martha said slowly, allowing Heather to take her hand, but not meeting her eyes. "Please, sit down."

Heather sat next to Martha on a large leather sofa. Though the temperature in the room was actually a bit warm, Martha pulled an afghan around her shoulders, shivering slightly.

Heather took a deep breath, then dove right in. "Martha, I said I enjoyed working for your brother—and that's true. I always felt like he was a generous and kind man, and a good boss." She paused. "Until yesterday, that is."

Martha looked up sharply. "What happened yesterday? Are you talking about the man Andy fired—the one they think killed him?" she asked.

"Dallas hasn't been named as a suspect," Heather said calmly. "He was a good reporter, and he really liked Andy. But yesterday, when Andy fired him out of the blue—without any kind of explanation—Andy was upset."

"I just can't imagine Andy doing something like that," Martha said firmly.

"Before yesterday, I couldn't either," Heather said then paused. "I think it's because of what Dallas wrote in the paper about your son, Tito."

Martha gave a short, bitter laugh. "Is that who wrote the article? I honestly hadn't made the connection."

Heather nodded. "Dallas felt like he was very fair in the article."

"I'm afraid I can't disagree with you on that. But I can tell you right now that that's not the reason. Andy and Tito were never close. Tito's father—Frankie—never liked Andy, and our son followed in his footsteps."

Puzzled, Heather slowly nodded. That was not what she'd expected to hear. But as she looked up, she saw that the other woman's face had suddenly grown very pale.

"Martha? Are you all right?"

Martha looked stricken. After a moment, in a soft voice, she said, "Oh, no."

"What is it?" Heather asked. From the look in her eyes and the way Martha was clutching the afghan, Heather worried Martha was on the verge of completely breaking down.

Finally, Martha said, "Did you know that Andy bailed Tito out of jail yesterday?"

"No," Heather responded carefully.

Martha continued, staring straight ahead. "I didn't either. At least until my husband told me before he left the house this morning in a huff. I was more than a little surprised that Andy had agreed to it, and the more I think about it, the more sure I am that he never would have, unless . . ." She appeared thoughtful for a moment. Then her gaze locked on Heather's. "I think my husband was blackmailing my brother."

Heather tried to contain her shock. "Over what?" she asked, anxious for Martha to keep talking.

"Over what he told me today . . ." She looked tormented.

"And yet I don't think Andy could have ever done what Frankie says he did."

"What did Frankie tell you?" Heather prodded.

Martha clammed up and crossed her arms over her chest defensively. "I don't even know if I believe him."

Heather shrugged and tried a different approach. "Well, maybe you're right—maybe your brother didn't do what your husband says he did but couldn't prove his innocence. In other words, maybe he was falsely accused."

"Yes," Martha said slowly. A light seemed to shine in her eyes for the first time. "Yes," she repeated. "I'll bet Luisa put Frankie up to it—she's an awful person," she said in a low voice, almost as if speaking to herself.

"Luisa?"

"Frankie's sister," Martha said, looking at Heather and seeming to shake herself from a daze. Straightening up, she motioned toward the door. "I'm sorry, but I shouldn't say more. I'm not thinking straight, and I'm a mess. I haven't even showered for the day yet."

Heather stood, knowing that if she pressed for more information now she'd probably only succeed in pushing Martha away. "I understand—thank you for visiting with me. And I am truly sorry about the loss of your brother."

"Thank you," Martha said, and Heather could see the sheen of fresh tears in her eyes. She quickly brushed them away and firmly said, "I hope that you will respect my wishes, Miss Scott, and not spread the rumor that Frankie might have been holding something over Andy's head. I don't think I could handle that right now." She paused then added, "Do I have your word?"

"Yes," Heather said. "I won't report rumors. But if you ever need someone to talk to, please call me. You have my card."

To Heather's amazement, Martha leaned forward and enveloped her in a hug. "Thank you," she said quietly. "And thank you for caring about my brother's death."

Back in her car, Heather mulled over what she had just learned. She hadn't unearthed anything she could include in an article for the paper, so in that regard her visit with Martha Maggio could have been considered a waste of time. However, she had come away with a growing suspicion regarding Frankie and Tito Maggio, as well as Frankie's sister, Luisa. She earnestly hoped that the police were heading down the same path and that someday soon Martha would be willing to tell her more.

CHAPTER 6

BETWEEN EL PASO AND SAN ANTONIO lay hundreds of miles of open, rolling desert and lightly traveled freeway. Vehicles were particularly sparse that sweltering Saturday afternoon as Dallas drove on, hoping an officer would not appear and recognize his truck.

As Dallas looked ahead down the long stretch of open highway, he could see a semitruck in the distance. As he drew closer, he realized that it was the same one he'd come across earlier. It was still traveling slowly. Dallas checked his rearview mirror and pulled to the inside lane. He was almost up to the rear of the trailer when a loud explosion shattered the drone of the tires on the highway, and the semi veered sharply into the inside lane. Dallas slammed on his brakes, and as he skidded to a stop he watched in shock as the huge truck began to slowly overturn. Then it was on its side, sliding into the median as its cargo of cars popped loose from the chains that had held them to the trailer and rolled in several directions, filling the median and the westbound lanes with tons of costly wreckage.

After several seconds that seemed to stretch for hours, the noise and commotion became still. At last Dallas was able to shake himself into action as he realized that the driver of the truck might need help. When he drove up alongside the truck, he saw that it was lying on its side in the median, barely off the pavement, passenger-side up. To his surprise the windshield was still intact. Dallas jumped from his pickup just as a man began to climb up through the passenger door.

"Hey! Give me your hand," Dallas called as he hurried over to help the man down. He could see blood seeping from several cuts on the young man's face, but he didn't seem to be seriously injured.

"My partner's still in there," the man said, bending over and resting his hands on his knees.

"I'll help him," Dallas said as he quickly scrambled onto the truck and peered inside. The second man was standing on the driver's-side door. To Dallas's relief, he was also bloody but didn't seem to be seriously hurt either.

Just as he turned to relay this news to the first man, he felt himself roughly shoved from behind. As Dallas stumbled forward, the man inside the semi grabbed him by the head and pulled. "What—"

His question was cut off as something solid connected with his head. Then darkness smothered him.

* * *

"Did you get his ID?" Nick called to Tito.

"Yep, I got it," Tito replied with satisfaction. "I got his keys and phone, too. And I grabbed your logbook and stuff like you said. Nothin' left in there to tie us to the truck." He glanced around nervously and swiped at a bleeding cut on his forehead. "Now let's get out of here. They'll kill us if they find out we lost this load of dope."

"They'll kill him," Nick said easily, waving back toward the truck. "They'll only kill us if they can find us. I don't know about you, but I'm not going back to El Paso."

As they got in the black Chevrolet, they watched as a car pulled over on the far side of the road, where the wreckage of the semi's cargo was completely blocking the roadway. A man and a woman jumped from the vehicle and began running toward the overturned semi. The woman lifted a cell phone from her purse and pressed it to her ear.

Nick slammed on the gas and sped past the couple, but neither seemed to notice. A few minutes later, once they had put several miles between them and the wreck, Tito opened the wallet he'd stolen and began going through it. "We got all kinds of good stuff," he said with pride. "Credit cards, cash, driver's license." He studied Nick. "He looks a little like you. You could use his license if you needed to," he said with a grin.

After stuffing the license back in the wallet, Tito pulled out more cards. "The guy's a Mormon," Tito said with disgust as he waved another card at Nick. "This is some kind of Mormon ID card. It says TEMPLE RECOMMEND on it."

He continued to thumb through the contents of the wallet. Suddenly, his eyes grew wide. He'd only skimmed over the name on the license and temple recommend, but now he did a double take. "Nick!" he said in alarm. "You won't believe this."

"What?"

"That guy the cops want for my uncle's murder—the guy who wrote the story about me. They said his name was Dallas Dixon on the radio, right?"

Nick shrugged. "Yeah, so?"

"We just put him in our truck!" Tito exclaimed.

"So, what do we care?" Nick asked.

"We *don't* care, but we've got ourselves a little problem now. The cops are looking for him and this truck." Tito pounded his hands on the dash. "If they find us driving it, we're through."

"Relax. All we gotta do is get us some different wheels. That shouldn't be too hard."

Tito rolled his eyes and spoke emphatically as if talking to a three-year-old. "But when they find this truck, they'll know it belongs to Dixon. They just might put some pieces together when they start wondering who the guy without ID is that we left in our semi." He thought a moment and then concluded, "We gotta get rid of this truck where nobody will find it for a long time. And we gotta do it soon."

"Fine, but I say we keep driving for a while. There's no place to get rid of a truck out here in the middle of nowhere. The wreck will keep the cops busy for a while, especially when they find all that coke."

Tito was silent. Then he squinted and asked, "What happened, anyway? What made us wreck?"

"It felt like the left front tire blew," Nick explained. "I couldn't hold the truck on the road. I never had anything like that happen before."

Tito grunted. "You just better keep this truck moving. Unless we get some serious miles behind us, we're dead."

"Quit worrying, kid. I'll keep driving. If cops try to stop us, we'll just have to send a little friendly fire their way," Nick said, patting his side confidently.

Tito hunched against the passenger side of the truck, silently cursing their bad luck. He knew this might be the final straw, one that meant he'd have to start a new life somewhere other than El Paso. The cops were already hounding him, and sooner or later they might figure out what he'd done there. Then he'd be in worse trouble than he already was.

CHAPTER 7

"Careful there," Kyle said. The paramedic was working alongside several others, trying to get the truck driver out of the cab. "This guy's unconscious. He could have a fractured skull—we don't want to make it worse."

His colleague and the two officers who were helping nodded. It was another five minutes before they had the driver out of the cab of the semi, and once they laid him down, Kyle bent over to examine the man. His brow crinkled as he studied him and glanced back into the cab of the truck. "This is strange," he said slowly.

"What is?" his partner, Mason, asked.

"You see the blood in that truck? Well, this guy hasn't got a single cut on him. The only injury that I can see is a nasty knot on his head."

"Do you think someone else was in there with him and got out and took off?"

Kyle nodded. "That's the only explanation I can think of." He gestured toward the officers. "We need to let them know what we found. The other guy could have been the driver. They might want to take some blood to check DNA," he suggested.

While Mason continued to care for the unconscious man in the back of the ambulance, Kyle walked back to the truck and approached Sergeant Trey Thain.

"What's up, Kyle?" Trey asked.

"We just wanted to let you know that it looks like the guy we found in the truck might not have been the only one in it," Kyle said.

"Why do you say that?" the sergeant asked, looking concerned.

Kyle explained, and Sergeant Thain nodded and said, "We'll be sure to follow up on that—thanks for the information. By the way, before you guys leave for the hospital, make sure you get us the guy's wallet so we can ID him."

Kyle shook his head. "Unfortunately we can't. There's no ID on him, no wallet or anything."

Sergeant Thain looked a bit surprised, but he nodded. "We'll check inside the truck. There's got to be something in there. They don't let people drive expensive rigs like this without all kinds of ID—logbook, driver's license, credit cards. We'll let the hospital know as soon as we figure out who he is."

"Thanks." Kyle moved to walk away, but he turned back when he heard another officer shout at the sergeant, his tone urgent. "Trey, you won't believe what's in the trunks of these new cars."

Sergeant Thain raised his head from the notes he'd been making. "What is it?"

"If it isn't cocaine, then I miss my guess," Officer Dick Bentley said in a much softer voice as he reached Trey.

The sergeant's expression hardened. "Are you sure?"

"No, I can't be sure until we test it," Officer Bentley said. "But I'd bet on it."

"Get the public away from the wreckage," Sergeant Thain barked. "This just became a major crime scene. I'm going to call for more officers."

"Yes, sir," the officer said and turned back to the wreckage.

Sergeant Thain turned to Kyle, "You heard that, I suppose?"

Without waiting for Kyle to respond, he continued. "I think we might have just found out why someone skipped out of here. Don't let this guy out of your sight, whatever you do—he's got some questions to answer. I'll have an officer meet you at the hospital."

* * *

Dallas struggled to open his eyes, squinting against the pounding in his head. It took a few moments before he realized he was in a hospital. He tentatively moved his arms and legs and then slowly sat up, trying to assess the extent of his injuries. Other than a bad headache and a lump that he discovered on the back of his head, he seemed to be okay.

After a few minutes, his head began to clear, and as it did he remembered the truck wreck. His pulse jumped as he recalled looking in the truck cab to see if the driver was all right and then being shoved forward. It was there that his memory ended.

He gingerly touched the back of his head, feeling both confused and angry. Whoever the man in the wrecked truck was, he had clobbered Dallas and left him there. But the anger faded to fear as he remembered why he had been out on the road in the first place. He had to get out of the hospital. He slowly got to his feet, steadied himself for a moment, and then crossed the room. As expected, he found his clothes in a small locker there.

Alert now, and finally in full control of his senses, he dressed quickly and prepared to leave before a nurse or doctor came back in. It wasn't until he was ready to walk out the door that he realized his wallet and phone were gone. Alarmed, he checked the locker again. They weren't there. A sinking feeling weighed down his chest. Could the men from the wrecked semi have taken his things? It seemed only too likely. *And what about my truck?*

Dallas had to fight off the urge to panic. But another thought amplified his worry. Maybe the cops had his wallet. If so, they would know who he was, and that would be a disaster. He stood for another moment, unsure what to do. Then he made a decision. Wallet or not, he was leaving this hospital.

Much to his dismay, as he stepped into the hallway, a police officer stood from where he sat in a chair beside the door and took hold of his arm. "You aren't going anywhere, buddy," he said gruffly. "The doctors haven't released you."

Dallas thought quickly. "Really, I'm fine. It's just a bump on the head. There's no reason for you to keep me here any longer," he said, trying to keep his voice even but fearing the worst. *I'm about to face a murder charge,* he thought with a sense of disbelief.

When the officer moved to escort him back into his room, Dallas held up his hands and played his last card. "Look, unless I'm under arrest for something, I think you have to let me go. And since I haven't done anything wrong, I'm pretty sure that's the case." The last part was true, but he knew he could very well be under arrest, despite his innocence.

"You're not—yet," the officer said.

"What?" Dallas asked, trying to appear puzzled. He glanced down at the officer's name tag. It read Taggert, and his badge identified him as an officer with the Fort Stockton Police Department.

"I'll let the state troopers discuss the matter with you," Officer Taggert said. "They're the ones who asked me to hold you here. But for now, you'll need to go back in your room."

Dallas knew resistance would only make matters worse, even though he had no doubt he could easily overpower Officer Taggert, so he grudgingly returned to his room. After the officer shut the door, Dallas stepped next to it and listened carefully. As he had expected, the officer quickly got on his radio. "This is Sam Taggert. Your John Doe drug carrier is awake," he said. "And he's anxious to get outta here."

Dallas stepped back to his bed and sat down, more confused than ever. Apparently the cops didn't know who he was—which meant they didn't have his wallet or his phone. That was a good thing. But for some reason they were accusing him of being a drug carrier. He groaned inwardly as he realized what must have happened. Whoever had been driving that semi must have had drugs hidden in it somewhere. They'd knocked him out, stolen his wallet and truck, and left him to take the heat while they got away in his pickup.

So far their plan had worked out pretty well. The only way out of this mess now would be to talk his way out of it. If he could just get out of this hospital, he knew he'd be okay for at least another few days. He'd learned a lot about the value of always being prepared while he was in Iraq, and so he carried a hundred-dollar bill and an emergency credit card in his shoe. Actually, he had one in each of his three pairs of shoes, but two of those pairs were in his stolen truck. Fortunately the third was now on his feet. He leaned down to check his right shoe just to make sure. The money and card were right where he'd put them. *At least one thing has gone right today,* he thought with a grim smile.

A few minutes later, two officers entered the room. After his encounter with the officer guarding him, Dallas expected them to be gruff, even menacing, but they seemed pleasant enough. The first officer to enter the room, a tall man with short brown hair and a thin, smiling face wore sergeant stripes on his sleeves. "Feeling better?" he asked Dallas.

"Yeah, I think I'm just fine," Dallas said warily.

"Nasty knot on your head," the second officer, a short man with a shaved head said.

"Yeah, that guy must have whacked me pretty hard," Dallas agreed.

"I'm Sergeant Trey Thain," the first officer said without acknowledging Dallas's statement. He pointed to the other man. "This is Trooper Dick Bentley. We're investigating your accident."

Dallas shook his head emphatically, causing a minor burst of pain. "I wasn't in an accident. I was assaulted and robbed when I tried to help two men who wrecked a semi," he said.

Sergeant Thain pulled a notebook from his back pocket. "Please, go on."

Dallas quickly explained what had happened when he had stopped to help the men in the semi.

"So the guys took your truck and left?" Trooper Bentley asked when Dallas had finished telling them what he remembered.

"I guess. I parked it within just a few feet of the wreck. And since you say it wasn't there, I can only imagine they stole it," he said. Not wanting them to know that he had overheard the officer's comment about drugs, he added, "Maybe they were worried about what their boss would say when he learned that they'd wrecked a bunch of new cars."

The officers glanced at each other. Then Sergeant Thain looked down at his notes. "We'll need a description of your pickup, and I don't believe you've told us your name yet. We can get the information out on the air to help get your belongings back."

"That would be great," Dallas said slowly, his mind spinning. He had no desire to lie to the police, but he knew that if he gave his real name he'd be hauled away then and there. Dallas Dixon was a wanted man, and if he was taken into custody he knew he would lose his only chance to prove his innocence. "My name is Drew Darlington," he said with a small twinge of guilt, keeping his initials but using the name of a soldier he'd known once in basic training. "I'm from California. I was on my way to New Orleans."

Sergeant Thain was busy writing the information down in his notebook "Would you describe the truck?"

As much as he wanted his truck back, there was no way he could give them an accurate description of that either. So he fabricated a description and make.

"License plate number?" Trey asked.

"I was afraid you'd ask that," Dallas said truthfully. "I've never memorized it."

Officer Bentley shook his head. "I couldn't tell you mine, either, come to think of it," he mumbled.

"It would also help if you could describe the two men who mugged you," Sergeant Thain suggested.

He described the man then said, "I'm afraid I can't tell you much about the other guy. The only thing I can remember is that as I leaned down into the cab I saw that he had brown hair."

The sergeant wrote the information down, and Dallas held his breath, knowing that the next few minutes could determine whether he would be a free man or whether he would remain in the company of police for a long time to come.

CHAPTER 8

TITO CHUCKLED AS HE AND Nick climbed back into the small blue Jeep they had hot-wired an hour ago. Once they had secured their new getaway vehicle, Tito had followed Nick into the desert south of Fort Stockton, where they had run Dallas's truck over the edge of a small ravine. They were certain it would be a long time before the truck was found in the remote area.

"I think we just sealed the deal," Tito said, brushing his hands together. "All we gotta do now is call Luisa and tell her the semi was stolen, and we'll be in the clear and Dixon will take the fall."

"Careful, Tito," Nick said, glancing sideways at him. "Luisa's smart—she'll wonder how one guy got the drop on both of us." He looked into the rearview mirror and then added, "She might be your aunt, but that don't mean she'll take kindly to being lied to. Remember that guy, Jaime, who pulled that stunt a couple years ago, taking more than his cut of the deal?"

Tito shuddered and was silent for a moment.

"That's right," Nick said and grunted. "Where he's at, he don't get no deals no more."

"So what do we do?" Tito asked, his good humor slowly melting to dread. He picked up the stolen wallet and began absently riffling through it as he tried to think. Suddenly, he stopped as his fingers rested on a business card for the *Chronicle*.

"I think I just got an idea," he said, grinning once more as he picked up the cell phone.

* * *

Heather didn't like the way Elliott was grinning as he swung into her cubicle just as she was preparing to leave for the night. He plunked himself down on the edge of her desk and announced, "I can't believe how dumb Dixon is. He's sunk."

"What do you mean?" Heather asked tiredly and began to pack up her briefcase. "Like I keep saying—there's no proof he had anything to do with Andy's murder."

"Oh, they'll get the proof. Rigo is a smart cop. But in the meantime—are you ready for this?—he's in custody for hauling a truckload of cocaine on Interstate 10." Elliott was as excited as Heather had ever seen him. She winced at the look on his face. *Does he really hate Dallas that much?* she wondered.

"What are you talking about?" she asked with a touch of anger.

"A story about a truck wreck on I-10 just a few miles west of Fort Stockton came across the wires a little while ago. The semi was hauling new cars. And get this, Heather. The trunk of every one of those new cars was filled with cocaine—millions of dollars' worth!"

"And what in the world does that have to do with Dallas?" she asked, growing increasingly impatient as she looked toward the door.

"Here's what. Dallas was driving the truck!" Elliott exclaimed.

"There must be some mistake . . ." She faltered, suddenly feeling faint.

"Oh, there's no mistake," Elliott countered. "They found him unconscious in the cab—he didn't have any ID on him. They took him to a nearby hospital. That's where he's at now."

Heather narrowed her eyes, suddenly suspicious. "If he didn't have ID and he was unconscious, how do they know it was Dallas?" she asked.

"They don't, but they will shortly," he said matter-of-factly. "Gordon is calling the Texas Highway Patrol as we speak."

"How in the world would *Gordon* know that the unconscious guy was Dallas?" she asked and pulled her briefcase onto her shoulder.

"He just got a call from someone who tipped him off— someone who said that Dallas was driving the truck."

Her brow creased. "Who?"

"It was an anonymous call, but that's beside the point. All they have to do now is fingerprint the guy, and they'll confirm it's him."

The story was sounding more far-fetched by the moment. "Elliott, what would Dallas be doing in a semi? Where's his truck and all of his stuff? It doesn't add up, and you know it."

"Maybe not right now, but I think it'll all come together soon," Elliott said confidently as he turned away. "And when it does, I'm assigning you to cover the story. After all, you're now officially one of the crime reporters for the *Chronicle*. I'll still help you guys out now and then of course, but my new responsibilities will keep me pretty busy."

A moment later, Heather could hear Elliott spreading the supposed news to another reporter. She gritted her teeth as she heard the smugness in his voice. *Unbelievable,* she thought with disgust. But what upset her even more was that he had planted the tiniest shred of doubt in her mind. Shaking her head, she tried to get Elliott's voice out of her head. In that moment, she determined that since nobody else seemed to be doing so, she would find evidence of Dallas's innocence. She grabbed her purse, adjusted her briefcase, squared her shoulders, and headed for the door.

* * *

"Sergeant Thain, I think we just made a big mistake," Officer Bentley said in a low voice as he hung up the phone.

"What's wrong?" Sergeant Thain asked in concern.

Officer Bentley shook his head. "An anonymous tip was just called in saying that our guy was in fact the truck driver."

"What?" Sergeant Thain thundered. "The physician who examined him told us he was certain that the guy's injuries weren't consistent with those he would have sustained in the wreck." The breath whooshed between his pressed lips in a whistle. "That was the only reason we let him go." He ran his hands through his hair, debating what to do now. "He just left a few minutes ago; he's probably still around."

Officer Bentley shook his head. "I have a feeling he's not. The caller had another tip. He said our 'Drew Darlington' is actually Dallas Dixon—who is wanted for questioning in the murder of that newspaper editor in El Paso. That was the lieutenant on the phone just now. He said that the new managing editor of the *Chronicle* got an anonymous phone call telling him that the driver of the semi that wrecked while hauling cocaine was Dallas Dixon. The lieutenant had already checked and found out that Dixon used to drive big rigs. He's even still licensed for it."

The sergeant still shook his head. "But it doesn't make sense. You and I were at the scene, and so were the paramedics. Somebody bled in that truck, and it wasn't the guy we had in custody."

"I don't get it either, but the lieutenant wants us to find him."

"And we will. We've at least got his fingerprints, so we'll have someone start checking them just to confirm he's who they say he is. In the meantime we'll dispatch some officers to start combing the area. He can't be far. He doesn't have any ID, money, or transportation. We'll find him."

* * *

"Thanks for the lift," Dallas said to the driver of a compact Chevy pickup as he settled into the seat.

"No problem. How far are you going?" the driver, a short man with a few strands of gray hair atop his balding head asked.

"San Antonio," Dallas answered. If he could get that far, he'd at least have a place to stay until he figured things out. He was sure Michael would help him.

"I'm headed just north of Junction. I'll be leaving the freeway there, but you can ride with me at least that far," the man offered.

"I appreciate it," Dallas said. "My car was stolen and I really need to get to San Antonio."

"Wish I could do more for you," the man said amiably. He hadn't asked Dallas for his name, nor had Dallas volunteered it. He felt guilty for leaving the hospital under less-than-honest circumstances, but he couldn't bring himself to be taken into custody for a crime he hadn't committed. He promised himself that he would do everything possible to put the pieces of this puzzle together, and then he'd let the police take it from there.

* * *

Sitting on a carved wooden bench beneath a large oak tree, Mason Huggins casually thumbed through a newspaper a client had given him a few minutes earlier. He'd just finished skinning and quartering a wild hog and didn't have anything to do until one of the hunters shot another one. Mason had been working at this hunting ranch southeast of San Antonio for several years, ever since he'd gotten too old to keep racing cars. His job was to skin, cut up, and freeze the wild game that was killed by those who had paid for the privilege of hunting on the ranch. He didn't mind the work, and the ranch provided him with a trailer to live in. He made enough money to buy whatever he needed, which wasn't much.

As he spat a stream of tobacco out of the corner of his mouth, Mason turned the page. A headline caught his attention. It was the name *Dixon* that stood out to him as if it were highlighted. He closed his eyes as the face of the girl he'd once loved came automatically to his mind. *Jeanne.* As it always did, a blanket of shame enveloped him as he thought of her. He'd bolted when she'd told him she was pregnant, but he'd never been able to forget her.

He let go of the paper with one hand and rubbed his thick head of greasy brown hair. Somewhere out there he had a child, a son. And even though he'd walked away—run, rather—from the prospect of fatherhood all those years ago, he hadn't stepped off the face of the earth. When he realized that Jeanne's son had become a newspaperman, he had gotten in the habit of watching the newspapers from southwestern Texas. However, he hadn't ever seen the name *Dixon* in a headline before.

As he frowned and glanced back to read the rest of the headline, a stiff gust of wind suddenly tore the paper from his hands—but not before the word *murder* jumped out at him. The paper ripped in two, and Mason scrambled after it as the wind scattered it in several directions.

He grabbed several pages and searched frantically through them, but the one with the headline he'd been reading wasn't there. The wind gusted again, and a few feet away he watched several ripped pages fly high into the air and blow to the east and out of sight. He gathered up the rest of the paper as the wind died away then returned to the bench beneath the large oak to search methodically through what was left of the newspaper.

The article that had caught his eye was gone. A rifle fired in the direction the paper had flown, and he forced himself to stay where he was, remembering that there was a party of four hunters out there. Going after the rest of the paper would be harebrained.

Mason sighed in frustration, thinking of his lost love and the son he never knew and wondering what kind of trouble that son could possibly have gotten into.

* * *

Martha rang the bell to Kate's house and waited for her to answer. Her emotions threatened to overwhelm her as she glanced at the familiar setting. Her brother had lived here. Her brother was dead.

When Kate answered the door, Martha looked at her red-rimmed, haunted eyes and without a word gathered her sister-in-law into her arms. The two stood in silence for a moment.

"Kate, we need to talk," Martha said after a moment.

Kate slowly nodded and led Martha into the kitchen, where the two women sat down at the table.

"I've been pacing back and forth in my living room, deciding whether to come over here or not, and in the end I decided I owed it to both of us," Martha began, focusing her attention on the edge of the lace tablecloth. "You know that Frankie and Andy never got along." When Kate nodded, she continued. "I never knew how much Frankie disliked him until today. He started saying the most awful things, lies about Andy . . ."

As Martha looked up, the expression on Kate's face stopped her midsentence.

"Kate? What's wrong?" Martha asked after a moment of silence.

"Maybe they weren't lies," Kate finally said, looking away.

"He talked about an accident . . ." Martha trailed off as Kate began to nod.

"It's true," Kate replied as the tears gathered in her eyes. And then the pieces of the puzzle began to unfold.

After the women had talked for more than an hour, Martha wiped her eyes and placed a trembling hand on Kate's shoulder. "We have to go to the police."

Kate's eyes widened and she stood up with a start. "Martha, no," she said frantically then began to sob once more. "All I have left of my husband is his memory. I'm barely hanging on as it is with all this press. If they knew what we know . . ." She shuddered. "That poor girl's family . . . I was so angry at Andy when he told me he'd kept it all a secret to keep himself out of trouble . . . but now . . ." Tears spilled down her cheeks. "It won't bring her back to drag his name through the mud." She fixed Martha with a pleading gaze. "We can't tell the police the whole story . . . not yet."

At Martha's skeptical expression, she shook her head emphatically. "I promise you, Martha, we'll tell them soon. I swear it. The girl's family deserves to know what happened. Just please, not yet."

Martha nodded slowly, her eyes red and puffy. "We have to do something, Kate." She paused then said, "I think I know someone who can help."

CHAPTER 9

Dallas hadn't slept well during the night, but at least there had been no nightmares, and he felt better than he had when he'd crawled into bed the night before. The driver of the little truck had dropped him off in the small town of Junction where he had rented a room for the night using cash he'd obtained from a nearby ATM. He'd registered for the room under an assumed name and stayed inside, watching TV until sleep came, trying to learn what he could from the news.

What he'd seen and heard worried him. The police were actively looking for him. He was now wanted for questioning regarding both the semi wreck and Andy's murder. Someone had made an anonymous phone call to Gordon Townsend—who was now apparently the managing editor of the paper—stating that Dallas had in fact been the truck driver. Dallas was certain the call had been made by the men who had stolen his wallet and his truck and left him unconscious. It couldn't have been anyone else.

Dallas's life was hardly recognizable to him. He was a fugitive, subject to arrest if a cop saw him. By the time he had showered and dressed in his clothes from the day before, Dallas had decided that a few phone calls were in order. He determined to make his calls and then get on his way, knowing that his location could eventually be traced with the credit card he'd used the night before once the police figured out that he had one.

The first call he made was to Michael Nugent at his paper in San Antonio. When Michael came on the line, his voice was urgent. "Dallas, what the heck's going on?" he asked.

"I wish I knew," Dallas said miserably then went on to explain what had happened since they'd last talked.

After he'd finished, Michael was silent for a long stretch. Finally, he said, "I'm afraid I can't help you much, Dallas. Your picture and story are all over the papers. What you need is a good lawyer and a top-notch private investigator."

"Neither of which I can afford—especially since my money, what little I have, is going to be hard to get to without some ID," Dallas lamented.

"I wish I could help, I really do," Michael said, and Dallas knew he meant it. "I know you didn't have anything to do with those crimes, but the police seem to think otherwise."

"Thanks, Michael," Dallas said, then mumbled a good-bye and hung up.

Once more he dialed. Having lost his cell phone, he had also lost his list of phone numbers. So he dialed a number he had memorized and hoped he didn't come to regret it.

* * *

The phone on Heather's desk rang, startling her from her thoughts. She debated letting the machine get it. She'd been swamped since coming in to the office a little before seven that morning. Elliott was pushing her to get an update written on the progress the police were making in Andy's murder, and she didn't have time for another call right now. But with a sigh, she picked up the receiver.

"Heather . . . it's me. Please don't hang up."

Momentarily caught off guard, she didn't respond right away to the familiar, deep voice, so he went on. "I'm sorry to call you at the office, but my cell phone was stolen, and I can't remember your cell number."

Heather inhaled quickly. She spoke softly so no one would overhear her. "Are you okay?" she asked.

"Physically, I'm fine. But otherwise . . ."

"I'm so sorry, Dallas. If it makes a difference, I believe you're innocent." Heather bit her lip. *Well, I do,* she thought, shaking her head. *Elliott's just getting into my head.*

"Thanks, Heather. That means more than you can possibly realize. Look, I'm sorry to put you in this position, but I didn't know who else I could trust. Soon I'm going to hire an attorney and turn myself in, but before I do that, I need to put a few of the pieces of this puzzle together myself. I feel like this is all a bad dream." He sighed heavily. "I have no alibi, the police think I have a motive for Andy's murder, and I had the rotten luck to be on the freeway at the same time as that semi."

Heather's heart tugged at the forlorn tone of his voice. "Write down this phone number," she said quickly. "Then call me in an hour or so, around eleven. I'll be leaving the office for a while then. I don't want Elliott to overhear me talking to you—and believe me, he's keeping a close eye on me, the snake." She then whispered the number and quietly replaced her receiver.

A few moments later, Heather's cell phone rang. Knowing it might be Dallas, she glanced up surreptitiously before answering, only to see Elliott leaning over an adjacent cubicle, staring at her. She felt a momentary panic as she dug her phone from her purse and opened it.

She repressed a sigh of relief when she saw that the caller was not Dallas but Martha Maggio. She waved a shooing hand at Elliott and answered the call, hopeful that Martha was ready to tell her more about what she'd brought up earlier.

"We need to talk," Martha said without a greeting.

"Hi, Martha," Heather said evenly, trying not to sound too anxious. "What's going on?"

Martha inhaled loudly then said in a barely audible voice, "I think we—Kate and I—know who killed Andy. We want to—" Before she could say more, her voice caught.

Heather's pulse raced, but she forced her voice to sound calm. "I'm glad you called. Can I meet you somewhere?" she asked. She thought about the three Maggio family members Martha had mentioned earlier—her husband, son, and sister-in-law.

"Could you meet us at Andy's house?" Martha finally managed to ask.

"Um, sure," Heather said, taken by surprise "Will both you and Kate be there?"

"Yes, we're here now," Martha confirmed.

Wanting to ask more questions but deciding it was best to just get there, Heather said, "All right, I'll be there in twenty minutes."

"Thank you," Martha said quietly, and the line went dead.

As Heather left the office a few minutes later, her phone began to ring again. She stepped outside before she pulled it from her purse. This time it was Dallas calling.

"I can't talk long, Dallas. I'm on my way to Andy's house. His sister wants to meet me there. I think she might have some information that will be helpful to you." She glanced around as she got in her car. "I'll let you know what I learn as soon as I can."

"Heather, I don't know if that's a good idea," Dallas said, sounding uncertain. "What if she's involved in this somehow?"

"I'm pretty sure Martha's harmless," Heather said. "But her family might be another story. I promise I'll be careful, and I'll call as soon as I can."

* * *

When Heather pulled up in front of Andy's house, she saw Martha standing in the doorway. Behind her stood another woman, who Heather recognized as Kate, Andy's wife. Heather felt a pang of sadness as she thought of her terrible loss.

Not bothering with small talk, Martha led Heather to the living room, with Kate following behind. Heather was bursting with questions, in particular why Martha had called her instead of the police, but she kept silent, waiting for one of the women to speak first. As she sat on the sofa, Martha looked directly at her, determination instead of fear now humming through her voice. "Thank you for coming, Heather." She paused then said, "I'm not sure who we can trust right now, but we're taking a chance on you. Maybe I'll come to regret it, but when you were here earlier I got the feeling you were a woman of your word."

"Thank you," Heather said, surprised. She hesitated before adding, "You do know, however, that I may have to tell the police what you tell me, right?" she asked.

Martha glanced at Kate, who at first appeared stricken then nodded slightly. Martha continued. "We understand that—which is why we've decided to leave certain matters . . . well, undisclosed for the time being."

Heather raised an eyebrow but nodded, and Martha went on. "What I'm about to tell you pains me a great deal." For the first time since Heather had arrived, Martha's voice broke.

Kate placed a hand on Martha's arm but remained silent, looking at the floor.

"Your friend Dallas is innocent," Martha finally said firmly.

Relief washed through Heather, and she waited anxiously for Martha to continue. "Please, go on," she said.

"I called Kate after I had spoken with you, and we put some pieces together." Martha's voice broke again, and she began to cry. "Frankie *was* holding something over Andy's head. Andy felt terrible about it, but he thought Kate would leave him if she knew . . . and that I would hate him."

Wanting to press for more information but knowing that doing so might cause Martha to rethink her decision to share any information with her, Heather held her tongue.

Just then, the front door of the Norton home burst open and a short, angry-looking man with black hair and an olive complexion stormed into the room. "What are you doing in this house, Martha?" he demanded as he parked himself in front of her, waving a finger in her face.

Heather knew then who the intruder was—Frankie Maggio. He looked to be about fifty years old, and despite the fact that he was short and a bit pudgy, Heather found him intimidating. His face was dark with anger, and his fists were clenched; he hadn't even seemed to notice Heather.

Martha's expression was calm and determined. Kate Norton, on the other hand, got up from the sofa where she had been sitting beside Martha and quickly backed away, fear masking her features. Frankie continued glowering at his wife, clearly expecting her to get up and leave the house.

Heather rose to her feet, and Martha followed suit, stepping away from the sofa. She remained where she stood, however, when Frankie advanced toward her. "I was in the middle of a conversation with my sister-in-law," she said. "Please leave now, Frankie."

Her words emboldened Kate, who took a step forward. "Martha will be on her way home shortly," she said.

Frankie shifted his malicious gaze from his wife to Kate. "You didn't know your husband as well as you thought you did," he said darkly.

Kate looked torn between crying and lunging at Frankie, but Martha stepped toward him. "You can stop being cryptic, Frankie. Kate knows everything. And so do I."

Frankie looked shocked. "You're lying."

"No, Frankie, she's not," Kate said. "What Andy did was terrible, but what you did was just as wrong."

Frankie's face again began to twist in anger. "You little . . ."

"Get out, Frankie," Kate said fiercely. "If it wasn't for you he'd still be alive!"

Frankie leaped toward her and shoved her against the wall. Heather gasped as Martha went after him like a mother hen. He let go of Kate and threw Martha onto the sofa. Instinctively, Heather stepped between him and the women he'd attacked. His fist shot out and caught her in the left eye. She saw flashes of light and stumbled back. Distantly, she heard Martha scream at him. "Get out, Frankie! I'll call the police!"

"Who are you?" Frankie demanded, grabbing Heather's shirt sleeve as she pressed a hand over her injured eye.

She jerked her arm away and saw his eyes drift to the notebook she held, which had the *Chronicle*'s logo stamped on the front.

"You a reporter?" he demanded. "What have you been telling her?" he roared, turning back to his wife.

"The truth."

Frankie's rage boiled over again. Heather tried to duck his fist, but he struck her again, splitting her lip and causing blood to pour from her nose. She cried out and tried to back away, but he was relentless, hitting her once more in the eye he'd already hurt. She flew backward, and as she crashed down she felt her head strike something hard. Pain throbbed through her body and head, and the room spun. She was aware of the women screaming in the background and wondered in a haze if Frankie would kill them all here and now. In desperation, she tried to get up, but she only got as far as her knees when Frankie kicked her in the ribs. Pain shot through her in paralyzing waves, and a moment later, she slipped into blissful unconsciousness.

CHAPTER 10

WHEN HEATHER AWOKE, SHE SQUINTED, willing her vision to clear. Through the haze, she could see a figure leaning over her, and she lashed out, knowing she didn't stand a chance against Frankie but determined not to go down without a fight.

"Hold it, lady! You're okay now."

As the scene in front of her came into focus, Heather saw not Frankie, but a familiar man leaning over her; after a moment she recognized him as Lieutenant Rigo Garcia. A little sob rose in her throat, and she slumped back, relief flooding through her.

"What happened? Where are Martha and Kate?" she asked as she tried to sit up.

Rigo placed a gentle hand on her shoulder to keep her from getting up. "Martha and Kate are fine, but I need you to lie still for me. You have a very black eye, a cut lip, a bloody nose, some very bruised ribs, and a lump on the back of your head—likely a concussion."

"I'm so sorry, Heather," Martha whispered as she came to kneel by Heather's side and put a cold cloth on her face. Her expression was filled with pain and shame.

"Are you and Kate really okay?" Heather asked, glancing between the two women.

"We're fine. Thanks to you," Martha looked tormented. "Frankie has always been hotheaded, but I had no idea he was capable—" Her voice broke, and she stopped.

"It wasn't your fault," Heather said and winced against the pain in her head. "What happened? What made him leave?" she asked.

"Luckily, I was only a short distance away when Martha called 911," Rigo said. "Frankie tried to get away when we rolled up, but he's safely under arrest and waiting outside to be taken to the station." He smiled grimly. "These two women told me what you did—it was pretty brave of you to stand up to him like that." He sighed. "I'm sorry I couldn't get here sooner—an ambulance is on its way for you now."

"What? I don't think I need an ambulance." Heather gingerly reached up to touch her face.

"I'd still like to have the paramedics check you out, especially if you've got a concussion."

Heather looked at Martha, torn between wanting to hear the information she had come for and wanting to respect Martha's wishes not to involve the police yet.

Martha met her gaze then took a deep breath and looked up at Rigo. Heather breathed a sigh of relief as Martha said, "Lieutenant Garcia, the reason I asked Heather here in the first place was to give her information about my brother's murder." She fiddled nervously with the edge of her blouse.

His head jerked up. "What information? And why would you call a reporter instead of the police?" he asked, his eyes narrowing.

Her eyes dropped to the floor. "It was a mistake . . ." she whispered, her gaze shifting back to Heather's injuries. "I couldn't bring myself to go to the police yet. Tito's so young . . ."

"Tito?" Rigo asked.

"Her son," Heather filled in, looking at Martha closely. "Do you think . . . Tito had something to do with Andy's murder?"

Martha's nod was barely perceptible. Kate took a step closer to stand by her side and placed an arm around her shoulders.

A siren's wail sounded in the distance, growing steadily louder, filling the brief silence that had descended on the room. Rigo looked from Heather to Martha. As he opened his mouth to speak, he was interrupted by a loud ringing sound coming from Heather's purse.

Realizing Martha must have turned her phone on to call the police, Heather quickly reached out to silence it. As she pressed the button, she noticed the *Chronicle*'s number displayed on the screen.

Grimacing apologetically, Heather answered.

"Where in the world are you, Heather?" a familiar, unwelcome voice demanded.

"I can't talk now, Elliott. But I'm okay, and I'll explain everything later," she said quickly.

"Do I hear sirens?" he asked, ignoring her comment.

"Yes," she said in exasperation. "But like I said, I really can't talk right now—"

"You'll talk to me now," he interrupted. "Gordon and I need to meet with you, ASAP."

"Elliott, I'm on a story," she said, omitting the detail that she was directly involved in this story and hoping the line would get her off the phone.

"Not anymore, you're not. Sorry, Heather, but you're off the crime beat," he said. "I'll send someone to take over. Gordon and I have been talking. We've decided Andy put you in a position you can't handle."

"What?" she exploded, torn between wanting to hang up and hearing what else Martha had to say before the paramedics arrived and wanting to give Elliott an earful.

"For starters, you're supposed to be reporting, not playing 'wild-goose chase' on the paper's time. Now get back in here. Gordon says if you don't, you'll be out of a job just like Dallas," he said.

At that moment the door opened and two paramedics entered. Rigo reached for the phone. "Let me take that for you," he offered.

Rigo signaled for the paramedics to begin examining Heather and then put the phone to his ear. "Elliott, it's Rigo. Miss Scott can't come to your office right now. She's been injured. The ambulance just arrived, and she'll be taken to the hospital momentarily."

Rigo listened for a moment then said, "I'm not releasing that information at this time. You'll have to talk to Heather later. And by the way, you've got one fine reporter in her. Watch her—you might learn something. Good-bye, Elliott."

Heather suppressed a groan as he clicked the phone shut. She suspected that she might be joining the ranks of the unemployed before the day was over, but found she didn't care. Another week of working with Elliott and she'd probably be turning in her notice anyway.

As the paramedics helped her onto a stretcher, Heather watched as Rigo took Martha by the arm and led her into the kitchen. Rigo looked back and nodded at her, and Heather tried not to feel too disappointed that she hadn't been able to hear more of what Martha had to say. She sighed, glad that at least Martha would be talking to the police.

The ambulance began to pull away, but as it did so, Heather heard a thumping sound on the side of the vehicle. After a moment, it stopped. A second later, one of the paramedics opened up the back doors and handed Heather her purse. "Might have missed this. Rigo ran it out," the man said with a smile.

Heather nodded gratefully as the vehicle began to move forward once more. She closed her eyes, mulling over the bits of information she had gotten out of this nightmare. *Tito.* Martha's son. *Wild-goose chase, my eye,* she thought, frowning slightly.

* * *

Rigo sat at his desk, idly flipping a pen over his fingers, lost in thought. He'd just returned from talking with Kate Norton and Martha Maggio, though he still found himself with more questions than answers. Both Martha and Kate had been rather tight-lipped, only reiterating that they suspected Martha's son, Tito Maggio, had been involved in Andy Norton's murder. Martha had indicated that she believed Frankie and Tito had been holding something over Andy's head, but she had refused to go into any further detail on the matter. Rigo was now attempting to make sense of it all with Detective CC Cornwell.

"Tito Maggio," CC mused. "We've certainly heard that name more than once around here, haven't we?"

Rigo looked up and nodded. "Yeah. But murder? Tito's never struck me as violent—just a punk under a lot of bad influences. You heard what his father just did, and his aunt's been on our radar for years."

"That car theft ring he just got busted for wasn't small beans," CC countered.

"I know. I just can't see the kid murdering his own uncle. What's the motive?"

"It doesn't take much with that type. You heard the report from the station. Tito and his uncle came pretty close to blows in the parking lot, and the guys said the conversation sounded pretty heated."

"I just think we should keep our minds open to all possibilities."

CC nodded. "On that note, let's talk about Dallas Dixon."

"Have you finished that report on his activities in the last few years?"

"Pretty much. Dallas was an Army Ranger in Iraq, then he worked as a truck driver before enrolling in school." He gave

Rigo a meaningful look. "Not just anybody knows how to drive a big rig, you know. Plus that tip we got about him being the driver . . ."

"Even if Dixon *was* the driver of that semi, it doesn't mean he murdered somebody," Rigo said, picking the pen back up from his desk and scribbling on a notepad in front of him.

"Maybe not, but it doesn't help his case any. Anyway, his bosses at the paper think he did it," CC argued.

"One of whom is Elliott Painter," Rigo said, rolling his eyes. "Elliott is a very good reporter—when he doesn't let his ego get the best of him. Right now he's definitely under the influence of his ego."

"Dixon did have a motive," CC reminded him. "Losing his job over what seemed like nothing could lead someone to murder."

"You've got a point," Rigo agreed and rubbed his chin thoughtfully. "But what about Frankie Maggio? Martha and Kate said he had been holding something over Andy's head. Maybe Frankie wanted to shut Andy up before he told his wife and sister what Frankie was up to."

"Maybe," CC said slowly and gave an exaggerated shudder. "That whole family gives me the creeps. Assaulting his own wife and his sister-in-law, not to mention that pretty reporter." CC smirked. "Good thing he's already in custody. What about his son, though? Has anybody tracked him down yet?"

"Nope. He's gone. His mother has no idea where he is, and even Frankie seemed genuinely worried about where he might be. We're trying to track down his whereabouts now."

CC stretched out his hands and cracked his knuckles. After a moment he said, "So is that all of them?"

"All of our suspects? I don't know," Rigo said thoughtfully. "I can't help but wonder if there's someone out there who would have somehow benefited from Norton's death."

CC shook his head. "Who knows? I'll bet he had a good life insurance policy. Maybe it was his own wife who killed him."

Rigo raised an eyebrow. "I guess that's a possibility . . . but my gut feeling tells me that's not the direction we need to go. Even so, let's run a check on Norton's finances and see if he had any large insurance policies on his life."

As CC nodded and stood to leave, Rigo raised a hand to stop him. "There is one more person I think we should investigate," he said. "When I asked Martha if she had any idea where Tito might be, she said she had no idea where he was—that she'd already checked the only place she could think of where he might be: his aunt's house."

CC nodded slowly. "Luisa Maggio."

"Exactly," Rigo answered. "Might be a coincidence, but maybe not. Anyway, it wouldn't hurt to check her out."

"Agreed," CC said briskly. "I'll get going."

CHAPTER 11

"GET A TAXI AND GO straight home and lie down," the nurse told Heather as she picked up her purse. The woman clucked her tongue. "I don't know how you talked them into releasing you so soon, but since you did, you be careful. With the pain medication they gave you, it won't be safe for you to drive until at least tomorrow."

Heather nodded obediently. It had been just over two hours since she had arrived at the hospital. Her cracked ribs had been taped and the cut above her lip from where a tooth had gone through had been stitched. When she'd been insistent about not wanting to be hospitalized, the doctors had reluctantly given her some pain medication and a prescription for more and allowed her to be discharged.

Walking toward the hospital entrance, Heather reached into her purse for her cell phone to call a taxi. She'd have to figure out what to do with her car, which was still at Kate Norton's house, later. She flipped open the phone and was momentarily surprised to see that it had been turned off. *Pacemakers,* she thought, realizing the paramedics must have turned the phone off.

The phone had only just powered on when a call came through.

"Heather, it's Rigo Garcia."

"Hi, Lieutenant," she began, more than a little surprised. "What can I do for you?"

"I'm glad you've got your phone turned back on. Listen, I know you don't have a vehicle, so I was wondering if you wanted me to send a couple officers to the hospital to pick you up and take you home since you insisted on being released."

"Really? That would be great," she said.

"They'll drop off your car afterward if you'll give them your keys." He cleared his throat. "Look . . . I know you're probably feeling pretty out of it right now, but I'd really like to talk to you, once you've had a chance to recuperate a little."

"I feel fine," Heather said firmly, ignoring the jolt of pain in her ribs. "I was hoping you might be willing to share some information with me as well."

"Fair enough," he agreed. "If you'll give me your address, I'll swing by in a couple of hours."

Heather gave Rigo her address and found a bench to wait on. A few minutes later another call came through.

"Heather! I'm so glad to hear your voice," Dallas said in a rush when she answered. "I started to get worried when I didn't hear from you after a couple hours. What did Martha and Kate have to say?"

"I didn't get to talk to them very long," Heather said. "Frankie, Martha's husband, showed up."

"What? What happened?" Dallas's voice took on an urgent tone.

Dallas didn't interrupt as Heather explained what had occurred at the Norton residence. When she was finished, the line was silent. "Dallas? Are you still there?" Heather asked.

"I'm so sorry," he said quietly. "And I'm sorry you had to be involved in this."

"It's not your fault, Dallas," Heather said gently. "I'm going to be fine, really. And Frankie is in custody, where he belongs."

She paused. "Listen, though, I did get a little information out of Martha before Frankie got there."

"What did she say?"

"She thinks that her son, Tito, killed Andy."

"She told you she thinks her own son killed his uncle? Does she have any proof of that?"

"Both Martha and Kate were pretty closed-mouthed about why they think so, but they seemed sure."

"From what I dug up in that article, I wouldn't put it past him. That kid is a piece of work."

"I gather that. If I were still on the crime beat, I'm sure I'd get pretty familiar with his name," Heather mumbled.

"If you were still on the crime beat? Don't tell me you got fired." He sounded angry.

"Not fired—not yet anyway. Elliott and Gordon decided Andy made a rash decision, and that's it. It's back to society stories for this girl." She looked up to see two uniformed officers approaching. "Hey, the officers are here to give me a ride, but please call me back in a little while, okay?" She suddenly felt a rush of loneliness, wishing he were here to talk to her in person. "It's good to hear your voice."

"You too. You have no idea . . . Please be careful, Heather. I'll talk to you later." And with that the line went silent.

* * *

Heather thanked the officer who had driven her home, then she walked up the drive to her house, pulling out her cell phone to see if she had missed any messages while it was turned off. She had a few messages, and wouldn't it be just her luck—the first message was from Elliott.

"Listen, Heather, I know I was pretty hard on you earlier. I hope you're okay, but you need to know that the decision still stands. Anyway, I was thinking that maybe we could meet tonight for dinner. My treat. Anywhere you want to go. Then we won't have to bother with a formal meeting tomorrow. Okay, call me. Bye!"

Heather shook her head. *That guy is unbelievable,* she thought as she opened her front door and skipped to the next message. *Good grief.* It was from Gordon.

"Heather, it's Gordon. Elliott told me what happened, but I don't want to hear any excuses about the meeting tomorrow. Be there."

As the clipped, angry voice cut out, Heather pulled the phone away from her ear, startled. "I guess that's what happens to you when Elliott is your assistant," she mumbled after a moment. However, the message was doubly puzzling. Elliott had said he'd like to have dinner instead of a meeting in the morning—why would he try to undercut Gordon?

She couldn't handle any more messages right now. So, leaving the others for later, she pulled an ice pack out of the freezer and stretched out on the sofa, trying to calm the pounding in her head, get her ribs in a reasonably comfortable position, and then attempt to untangle her jumbled thoughts.

* * *

Dallas's last conversation with Heather had been the clincher. He couldn't keep running—not when someone he cared about had been hurt on his account. And not when he knew that there was a possibility that if he'd just turned himself in and gotten a lawyer when he'd first heard the radio report, none of this would have happened.

Filled with determination, he dialed Michael Nugent's number.

"I can't talk now, Dallas. I'm on a story," Michael said cautiously when he answered after a few rings.

"I understand—and I know I'm asking a lot by calling you again," Dallas replied and hurried on. "But I want your help finding an attorney."

"I'm happy to hear that," Michael said, sounding relieved. "I've been worried about you. Hey, I'll be back in the office in about an hour. Let me see what I can do for you then."

"Thanks, Michael," Dallas said. "It means a lot that you're willing to help me out."

"I'm glad I can help—and glad you decided to get an attorney," Michael added. "Is there a number you can give me for where you're at? It might take me a little time to get in touch with somebody, but I'll call you as soon as I do."

After giving Michael the number printed on the phone on the nightstand and hanging up, Dallas got up and walked to the window. "I sure hope that was the right call," he murmured as he stared out at the street below. "Maybe I should just change my name to Huggins and start a new life," he added with a grim smile. "That name seems to go pretty well with disappearing."

It was easy to let his thoughts drift somewhere other than his current situation, and his mind turned to his father. Dallas was twelve by the time his mother finally told him Mason Huggins's name, and ever since then Dallas had tried to picture the man who had left before he was even born.

His mother had told him that they had met in a bar and that she'd fallen instantly in love with the dashing young man. She hadn't even known where he came from or met any of his family. She'd told him on several occasions that his father loved cars, that he was a good mechanic, and liked to drive fast. But she'd also said that being a father had frightened him, as he was a restless and carefree man, and so he'd left her to care for their unborn child on her own.

Dallas's mother had worked odd jobs to support herself and her son, but their life had been difficult, and she had often turned to drugs and alcohol to deal with the stress and loneliness of life as a single mother. When she was only thirty-four years old, her lifestyle caught up with her and she died from cirrhosis of the liver. And so, at age fourteen, Dallas went to live with his maternal grandparents. He was eternally grateful to them—not only for raising him and teaching him the value of work on their farm, but for allowing him to become friends with several LDS kids. Those kids had influenced his life in ways that had made him who he was. Because of their example, he had been taught the gospel and baptized, and eventually he'd served a mission. His grandparents, even though they were not members of the Church, had been religious people, and they had decided that he would be better off a Mormon than a druggie like his mother or a runaway dad like his father.

Dallas was pulled from his reverie as he looked up and noticed several figures standing on the street three floors below. One of them, a man with a dark complexion and hair combed straight back tight to his scalp, was pointing toward Dallas's hotel window. None of the three looked familiar, and Dallas took a small step backward as the man who had pointed began speaking into a cell phone. The other two men, who were both wearing tight-fitting black T-shirts and loose jeans, began walking toward the hotel.

A growing sense of alarm pounded through Dallas's veins as he looked back toward the first man, who was still staring in the direction of his window. These men obviously weren't police— they had the wrong look. It was time to get out of there. Peering out the doorway and seeing no one in the hallway, he slipped out and quickly ran down the stairway.

On an impulse, he stood behind the stairway door and watched through the crack for a moment. When the elevator door opened, the two men he'd seen walking toward the hotel, along with another man he hadn't seen, stepped off. The two men in black T-shirts, who appeared to be Hispanic, led the way. The other man, a Caucasian, followed. They walked directly to Dallas's room. One of the Hispanic men knocked, pulling a handgun from inside his belt and sliding it behind his back.

Dallas had seen enough. He rushed down the stairs, arriving at an area adjacent to the lobby. His heart thumping erratically, he peered through the doorway and froze. The man who had stayed outside was entering the lobby, his cell phone pressed to his ear. He was rapidly striding toward the stairway door.

Easing the door shut, Dallas took a deep breath and waited. His time in Baghdad had taught him to be alert to any possibility, any danger. He was alert now. As the door flew open and the man entered, Dallas's training in hand-to-hand combat took over. He grabbed the man by the sleeve and swung him around.

The man's mouth formed a surprised O as he registered what had just happened, but he quickly jerked away and reached inside his suit coat. Dallas automatically grabbed the man's wrist and gave it a violent snap. The gun clattered to the floor as Dallas felt the wrist break.

The man let loose a scream, and Dallas let go of his arm and hit him hard in the face, cutting the scream short and sending his attacker reeling backward. He slid to the ground with a dull thump and lay still. Breathing heavily as the adrenaline coursed through his veins, Dallas picked up the gun, shoved it in his pocket, and again cracked open the door, praying that the commotion hadn't been overheard.

To his relief, he saw no one in the lobby. Even the attendant that only moments before had been standing at the registration desk had disappeared. Dallas darted across the lobby and spun to his left and into a short hallway. At the end of the hallway he found a door that led outside and to the side of the hotel. Glancing around furtively and again seeing no one, he put his head down and quickly walked through the parking lot and continued for several blocks

As he walked, he looked for somewhere to hide. Once it got dark he could worry less about being seen and could probably catch a ride out of town, but until then he couldn't take the chance. He knew Michael would be calling him back at the hotel soon, but there was nothing he could do about that now. He'd gotten lucky getting out of there when he had—he might not have the same luck if he ran into those men a second time.

He finally settled down in a grove of trees where he could stay out of sight but still have a decent view of the street. After sitting on the ground for a few moments, he shifted to a kneeling position and bowed his head. As he prayed he felt the same peace he'd felt on many difficult and dangerous occasions in Iraq. He knew there had to be a way out of this mess, but he also knew he needed help—and a lot of it.

* * *

Michael sighed and hung up the phone. It was his third failed attempt to reach Dallas, and he was starting to get worried. He was sure Dallas had meant to stay where he was until he could talk to an attorney and get some legal advice. Michael shook his head and dialed again.

Lincoln Graves, a sixty-two-year-old African-American and highly respected defense attorney, answered on the first ring. When Michael explained that he had been unable to get back in touch with Dallas, Lincoln made a grumbling sound in the back of his throat and said, "You let me know as soon as you do get in touch with him. If I'm going to represent him, I'll need to talk to him soon." He thought a moment then added, "It would help get things moving if you could come to my office and fill me in on more details of Mr. Dixon's present circumstances." He paused. "You should know, though, that if I decide to take on the case, I'll need at least a small retainer from him to make my representation official."

"I'll be right over," Michael promised. "And I'll bring my checkbook. Hopefully I'll hear back from Dallas in the meantime. This isn't like him."

"I hope so too," Lincoln agreed. "How soon can you be here?"

"I'll be over in fifteen minutes."

Michael had seen Lincoln in court on several occasions, but he'd only actually spoken to the prestigious attorney three or four times. As he was ushered into Lincoln's plush office in a small office building near the edge of San Antonio, he felt the same sense of awe he always did. The attorney's stark white, short-cropped hair, his imposing yet dignified six-foot-four frame, his piercing black eyes, and his firm handshake all combined to make Lincoln an impressive figure.

"Mr. Nugent," Lincoln said in a booming voice as he finished crushing Michael's hand, "it's good to see you again. Please, sit down. I'd like you to tell me a little more about your friend's situation."

Michael proceeded to fill the attorney in on the details he knew about Dallas's predicament. As he finished, he added, "Dallas was one of the finest soldiers that I had the privilege of working with. I truly do believe he's innocent of any wrongdoing."

"I see," Lincoln responded as he shifted a legal pad in front of him and leaned back in his plush leather chair. He looked thoughtful for a moment, then smiled at Michael. "This is highly unusual for me—agreeing to represent someone without even meeting him. But your friend's story is quite compelling. If you leave me a check for, oh, let's say fifteen hundred dollars, I'll take his case."

"Thank you, sir," Michael said sincerely without blinking an eye as he pulled out his checkbook.

As Michael stood to leave, Lincoln said, "I'll expect you to let me know the moment you locate your friend. In the meantime, I'd like to talk to the woman at the *Chronicle* you mentioned—the one who believes Dallas is innocent."

"I don't have a phone number for Heather," Michael said apologetically.

Lincoln shrugged and smiled. "That's okay. In my line of work you learn how to dig up information."

CHAPTER 12

Heather awoke to the sound of her phone ringing. Groggily, she sat up on the sofa and reached over to pick it up without first checking the caller ID. She regretted that almost instantly.

"Miss Scott, I understand you left the hospital nearly two hours ago," Gordon Townsend's too-loud voice greeted her. Wincing at the pain in her head, she pulled the phone farther from her ear. However, before she could respond, he added, "I find it extremely disrespectful that you haven't bothered to check in with me yet. I know I'm new at this job, but I am the managing editor."

"I—I'm sorry. I think the medication they gave me at the hospital knocked me out. I've been resting since I got home. I had no idea you expected a call," Heather replied, feeling her cheeks flame with embarrassment and anger.

"It seems common sense might have told you that," he muttered. Then, seeming to suddenly switch modes, he asked, "Are you going to be all right?"

"I think so," she said slowly. Then, on impulse, she added, "Elliott is probably upset I haven't called him back too—about dinner."

"Your personal life is your business," Gordon replied dismissively. "I'll see you in the—"

"Dinner to talk about my assignment . . . instead of the meeting tomorrow morning," Heather interrupted. What she was doing was reckless, she knew that, but she found that she didn't care at this point. If she drove a wedge between Elliott and Gordon, so be it. She didn't care for either one of them at the moment.

Gordon was slow in responding. When he finally spoke again, he said, "You must have misunderstood him. We plan to speak to you together in the morning. You won't need to call him back."

"Great," Heather said without missing a beat. "I should stay in bed anyway." *And thank you for confirming my suspicions,* she added silently.

"You do that," Gordon said. "I'll see you in the morning. Ten o'clock."

Heather hung up the phone and exhaled loudly as she lay back down on the sofa, grimacing when she jostled her hurt ribs. Just as she closed her eyes, the phone began to buzz again. Groaning, she grabbed it, this time looking at the caller ID. When she didn't recognize the number, she almost didn't answer. But with a sigh, she finally pressed TALK.

"Miss Scott," a deep voice began, "my name is Lincoln Graves. I've been retained to represent Mr. Dallas Dixon."

"That's wonderful," Heather said, relief flooding through her. She shifted to sit up. "I didn't know he'd hired an attorney. I've been so worried about him—where is he now?"

"Unfortunately, I don't know," the caller said.

"But . . . I don't understand," Heather fumbled.

"I was retained by one of Mr. Dixon's friends," the attorney told her. "However, he seems to have temporarily lost contact with him. That's part of the reason I'm calling now. When was the last time you talked to Dallas?"

She thought a moment. "About an hour and a half ago."

"If you could give me a little more information, it would help me. Could you tell me what you two talked about?"

Heather gave Lincoln the details of their conversation as well as a brief summary of the events that had taken place earlier in the day. As she finished, someone rang her doorbell.

Expecting Rigo, Heather asked Lincoln to wait a moment while she let him in. However, when she opened the door, she found not Rigo but Elliott Painter standing on her porch.

Working hard to control her expression, she let him in, knowing she didn't have much choice at this point.

"Lincoln, I'm sorry but I've got to go. One of my bosses just got here," she said regretfully.

"That's fine, but if you wouldn't mind, I'd like to talk to you more later," Lincoln said. "If I give you my number will you call me back when you have a moment?"

"Of course." Heather scrambled for a pen and paper as Elliott advanced toward her. She quickly wrote down the number and disconnected.

"I'll take that," Elliott said as soon as she had hung up the phone, reaching for the small notebook she'd just written the number on.

Heather ignored him, snapping the notebook shut and placing it in her purse.

Elliott's eyes narrowed. "I'm sorry, but now that you're not on the crime beat, I'm going to need you to hand over all of your notes—especially ones related to the murder."

"This is private business," Heather said. "It has nothing to do with the paper."

Elliott caught her off guard as he grabbed for the purse.

"Elliott! You're way out of line," Heather cried angrily, pulling the purse out of his reach and wincing in pain as she felt her tender ribs. She'd always known Elliott could be difficult to deal with, but this was overboard, even for him.

"If it doesn't have anything to do with the paper, why are you so worried about me seeing it?" he asked peevishly.

"I think it's time for you to be going," she said and marched toward the door.

He held up his hands, suddenly appearing repentant. "I'm sorry," he said. "You're right. It's just that Gordon is really upset. He's convinced you've been going behind our backs with your work. I've tried to tell him you wouldn't do that, but he's not buying it. He was thrust into his new position rather abruptly, and he simply wants to see to it that things go smoothly, that the board is happy with him. You've got to cut him some slack."

Still fuming, Heather crossed her arms over her chest and glared at him. "You're right, I wouldn't do that. But I do have a personal life, and what I do with my time is my business. I'm sorry that Gordon is in a tough spot. I don't envy him. But I'm not trying to cause him any problems."

Elliott stood looking at her for a few seconds then said, "You look awful." It was his first reference to her battered face since he'd stormed into the house.

"Thanks," Heather said irritably. "And I feel even worse."

"Hey, I didn't mean it that way, and you know it," Elliott said.

She shrugged and picked up the cold pack next to the sofa, applying it to her swollen eye, which was aching terribly.

Elliott's brow creased. "So, why didn't you return my call?"

"As you might be able to guess, I don't feel very well," Heather answered. "We're meeting in the morning anyway. I think that's plenty soon."

"I'll take a rain check, then," he said. "What's that now, two, three?" He grinned. "And about that meeting—I'd suggest you be there at ten on the dot. Gordon isn't going to want to listen to excuses if you're late."

"I'll be there," she said, her patience at an end.

"Good, I'll see you then," he said, and he turned toward the door, which had been left hanging open. But he'd only taken a few steps before he stopped and turned back. "About that call you were on when I came in. I hope it wasn't Dallas Dixon you were talking to. He's a wanted man, and if you know where he is, I think it would be wise if you let the cops know."

Heather bristled all over again. "It wasn't Dallas," she said angrily. "Now I'm asking you one more time, please leave."

"Then who was it?" he asked, refusing to be deterred.

"Hello?" came a voice from the open doorway. Heather looked up with relief and saw that it was Lieutenant Rigo Garcia. She almost wished he'd arrived a few moments earlier to see Elliott trying to snatch her purse.

"Come in, Lieutenant," she called.

"What are you doing here?" Elliott asked Rigo suspiciously.

"Heather has been the victim of a violent crime," Rigo said shortly. "I need to talk with her."

"Well, okay . . ." Elliott said reluctantly. "Just so you know, until Gordon and I make some reassignments, I'll continue working on the crime beat for a little while. I'll call you in an hour or so for your statement about what happened."

"Yes, you do that," Rigo said.

"Or, better yet, I could just listen in. That would save us both some time," Elliott suggested.

"That won't work," Rigo said shortly. "Sorry."

Looking annoyed, Elliott finally left. Heather couldn't help but heave a sigh of relief. When the door had closed, Rigo turned and asked, "How are you feeling?"

Heather removed the ice pack and shrugged. "I've definitely been better."

Rigo looked closely at her eye and shook his head. "I'm sorry this happened to you. I hope you get feeling better soon. Do you feel up to discussing a few things?"

"I'll be okay, yes. Please, sit down."

CHAPTER 13

DALLAS'S THROAT BURNED FROM THIRST. He had been hiding in the grove of trees for three hours now, but it felt more like three years. Despite the fact that he was in the shade, the heat was almost unbearable. He swallowed and glanced around him for the hundredth time. Although he was reasonably sure that he was well hidden, his senses remained on high alert. Once again, his military training and experience came to bear. Even though he was thoroughly miserable, he'd suffered worse. He'd spent some days in Iraq where the heat and tension were many degrees higher than this, and he'd endured it. He would endure this.

A number of cars had passed by Dallas's hiding spot, but as near as he could tell, none of them had been occupied by the men who had stormed his room. Over and over again the questions raced through his mind. *Who were they? Why were they after me?*

Dallas pulled the gun from his pocket where he'd shoved it after fleeing the stairwell. He looked at it closely as he turned it over in his hands. He flipped the clip out and saw that there were fifteen rounds inside and shivered despite the heat as he slapped the clip back in place and returned the weapon to his pocket.

After all Dallas had been through in Iraq, he'd at first felt insecure and nervous without a firearm by his side. Shortly after being discharged, he'd obtained a concealed weapons permit and purchased a pistol and holster. But he'd soon regained his sense of security and sold the weapon, a small .38 caliber revolver. At the time, Dallas had hoped he'd never feel the need to carry a gun again. He'd experienced enough violence and killing to last a lifetime. Yet here he was with a lethal weapon in his pocket, one he knew he could use with deadly accuracy if he had to.

And he wasn't about to part with it until this nightmare was over.

* * *

Heather breathed a sigh of relief. She had been comparing notes with Rigo Garcia for an hour now, and it sounded like the focus of his investigation had shifted from Dallas to Frankie and Tito Maggio.

Thinking of a question she had meant to ask some time ago, Heather said, "What do they know about the murder weapon?"

"Mr. Norton was shot with 9mm, hollow-point bullets. Our lab technicians believe they were fired from a SIG Sauer P226," he said, shrugging. "If that means anything to you. Of course, we'll have to get ahold of the murder weapon itself to make an exact match. Detective Cornwell is working on obtaining a search warrant for Frankie Maggio's place right now. Maybe we'll get lucky and find the weapon and wrap this thing up tonight."

"I sure hope so," Heather said, gazing out the window. *Hold on, Dallas,* she thought. *And please, be careful, wherever you are.*

* * *

Dallas breathed a sigh of relief as the sun finally sank below the horizon and darkness began to descend. It had been hours since he'd spoken with Heather or Michael, and he knew they'd be worried. He'd had plenty of time to worry himself, especially knowing what had happened to Heather.

Under the cover of darkness, Dallas slipped out of his hiding spot and made his way toward the freeway. He kept a sharp lookout for anyone who resembled the men from the hotel, but he saw no one before he caught a ride with a semi driver and headed east on I-10.

* * *

"What do you mean he got away?" Luisa hissed as she looked unsympathetically at Marco's newly casted wrist.

Fear sparked in Marco's eyes for a moment, but just as quickly it was gone. "He was expecting us," he said evenly.

"I don't see how that's possible," Luisa replied, her voice deceptively calm. "There were four of you. *Four.* You were armed." The corner of her mouth twitched, and she glanced toward the door.

"I told you I'd get the job done and I will," Marco said, clenching his jaw.

"For your sake, I hope that's the case. I don't want to think that you're getting sloppy on me," Luisa said coolly as she stood and turned away from him. "Dixon can tie Tito and Nick to the truck—and that puts me in jeopardy. Besides that, he's a nuisance." She paused. "The same goes for Tito and Nick. I don't know how Dixon managed to take over their truck, but it doesn't really matter. When you find them, I want both of them to disappear."

"Even your nephew?" Marco asked, his eyes widening slightly.

"Marco, I'll be honest with you," Luisa said as she turned back around. "I've always liked Tito, but we both know he's made some big mistakes recently. I've had it up to here with his incompetence, and you know how I feel about incompetent men. I don't tolerate them. And yes, I like Tito, but not enough to make up for the millions I would have gotten for that load that the cops now have. He failed for the last time, and so did Nick," she said matter-of-factly. "I don't want to see either of them again."

* * *

The search of Frankie Maggio's home and body shop had turned up nothing. The man had a couple of rifles, but he possessed them both legally and was otherwise clean. However, when Rigo called Martha at Kate Norton's house before going to the Maggio residence, she'd indicated that although she'd never seen Frankie with a pistol, she suspected Tito might have one. But who knew where it was? Probably wherever Tito had gone.

When Rigo and CC arrived back at the jail, they had the staff escort Frankie Maggio to an interview room.

"I want my lawyer," Frankie said the moment he saw the two detectives and the recording device that sat on the table in front of them.

"Fine, we'll call him," Rigo said. "And then we need to talk. We just finished conducting a search of your home and business, and we'd like to discuss some things with you."

"What?" Frankie asked, his eyes darkening.

"Here's a phone," Rigo said, sliding it across the table. "Let's get your attorney here first. I'm sure he'll want to hear this."

"I'll call him in a minute," Frankie said. "First tell me what you want to talk about."

"Without your lawyer?" CC asked, raising an eyebrow.

"Yes, without my lawyer," Frankie spat.

"Okay," Rigo said as he cast a sidelong glance at CC. "Then I guess you already know what this is about," he added, bluffing in hopes that Frankie would keep talking.

Frankie set his jaw and looked from one man to the other before finally muttering, "You talked to Martha and Kate. You know about Andy getting Tito outta jail, right?"

Without missing a beat, Rigo nodded and said, "We know. We'd like to talk to you about why Andy agreed to do that."

Frankie gave a short, bitter laugh. "I coulda guessed as much—Kate and Martha didn't tell you the whole story. Why they'd want to protect that scumbag, especially now that he's dead, is beyond me."

"Kate and Martha only told us that you—and Tito—had been holding something over Andy's head," Rigo said, leveling with him. "In legal jargon, that's known as blackmail. And it is illegal. It might help your case if you cooperate with us here and give us the information we need."

"Gladly," Frankie said with a smug smile. "Poor dead Andy was a killer."

* * *

Rigo stood outside the questioning room, waiting for CC to return before going back inside. He ran a hand through his short brown hair and then swiped it across bleary eyes. Now he knew why Kate and Martha had been so hazy on the details surrounding Frankie and Tito's blackmail. As soon as the whole story had come out, CC had left to get a couple of detectives started on searching for information about the girl who had been killed, since the only information Frankie knew about her was the year she had died. The next step would be to find her family and give them the closure they'd undoubtedly been seeking all these years. He shook his head. They would withhold the information from the press for the time being, but it would all come out eventually.

Rigo looked up as CC returned. Without saying a word, CC

nodded toward the door, and the two men once again sat down in front of Frankie.

"So can I go now?" Frankie asked impatiently. "The information was good, wasn't it?"

"Yes," Rigo said tiredly. "But it's not a get-out-of-jail-free card. It doesn't erase what you did to that reporter, and you had a part in covering up what happened to that girl all those years ago. We'll take your cooperation into consideration, but it doesn't make everything all right."

Frankie's eyes seemed to bulge, and Rigo watched as his hands clenched into fists. "You lied," he hissed.

"That's not true, Frankie," CC said quietly. "It will help your case that you're cooperating with us now. Besides, even if the hit-and-run hadn't happened, and even if you hadn't assaulted a woman earlier—big ifs, but still—we couldn't let you go. We're investigating a murder here, and, unfortunately for you, you're a key person of interest."

Frankie looked from CC to Rigo for a few moments, his jaw clenched tight. Finally, he looked down and muttered to himself, "Why should I be the fall guy?"

When neither cop replied, he looked up with a tight-lipped, bitter grin. "I got more information for you. But I ain't gonna share it unless we cut a deal here. Something in writing."

"I don't think you're in much of a position to be brokering deals right now, but keep talking," Rigo said. "We'll listen to what you want."

"I want you to leave me alone when it comes to prosecutin' the case of that dead girl. I wasn't driving, and it wasn't my idea to run."

"I'm assuming there's more," Rigo said.

"Make me a deal."

Rigo glanced at CC. "I can't give you anything in writing, Frankie. But I can promise you that if the information you give us helps us, let's say, identify the girl so her family can have closure, we'll see what we can do to get you a more lenient sentence. I want to figure this thing out, Frankie. Help us help you in this matter."

Frankie rolled his eyes, and for a few moments he didn't say anything. Then he shrugged, looked Rigo in the eye, and said, "I wasn't the only one who knew about the accident."

When he saw the look in Rigo's eyes, he added, "Yeah, Tito knew too, but only for the last three of four days."

"Did anyone else know?"

"Nope, just me and the boy. But there is something else I should tell you."

"Okay, keep talking," CC encouraged.

"Why not," Frankie said with a short bark of a laugh. "If she knew I was talking to you, she'd kill me. But then again she might kill me anyway just to be safe, since she knows I'm gonna get questioned in here."

"Who's *she*?" Rigo asked.

"My sister, Luisa."

"She'd kill her own brother?" Rigo asked, narrowing his eyes.

"You better believe it. She's one mean lady. I didn't learn this blackmailing thing by myself. She taught me."

"So she also knew about the hit-and-run?" CC asked.

His expression darkened. "No, there was no way I'da told her. But I did make a little mistake a long time ago, and I've paid for it ever since. She's nearly bled me dry."

"What did you do?" Rigo asked.

"That I ain't saying. I think the statute of limitations has run out—I ain't sure. But what happened had been mostly her doing. Course, she always told me that if I didn't cooperate, she'd find a way to make it look like it was all my idea. I'm telling you, my sister can be mean."

"Sounds like it," CC said with a straight face.

"When Andy told me he was going to confess to Kate, I lost it. If Luisa found out about my part in Andy's crime, she'd hold that over me, too. She's like that." He shook his head as Rigo and CC continued listening in silence. "She's never liked me all that much—her own brother. But she always did have a soft spot for my boy, Tito."

Rigo nodded then said carefully, "When I talked to your wife, she told me she was very worried about your son. In fact . . . she believes he may have had something to do with Andy's murder. Is it possible that Tito is with Luisa?"

"No," Frankie said, his eyes narrowing. Then his voice faltered. "I . . . I haven't heard from Tito since he got outta jail. He's always over at *her* place . . ." Suddenly he looked pained. "My Tito was a good boy until he started going over there so much. The night Andy died, I called Luisa when I couldn't find Tito. Asked if he was over there. She said he wasn't . . . but I think she lied to me."

"So do you think—" CC began.

"I don't know what I think," Frankie said testily. "But if Tito did have anything to do with my idiot brother-in-law's death, you mark my words: Luisa put him up to it."

"I can promise you we're looking at Luisa very closely," Rigo said. "It would help, though, if you could tell us a little more about her activities in the past while."

Frankie shrugged. "She's been real into this trucking business she started a few years back. I think she uses it as a cover."

"A cover for what?"

Frankie looked wary. "I don't know. But I heard about that big rig full of drugs they found the reporter in. Wouldn't surprise me if it was one of Luisa's. But I can't prove anything like that. I just wouldn't put it past her, that's all."

* * *

After another twenty minutes of questioning, Rigo felt like he'd gotten all the information he could from Frankie for the time being. He was now convinced that Luisa and Tito Maggio were the prime suspects in Andy Norton's murder.

When he and CC returned to the police station, there was a message from Sergeant Trey Thain of the Texas Highway Patrol waiting for them. Dallas Dixon's pickup had been found. It was being towed into Fort Stockton, and Sergeant Thain wondered if they wanted to be there when it was inventoried.

"We need to follow up on Luisa Maggio and do a search at her home and business as soon as we can get a warrant," Rigo said to CC. "But I think in the meantime we should head over to Fort Stockton. Dixon's not in the clear yet."

Rigo placed a call to Sergeant Thain. "We were planning to do the inventory as soon as we get the truck into the station," Sergeant Thain said. "But if you want to be there, we can hold off a little bit."

"I'll be there," Rigo said. "I'll see if I can get the department plane to fly me down. Can you have someone meet me at the nearest airport?"

"You can fly into Fort Stockton. We have an airport here. I'll meet you at the airport. Just let me know what time you'll be there."

"I'll call you back in a few minutes," Rigo said and hung up. "CC, get to work on those search warrants. I'll be back as soon as I can, and then we'll see if we can find out what Luisa Maggio has up her sleeve."

CHAPTER 14

DALLAS BREATHED A SIGH OF relief as the driver he'd hitched a ride with pulled into a truck stop to fuel up and eat. They were about a hundred and twenty miles outside of Junction, and Dallas felt his fear of being apprehended by the men who had come after him beginning to subside. After a quick meal, he turned to the truck driver, a tall lanky man, and said, "George, I need to make a phone call. I'll meet you back at the truck in a few minutes."

Dallas found a pay phone outside and dialed Michael's number. It was late, but he knew Michael wouldn't mind under the current circumstances.

"Dallas, where in the world have you been?" Michael asked in a rush as soon as he heard Dallas's voice on the line.

"I wish I could tell you the whole story, but I don't have much time." He took a breath. "Unfortunately, the cops aren't the only ones after me. I think somebody's pretty upset about losing their cocaine. To make a long story short, I'm lucky to be alive." He glanced toward the truck stop. "I found someone who was willing to give me a ride to San Antonio."

"Lucky to be alive?" Michael muttered. "You've had quite a day, haven't you? I know you have to go, but listen, I retained an attorney for you, Dallas. He told me he needed you to call him—no matter what time I heard from you. His name is

Lincoln Graves. He's the best there is," Michael assured him. He then proceeded to give Dallas Lincoln's home and cell phone numbers.

"Thanks, Michael. I don't know what I'd do without you. I'll call right now. And I'll be in touch," Dallas promised.

"Lincoln Graves," a deep voice said, interrupting the third ring after Dallas dialed the attorney's home phone number.

"Mr. Graves, my name is Dallas Dixon," Dallas began tentatively. "Michael said you wanted me to call you no matter what time it was. I'm sorry it's so late."

"Are you all right?" the attorney asked.

"I'm fine at the moment. But it's been a rough day, to say the least. I need to know what to do," Dallas said. "Did Michael tell you what's going on?"

"He did," Lincoln said and then paused. "He believes you're innocent. But we need to get one matter squared away right off the bat. Whether you are or not, I've agreed to defend you, and I need you to be honest with me. So, to begin with, I have two questions for you."

"Okay," Dallas said. "I'll tell you whatever you need to know."

"Good. Did you kill Andy Norton?" Lincoln asked bluntly.

"No," Dallas said firmly.

"Did you wreck that semi that was carrying a load of cocaine?"

"No again. I was trying to help the guys who did wreck it. They knocked me out, stole my ID and my truck, and left."

"Where are you now?"

Dallas told him as George leaned out the doorway of the rest stop and shouted that he was leaving now.

"Can I call you in the morning when I get to San Antonio?" Dallas asked quickly, waving toward George, indicating he was coming.

"You do that. I'm going to arrange for a press release first thing in the morning, simply stating that you are not guilty and that I'll be representing you. We'll take it from there when you call me tomorrow."

Despite the late hour and his hurry, Dallas had one more phone call he wanted to make. But as he dropped more change into the phone, George honked his horn and began to inch forward. Hoping that Heather would understand, he hung up the phone and ran to the already-moving truck and climbed aboard.

* * *

Despite the pain medication's label—WARNING: MAY CAUSE EXTREME DROWSINESS—Heather couldn't fall asleep. Shortly after midnight, she finally gave up on trying to sleep and got a glass of milk from the refrigerator.

She didn't need to look in a mirror to determine that her eye was still swollen shut. Try as she might, she couldn't open it. Gingerly, she touched the tape over her ribs. She winced, and her tongue sought out the stitches in her lip. It would be a while before she was back to her old self again.

As she sipped her glass of milk, she stared out the dark kitchen window, seeing only a few stars bright enough to overcome the city lights. She glanced at her cell phone lying on the table and chided herself even as she picked it up to check just once more to make sure she hadn't missed any calls. She hadn't.

"Get ahold of yourself, girl," she whispered and shook her head. "Dallas can take care of himself." But believing those words was another matter, and it was a long while before sleep came.

* * *

"It's definitely Dixon's truck, but how did it get to where we found it?" Sergeant Thain mused as he and Rigo began the inventory.

"I don't know, but we'll definitely want to process it for fingerprints," Rigo said. "If I had to make a guess, I'd say it was stolen from him. The fact is, Dallas couldn't have driven his pickup out here at the same time that he was driving, or even riding, in the semi. He couldn't have done both."

"Do you mean his truck was stolen by the guys he claimed were actually driving the semi?" Officer Dick Bentley chimed in.

"That would make sense. But there's still the call to the editor of the *Chronicle* to consider. Whoever placed that call said Dixon was the driver," Trey noted.

Rigo looked up. "I've never been one to put too much stock in anonymous callers. By the way, do we know who else might have touched Dixon's truck? Did the people who found it touch it?"

"Oh, no, they were in a small plane. If they hadn't flown over the area, it might have been weeks before anybody stumbled onto the truck. The pilot radioed in because of the remoteness of the location and the odd position the truck was in—it looked like a crash. It took a tow truck to get it out. And as you can see, there was some damage to the front end," Sergeant Thain said.

Rigo nodded. "Let's get on those prints."

As he turned back to the truck and shuffled through some loose papers in a briefcase, one caught his eye. He separated it from the others and looked closer. It was a memo from Gordon Townsend to Dallas Dixon. Rigo read it. Then he read it again, his brow furrowing deeply.

He pulled his notebook containing notes from his conversation with Heather Scott out of his pocket and scanned them quickly. When he found what he was looking for, he glanced back at the date stamped on Gordon Townsend's memo. He frowned. The memo was dated the day before Dallas's article about Tito Maggio had come out in the paper. In the memo, Gordon specifically instructed Dallas to drop the story. It stated that Tito Maggio was Andy's nephew and that it would be better for the *Chronicle* to leave the story alone.

Rigo sat looking at the memo. Dallas had specifically been instructed in writing to ignore the story that had been the start of all of this. And yet he'd gone ahead anyway. That meant he'd lied to Heather, since she'd told him that Dallas had had no idea that Tito was Andy's nephew. *What other lies had Dallas told?*

He looked more closely into the briefcase. At the bottom, beneath some papers, writing pads, and pens was something that was totally out of place. With his gloved fingers, Rigo pulled out two bullets. Both were 9mm hollow points. *The same caliber and type of ammunition that had ended Andy Norton's life.*

"I'll need to take these items with me," Rigo told Sergeant Thain and explained their significance to his homicide investigation. "I'll give you a receipt for them before I go."

A few hours later as they were finishing up the inventory, the report came back on the fingerprints that had been lifted from the steering wheel, the door latches, the jockey box, and the dash of Dallas's pickup. As expected, most belonged to Dallas Dixon. Several could not be identified. But several, which had been taken from the passenger door, the dash, and the jockey box, were conclusively identified as belonging to Tito Maggio.

As Rigo and his detectives assembled the next morning, he briefed them on the evidence he'd collected during his overnight trip to Fort Stockton. That done, the officers proceeded in two groups to the headquarters of Luisa Maggio's trucking company and to her home. Rigo fervently hoped they'd learn something that would be the key to unraveling the mystery that seemed to grow more convoluted at every turn.

* * *

It was a quarter after ten that Thursday morning before Gordon Townsend's secretary told Heather she could go in. As she entered the office, Gordon looked up and scrutinized her face, obviously studying the bruises, but he said nothing. Elliott smiled at her from a chair beside the desk.

A little taken aback that neither man had shown the courtesy of standing when she came into the room as they typically did, she felt the knot in her stomach tighten. Whatever hope she'd had of coming out of this conference with her job intact was rapidly dissolving.

"Do you have your cell phone with you?" Gordon asked without a greeting.

"Yes, why?" she asked.

"We don't want any interruptions. Please turn it off, and then we'll talk."

* * *

A small TV with a grainy picture was turned on with the volume just high enough that Mason could hear it as he cleaned a doe. He'd never found the missing page to the newspaper he'd been reading, and he'd been keeping the television on when he had the chance, just in case he might hear something.

He'd come to hope that sometime, somehow, he would be able to learn of the whereabouts of his son. He even dreamed about meeting him. However, Mason was realistic enough to know that Dallas probably wouldn't want to have anything to do with a father who had deserted him and his mother before he was even born.

He whetted his knife for a few moments. As he did, he

distantly heard a new voice begin speaking on the TV. Suddenly, Mason jerked his head up. *Did he just say Dallas Dixon?* He quickly reached forward to turn up the volume. He saw a tall black man with snowy white hair and a perfectly tailored suit fill the screen.

"Yes, I have been retained to represent him. No formal charges have yet been filed against my client, but I am, in his behalf, denying all allegations that have been or might be made. As soon as I determine the best course of action for Mr. Dixon, I'll file the appropriate motions in the court in El Paso," the attorney said. "Rest assured that we will cooperate with the authorities."

"Where is Dallas Dixon now?" a reporter asked.

Mason's heart nearly stopped.

The man, who a banner caption on the screen identified as Lincoln Graves, spoke again. "I'm not going to disclose that information at this time."

"Are you saying he's not in police custody?" the reporter asked.

Lincoln ignored the question. "Any further statements about Dallas and his whereabouts will come from my office as we deem them to be appropriate."

"Do the police in El Paso know you're representing him?" The reporter was persistent, and Mason smiled a little as he saw the scowl on Lincoln Graves's face.

"Yes. I've personally talked to the lead investigator, Lieutenant Rodrigo Garcia. As I said, we're cooperating with the authorities in every way we can. That will be all for now," Lincoln concluded.

The news anchor came on the screen then and reiterated that Dallas had not been charged with any crime at this time but was still simply a person of interest in the case. He also said that anyone who saw Dallas should report the information to the nearest police office. He then gave a brief description of Dallas and even showed a photograph of his face. Mason shivered slightly. It could have been a picture of himself at that age.

Mason almost went back to cleaning the deer when it occurred to him that Lincoln Graves might have held the news conference at his office. Maybe he'd be there for the rest of the day. He laid his knife down and hurried to his trailer.

* * *

Dallas picked up the remote and turned off the news conference. He lay back against the hotel bed and stared at the now-quiet, sparsely furnished hotel room. George had dropped him off here several hours ago, and he had managed to get a bit of sorely needed rest. He sighed. It was time to call Lincoln Graves again. The attorney Michael had retained for him had given him the first real inkling of hope he'd felt since this whole mess had begun.

"Stay where you are; I'll come by to pick you up in about thirty minutes," Lincoln said when Dallas got ahold of him. "Then we'll talk."

When Dallas hung up, he tried to call Heather but got her voice mail. Disappointed, he hung up the receiver and walked to the window, where he stood waiting for Lincoln Graves to arrive. He kept the 9mm pistol in his pocket. He didn't want to be surprised again.

* * *

When Lincoln Graves's secretary answered the phone, she told Mason that Mr. Graves wasn't taking any calls. When he attempted to persuade her that this was an important matter, she curtly told him that she could take a message. He quietly told her no, and she broke the connection. Disappointed, he went back to his work for a few minutes. Finding himself unable to concentrate, he stopped, washed his hands, and went to the headquarters building to request permission to leave for a while.

Back in his trailer house, Mason cleaned up as well as he could. He shaved, combed his hair, and put on his best clothes. That wasn't saying much, but at least the slacks and shirt were clean. Then he headed for his pickup to start the drive to San Antonio.

* * *

Marco's wrist throbbed, but he ignored it. He'd finally gotten a break, and he felt his breathing come easier. Marco had spent the last five hours keeping tabs on two dozen men he had dispatched to every truck stop and service station scattered across the highway for a hundred miles west of the San Antonio area. Their job had been to watch for anyone who came even close to fitting Dallas's description and to talk to others to see if anyone else might have noticed him.

A lot of false leads had come in, but at last his hard work had paid off. One informant had seen a man who resembled Dixon getting out of a semi at a gas station in San Antonio. The man had disappeared before he could catch up with him, but the source had confirmed enough details that made Marco certain it was Dixon.

That sighting, coupled with the information that an attorney had been retained to represent Dallas, sent Marco roaring east. The sleek black Escalade pushed the speed limit, and Marco's temper simmered near the boiling point. His orders were to find Dallas and remove him. If he had to go to Lincoln Graves's office to accomplish that, then that's what he would do.

CHAPTER 15

HEATHER BREATHED A SIGH OF relief as she exited Gordon's office. Yes, she had been taken off the crime beat. But she still had her job, and she hadn't been suspended for any supposed breaches of policy. However, Gordon and Elliott had presented a united front in ordering her to take two weeks off with pay to recuperate from the injuries she had received. That was okay with her, though. Right now, all she wanted to do was go home and get some more rest.

As she walked to her car, she checked her cell phone for messages. Her heart skipped a beat when she heard Dallas's voice come on the line.

"Heather, I hope everything's okay. I just wanted to let you know I'm . . . okay." He hesitated a moment longer, and she frowned, knowing he was anything but okay. "I'll be in touch as soon as I can. I'm headed to my attorney's office. Wish I could see you too."

She offered a silent prayer of gratitude that he was safe. She closed her phone and looked up, only to see that Elliott had come up behind her.

"Hey, Heather. I'll give you a call in a couple of days, okay?" He raised an eyebrow at her. "Don't forget, we have a dinner date coming up. I only give so many rain checks." He waggled a finger at her. "But for now, you get feeling better."

Forcing a smile, she said, "Thanks, Elliott. It'll be nice to have some time off. I need it."

"Just so you know," he said, apparently annoyed she'd brushed off his comments about dinner, "you owe me. Gordon wanted you suspended without pay. I talked him out of it."

Heather just looked at him for a moment. "You're a pal, Elliott," she said flatly and stepped past him, determined not to let on that his comment had unsettled her. *What did Gordon have against her?*

"Wait, Heather."

Gritting her teeth, she stopped and turned. "Yeah?"

"You really do need to stop wasting your time on Dixon. I know that's Gordon's main concern too. I talked to Rigo a couple of hours ago, and there's another nail in Dallas's coffin."

When she didn't respond, he went on. "They found his truck, and guess what they found inside? A memo from Gordon. Telling him *not* to write about Maggio."

With that, Elliott gave her a self-satisfied smile and walked away.

Brushing back tears, Heather again headed for the parking lot. Though she was now sure that Dallas wasn't involved in Andy's murder, she wished more than ever that she could talk to him, or, better yet, see him, to put the pieces of this puzzle together with him. As she reached her car, she looked back at the *Chronicle,* not at all certain she'd ever set foot inside again and not sure she even wanted to.

* * *

Luisa stood in the doorway of her home, her hands clenched into fists, the only outward indication of anger. Her sharp red fingernails dug into the palms of her hands. She watched as Rigo Garcia and his detectives got into their vehicles and drove away.

As they did so, Luisa slowly and deliberately punched a number into her phone. When Marco answered, she said softly, "My home and office have been searched."

He waited a moment, and she thought she heard him swallow. "They didn't find anything, did they?"

"What's to find?" she replied calmly. "How close are you to finding Dixon?"

"Soon," Marco promised.

"Soon had better be *now* the next time I talk to you. Oh, and before you get rid of him, you had better make sure you've got enough evidence planted against him to get the cops to quit looking my way. Do you understand me?"

"Of course."

"I'm counting on you, Marco. Find Dixon and then Tito." She hung up the phone with a decisive click.

* * *

"You need to go home and get some shut-eye, Rigo. You look like a walking dead man," CC said as they returned to the office.

"I know. That's about how I feel," Rigo said as he rubbed his tired eyes. "But there's still plenty of work to do. Both Dallas and Tito are still out there somewhere, and they both have a lot of questions to answer."

"As for Dallas, I think his attorney will turn him over to us," CC replied. "The guy seems pretty sure that he can get him off. Off course, he doesn't know about the memo from Gordon Townsend or the ammo in his briefcase. All we have to do is wait a little longer."

"What about Tito?"

"We can get a picture of him from the jail and send out a nationwide alert. By the way, what are we charging him with?" CC asked.

"Auto theft, maybe? We know he was in Dallas's truck some-time before it was abandoned, and he and Dallas aren't exactly buddies," Rigo said. "I think that'll give us enough to get a warrant." He thought for a moment. "Back to Dixon, though. I think a call to the San Antonio police is in order. They need to know about his meeting with Graves—just in case he decides to run again."

* * *

The interview with Lincoln Graves took nearly two hours. As their conversation wound down, Dallas once again felt a wave of gratitude that the man was on his team. And best of all, Lincoln believed him when Dallas said he was innocent.

"So what's the next step?" Dallas asked.

"The safest place for you right now is in police custody," Lincoln said. "I know that's not a pleasant thought, but whoever came after you in Junction isn't likely to give up so easily."

Dallas nodded and felt a small pang of guilt. He'd kept one piece of information from his attorney—the pistol he'd taken from his assailant. He had almost told Lincoln that part of the story, but at the last moment he'd kept silent. He knew that if he did so the gun would be confiscated immediately, and he couldn't bring himself to turn over his most reliable form of protection. Once again, the training and instincts he'd acquired in Iraq had come back to him with surprising force. He prom-ised himself that when they arrived at the police station, he'd tell Lincoln the rest of the story and give him the gun, but not until he was there safe and sound.

"We won't tell them we're coming," Lincoln continued. "To the station, I mean. I don't want the media catching wind of this. But I would like to make a call to Lieutenant Garcia so he can start making plans to get you back to El Paso. I'd also like to call my friend Sam, if it's all right with you. He's a private eye—one of the best. Hopefully, he'll be able to sniff out the trail of the guys who were after you."

Dallas nodded in agreement as Lincoln picked up the phone. When he finished the conversation and replaced the receiver, he turned to Dallas and said, "He's going to fly here. He'll leave as soon as the plane and pilot are ready. We'll call Sam from the police station."

"Great," Dallas said, attempting to sound sincere. He knew he was innocent. Fortunately for him, Lincoln believed it as well. He knew he had to let the justice system take its course. He couldn't run anymore. But his stomach churned as he wondered how many innocent men had gone to prison.

* * *

Mason Huggins hoped he wasn't too late. He'd blown a tire and it had taken him a few minutes to change it. Then, to make matters worse, his spare had been so low that he'd had to stop at a service station and get both tires repaired. Finally, though, he'd arrived. He parked his truck across the street from Lincoln Graves's office and studied the rust-colored building. It wasn't a large office building, but the small parking lot adjacent to it was almost full of vehicles.

His mind spun as he tried to think of what he should say. He was sure the same woman who had answered the phone earlier would still be protecting Mr. Graves from superfluous visitors. Maybe if he waited right here in his truck for a few minutes, Dallas would come out. If he did, even if he was accompanied by his lawyer, Mason could simply approach him and see if Dallas was willing to talk. If he wasn't, then that would be that.

* * *

Dallas kept his eyes focused straight ahead as he accompanied Lincoln out of the office toward the parking lot. "Things will work out one way or another," the attorney said quietly, patting Dallas on the shoulder as he opened the door to exit the building.

"Thanks," Dallas replied, mustering a smile. "I really hope so."

When Dallas's gaze shifted back toward the parking lot, he saw a black SUV driving slowly toward him and Lincoln. The windows were tinted, making it impossible to see the occupants. He watched as the vehicle drove past them and pulled into a parking space.

Dallas pulled his gaze away and was about to ask Lincoln a question about whether he would be allowed to make any calls once Rigo Garcia arrived when his breath caught in his throat. Out of the corner of his eye he saw that two men in dark suits and glasses were exiting the vehicle and walking rapidly toward him.

Dallas tried to keep his panic at bay and did his best not to let on that he had seen the men. However, he saw a sudden movement from the west side of the parking lot. Another man in a dark jacket and tan slacks was walking toward him and Lincoln. A wave of nausea threatened him as the man's jacket sleeve lifted slightly and he saw the whiteness of a cast on his arm.

There was no longer any doubt as Dallas watched the three men quickly converging. They had found him.

"Get down!" Dallas shouted, shoving Lincoln to the ground just as a shot rang out. Then he dove for cover himself.

The two men who had exited the vehicle sprang into action as the man with the broken wrist abruptly ducked down below the nearest car, shielding himself from view. One of the men fired a shot that missed its mark, exploding against the side of the car above Dallas's head. The man cursed and aimed again, but not before Dallas had pulled his own weapon from his pocket and fired.

The man from the SUV who had fired let out a strangled cry, and Dallas heard him fall to the ground with a dull thud against the pavement. He heard shouting coming from the other end of the parking lot and turned to see three uniformed men leaping from a blue sedan.

"Police! Drop your weapons!" The second man from the SUV began firing in their direction. The police returned fire but he had already found cover behind a car.

Dallas's breath came in quick spurts as he looked around him methodically, adrenaline pumping through his veins. He saw that Lincoln had managed to crouch against a parked car, slumped over and holding his bleeding shoulder.

One of the police officers cried out just as another loud pop of gunfire sounded, and Dallas turned in their direction, attempting to see if the officer was down.

At that moment the second man from the SUV darted out from behind the vehicle next to where Dallas was crouching, his gun aimed in Dallas's face. He grinned maliciously, and Dallas wasn't sure he'd have time to react. But just then one of the officers fired, hitting the man in the shoulder and sending him spinning to the pavement. Dallas scurried away from the writhing form on the ground, willing himself to keep calm, to keep moving.

As he looked back to see if Lincoln had followed, he heard the sound of an engine gunning. Whipping around, he looked up to see an old pickup barreling toward him. Just as he was about to dive toward the next row of cars, the truck screeched to a stop and a man flung open the door and extended his hand.

"Get in, Dallas! I'll get you out of here."

Stunned, Dallas looked into the face of the man who had just called him by name. He'd never seen this person before in his life, but there was something familiar about him. He didn't dwell on this fact, however, as at that moment a bullet exploded next to his foot. The man with the broken wrist had surfaced a few cars over and was aiming again, his mouth drawn in an angry frown.

With one last agonized glance toward the area where Lincoln was still hunched over in obvious pain, Dallas dove through the open door of the truck. Then they were off. He couldn't believe the way this man drove. If there was anyone after them, they would soon be left behind.

* * *

Lincoln Graves hunched farther against the parked car, gripping his shoulder. He'd been struck by a bullet, and though he wasn't in a position to see the wound clearly, he could feel the blood seeping through his shirt. His head throbbed from where he'd hit it when Dallas had pushed him to the ground, but his thoughts were clear as he tried to process what had happened in the last few minutes. He realized that he'd unwittingly led his client into an ambush and that these men were probably the same ones who had attacked Dallas in Junction. Lincoln also knew that Dallas's quick thinking and actions had likely saved his life.

He peered around the tire's edge, then jerked back as another shot rang out. The questions continued to pile up. Where had Dallas gotten a gun? Had he had it all along? What did these men, who were willing to engage the police, want with Dallas?

Several minutes went by, and all was silent. Then Lincoln heard footsteps. He tensed and moved closer to the tire.

"Mr. Graves? It's okay. I'm Sergeant Daryl Everton."

Lincoln exhaled loudly and looked up in relief. The officer peered down at the blood pooling near Lincoln's arm.

"We've got help coming. You just hang in there."

He nodded. "Where's my client?"

The officer shook his head. "We haven't found him yet."

Lincoln's forehead creased in concern. "Were any officers injured?"

"One, yes, but luckily he was hit in the vest. He'll be okay. We got lucky. One of the assailants was killed, and another was injured—he's in pretty bad shape. As for the third, we've got officers combing the area now. He managed to get away in the SUV."

"They're after my client," Lincoln said urgently. "I believe they'll kill him if they find him."

The officer nodded slowly. "We're looking for both Dallas and the guy in the SUV now." He shook his head. "Your client sure does seem to be able to handle himself, though. The guy who died—that was Dallas's doing."

Lincoln sighed. "I had no idea he was carrying a weapon."

Sergeant Everton raised an eyebrow. "He not only had a weapon, but he knew how to use it pretty effectively."

"He's an Iraq vet, an Army Ranger," Lincoln said, then looked the officer in the eye. "Like I said, I don't know how he ended up with a gun, but I do know one thing. His quick thinking and swift action almost certainly saved my life."

The officer nodded slowly. "In all honesty, he probably saved ours as well. The last thing we were expecting was an ambush," he admitted.

Lincoln thought for a moment then said, "I heard a vehicle roar by during the shooting. Was that the man who got away?"

"I don't think so; the SUV took off down the street. I know what you're talking about, though. Another vehicle did come through here, but I was so focused on the shoot-out that I couldn't tell you what it looked like. It was probably someone trying to get out of the way. We're lucky no bystanders got caught in the crossfire."

"Maybe, but it also could have been reinforcements for the attackers. And if that's the case, I'm certain that vehicle is after Dallas as well," Lincoln said, his expression grave.

Sergeant Everton keyed the speaker to his portable radio, relaying the message that a second ambush vehicle may have followed Dallas through the parking lot toward the south entrance.

As the officer signed off, Lincoln struggled to stand up. There was work to do; he needed to get busy doing it.

Sergeant Everton tried to keep him down but when Lincoln shot him a glare, he meekly held out his arm to help him up. "You'll need that shoulder attended to, Mr. Graves. Please, will you just wait here until paramedics arrive?"

"All right," Lincoln grumbled. "But as soon as I get bandaged up, I need to get back to my office. My client is in worse trouble than I thought."

CHAPTER 16

"How . . . did you know my name?" Dallas asked once the old truck they were in had finally slowed down, and he'd released his grip on the dashboard. The man driving the truck hadn't spoken since he'd roared away from the parking lot. His entire attention was focused on driving, which Dallas was grateful for. He drove like no one Dallas had ever ridden with. He glanced nervously toward Dallas as the vehicle continued eastward.

"Well, Dallas . . ." He swallowed, and another minute passed in silence.

Dallas's forehead creased in confusion. "Listen, I appreciate you helping me out back there . . . I just . . . do I know you?"

"Well, uh, sort of." He shook his head then blurted out, "Darn it, Dallas, I'm just going to come out and say it. My name is Mason Huggins. I'm your father."

Dallas simply stared. *Mason Huggins.* His father. He opened his mouth to speak and then closed it again.

"Maybe you're not so glad I picked you up back there after all." Mason forced a laugh as Dallas remained speechless. "And I hope I didn't scare you too badly the past few minutes. I just wanted to make sure no one followed us."

Dallas ran a hand over his face. As improbable as it all was, he believed this man was telling the truth. He remembered the sense of familiarity he'd felt when he'd first seen the man and wondered now if he maybe resembled him. "I don't even know what to say." He narrowed his eyes. "I guess the first question that comes to mind is why in the world were you in that parking lot?"

Mason shrugged. "I saw you on TV, and . . . well, I wanted to meet you. I've wanted to meet you for years." He scratched his chin and glanced at Dallas. "I know I did you and your mama a terrible wrong. I've wanted to tell you I was sorry for a long time," he admitted with a sigh. As Dallas moved to speak Mason held up a hand as he stared ahead at the highway. "I want you to know that I have no intention of asking for your forgiveness. Don't deserve it after what I did. But whether you decide to jump outta this here truck at the next stoplight or talk to me a little more, I'm glad I was where I was today."

Dallas was too, but he kept silent, his mind whirling with the recent turn of events. Part of him wanted to ask his father the thousand questions he'd had for as long as he could remember, and part of him wanted to put his head between his knees and breathe into a paper bag to keep from passing out. He was wanted for questioning in a murder and a drug bust. He'd just killed a man. His long-lost father was back. And he'd just had the craziest ride of his life. *What's next?* Dallas wondered as the absurdity of it all gave him the sudden impulse to laugh out loud.

Dallas looked out the window and tried to process everything that had just happened. With a sinking feeling, he realized he was on the run again. He was sure that the local authorities would charge him with something for shooting the man despite the fact that he had probably saved the lives of his attorney and some officers.

This thought failed to provide Dallas with much comfort. He'd killed a man. Granted, he hadn't checked to make sure the guy was dead before he fled the scene, but he knew the moment he'd fired that it was a lethal shot. He didn't miss. But already he was second-guessing his actions. It was true that he'd had to kill in Iraq, but it wasn't the same. He knew that in a sense he was at war now—a war being waged against him by some unidentified person, either Andy's real killer or someone else who wanted him framed for the crime. A hollow, hopeless feeling filled his chest. His attempt at turning himself in had failed at the expense of a man's life—and likely more, since the assailants had been shooting at the officers.

His thoughts were interrupted by Mason clearing his throat. "Uh, Dallas, anytime you feel like talking, I'll be here listening," he said hesitantly.

"Thanks," Dallas said and shifted in his seat. He finally thought to ask, "Where are we going?"

"To a safe place, if you're willing to go there with me." Mason said firmly. "Ain't nobody going to find you there if you don't want 'em to."

Dallas hoped that was true, but he had serious doubts. The men who were after him weren't giving up—they'd made that evident today. But maybe he'd at least have a temporary reprieve from having to constantly look over his shoulder. He leaned back and closed his eyes. Then he thanked the Lord for once again preserving his life even as he wondered how many times he would be offering similar prayers. He also prayed for Heather, asking that he'd be able to find a way to get in touch with her soon. And for her safety.

Finally, he prayed that he could somehow find it in his heart to forgive this man, his father, who he had resented his entire life but who was there for him today at a critical time.

* * *

The Cessna Skyhawk shuddered in some sudden turbulence, briefly interrupting Rigo Garcia's train of thought.

"Sorry about that, Rigo," the pilot, Sergeant Will Cullen, said into the mouthpiece of his headset with a grin. "Didn't expect that. It's been smooth all the way here until now."

"Don't worry about it. I was just thinking about this darn case."

Will nodded and offered a sympathetic smile before turning his attention back to the plane's instrument panel.

Rigo sighed, once again lost in thought. He'd been immensely relieved when Dallas Dixon had agreed to turn himself in, and he was anxious to interview him—particularly in regard to the memo and the bullets. *Maybe this interview will give us the break we need,* he thought hopefully.

Just then a call came in on the aircraft's police radio, and Rigo listened as Sergeant Cullen responded. He narrowed his eyes as Will said, "Are you kidding? That's a rotten break." He shook his head and ended the call. When he got back on the intercom he said, "Apparently your bird just flew the coop, Rigo."

"You've got to be kidding me," Rigo said as he stared back at his pilot. "What happened?"

Will shook his head. "The report of what happened is still coming in. But there were some casualties. I'm assuming that Dallas wasn't one of them, or he wouldn't have gotten away."

Rigo's eyebrows rose. "Casualties?" He put his head in his hands and groaned. "Radio back and tell them we still want to meet them at the airport. I want to know exactly what happened down there."

"Sure thing," Will agreed. "In the meantime you might try your cell phone, see if you can get in touch with someone on the ground who knows a few more details."

"Can I get a signal up here?" Rigo asked in surprise as he pulled his cell phone out.

"You should be able to. We aren't nearly high enough to start running into problems," Will told him.

Rigo took off his headset and dialed a number. He couldn't imagine what had gone wrong, but whatever it was, it had clearly complicated this case worse than it already was.

Five minutes later he closed his phone. "What did you learn?" Will asked after he had put his headset back on.

Rigo's voice was solemn. "One man is dead and three are injured, including an officer and Dixon's attorney. Three armed men ambushed Dixon and Graves as they left his law office. One of them was killed, one was injured, and the third managed to get away in an SUV. There was also a second vehicle, but the officers aren't sure of its involvement. Dallas is missing, and so far they haven't found a trace of him."

"Were the officers already at the scene?" Will asked.

Rigo nodded. "Yes, because of my call asking them to be there," he said with a sigh.

"Good thing, too. Otherwise that call might have been to tell us that Dixon and his attorney were gone for good."

"That's not exactly how it came down," Rigo said slowly. "The guy who died? Dallas Dixon shot him. Direct hit with one bullet. The officers said his attorney didn't know he had the gun."

"Sounds like he sunk himself now," Will said.

"I don't know," Rigo replied thoughtfully. "The sergeant I just spoke to said that if it hadn't been for Dixon, there probably would have been a lot more casualties. Lincoln Graves believes that Dixon left the immediate scene in an attempt to draw the second vehicle away. The sergeant I spoke with—Everton—went so far as to call him a hero."

"Wow. That's quite a story," Will mused, pursing his lips. "What about the attorney? How bad's he hurt?"

"He took a bullet to the shoulder and has a lump on his head. Nothing too serious according to the paramedics. Dallas actually shoved him down as the first bullet was fired."

"And they have no leads as to where Dixon is now?"

"Not a one."

"Well, there might be one silver lining to all this," Will suggested.

"And what would that be?"

"Ballistics. Maybe the gun Dixon used happens to be the same one that killed Andy Norton."

Rigo gave a grim smile. "That's true. And I'll be waiting on pins and needles for the report to come back, because get this— from the entrance wound, they're pretty sure the bullet was a hollow point. Andy Norton was shot with 9mm hollow-point rounds."

* * *

After they had driven for a little more than an hour, Mason Huggins pulled down a short dirt lane and stopped at a locked gate. The adjoining chain-link fence disappeared into tall trees running as far as Dallas could see. A nearby sign identified the place as a private hunting preserve.

Mason got out and unlocked the gate, and they drove through. He then locked the gate behind them and drove on. After about a quarter of a mile they came to a large clearing with a cluster of buildings.

"We're home," Mason announced with a grin as he pulled to a stop in front of a mobile home. "I clean and cut up wild game, mostly hogs," he said with a touch of pride as he got out of the truck. "Come on in and make yourself at home."

Dallas wordlessly followed Mason into the trailer. It was sparsely furnished but clean and orderly. "I never did get married," Mason said with a shrug. "So this is all I have to show for the past thirty years. It's not much, but you can stay here as long as you need to."

"Thanks."

Mason nodded, and his expression turned serious. "That gun in your pocket. Don't let anybody here see it. The only time our clients are allowed to carry firearms is when they go out hunting. The rest of the time they gotta keep 'em in their vehicles."

"That's fine; I'll keep it out of sight. But I am keeping it," Dallas replied firmly.

"I wouldn't expect you not to after what you been through."

Dallas relaxed a bit and gave the little mobile home a closer inspection. "So everything you own is right here?"

"I'm afraid so," Mason said. "Not much, is it?"

"No, it's nice," Dallas said. "What are the trophies on that bookcase?"

"I used to race a little," he said modestly. "I got lucky and won a time or two."

"After riding with you today, I can believe it." He looked around some more, then he cleared his throat and said, "I just wanted to know . . . well, I just wondered if you had anything here that shows . . . you know . . . that you're my father."

Understanding flickered in Mason's eyes, and without a word he walked over to a small desk and opened a drawer. He withdrew an aged, yellowing envelope. From inside he pulled some photos, the kind that come out in a strip from a photo booth. Mason handed them to Dallas.

They were poses of a young couple, laughter shining in their eyes. The woman, Dallas's mother, had a teasing look on her face as she stared at the man—who looked just like Dallas.

"You look a lot like I used to," Mason said with a grin. "Better actually. You got some of your mom's good looks."

Dallas felt the sting of tears in the back of his eyes and held the photos toward his father. "Yeah," he said. "Mom was a beautiful woman. Even in the last few years of her life when things were really bad . . ." Dallas said and choked up. He shrugged. "She did the best she could."

An uncomfortable silence enveloped the two men. Finally, Mason said, "I need to go let the others know you're here and that you might be staying for a while. I won't offer up any details." He looked at the ground then added, "Maybe, if it's okay, I'll just tell them you're my son and that you've come to visit."

"That's okay," Dallas said quietly. His father nodded, put the old photos back in the drawer, and then walked to the door. Before he opened it, Dallas looked up and said, "Thanks for being there today."

Mason shook his head sadly. "I should've been there long before today. I'm sorry, Dallas."

He turned to go, but Dallas spoke again. "What should I call you?"

"You can call me a no-good so and so if you want to. I certainly deserve it. I assume you don't want to call me Dad." He paused. "So you can call me Mason."

With that he gave a quick nod and stepped out the door.

* * *

"Are you sure you'll be all right, sir?" Lincoln's secretary asked, her brows furrowed as she stood in his doorway.

"I'm almost as good as new, Shelly," Lincoln said and patted his shoulder, where a bulky bandage lay underneath. That effort made him wince. He'd spent the past hour in the emergency room a few blocks from his office, where he'd been stitched up and given pain medication. "Go to lunch. Hopefully Dallas will have called by the time you get back."

With a reluctant nod, she left the room, and Lincoln settled back in his desk chair. Just as he picked up a pen, the phone rang. He quickly reached for the receiver.

"Mr. Graves," began an agitated voice that he immediately

recognized as belonging to Michael Nugent. "I heard you ran into some trouble. Are you okay?"

"I'll be fine, Michael. But I'm worried about Dallas," he said.

"Do you have any idea where he is?" Michael asked.

"We were caught completely off guard. I underestimated the men who were after him," Lincoln admitted. "Fortunately, I also underestimated Dallas. He may well have saved my life, as well as a few officers'."

"That's what I heard," Michael said. "And I'm not surprised. I also heard that he might have been taken by some of the men who ambushed you."

"I certainly hope not. I'm waiting by my phone, hoping he calls. Your young friend does seem to know how to handle himself in a tight spot."

"Dallas had some pretty close calls in Baghdad. He was an exceptional soldier, and I know every man in his unit respected him," Michael said. "Listen, I was wondering if you could call me if he contacts you. I mean as a friend, not as a reporter. I won't print anything unless you specifically ask me to."

Lincoln glanced at the red light flashing on his phone. "I'll call you," he promised, "but I need to go now. There's another call coming in."

A young woman's voice came on the line. "Mr. Graves? This is Heather Scott. I just heard what happened. Have you heard from him?" she asked in a rush, her voice full of emotion.

"I'm afraid I haven't. But I'm hopeful he'll call soon."

"Will you—"

"Call you if I hear from him? Of course," Lincoln said with a smile. "It's the least I can do for Dallas. You know, he spoke very highly of you, Miss Scott. And he told me what happened to you. Are you all right?"

"I still can't open one eye, and my ribs hurt like crazy whenever I move just wrong, but I'll be okay." She hesitated. "Thanks for offering to keep me updated. I know you're busy . . . but it means a lot to me. I won't bother you anymore right now, though," she said. "I really hope I hear from you soon."

As Lincoln put the phone down a moment later, he rubbed a hand through his wiry white hair and sighed. He'd defended many murder suspects throughout his career. Most had been guilty as charged. Lincoln had come to develop almost a sixth sense about the innocent ones. And he'd never felt so strongly about a man's innocence as he did now. And he intended to do whatever it took to prove that.

CHAPTER 17

WHEN MASON REENTERED THE TRAILER a few minutes later, he nodded toward Dallas and said, "I need a cup of coffee. How do you take yours?"

"No thanks," Dallas said. "I don't drink coffee."

Mason gave him a strange look but shrugged and went about making the pot of coffee.

"I could use a phone, though. I really should call my lawyer."

"I have a cell phone, but are you sure you want to call right now?"

"No, but I also don't want him to worry needlessly. And I want to make sure he's not hurt too bad," Dallas explained. He paused and looked thoughtful. "Actually, maybe it's not such a good idea to call Lincoln directly. I'm not crazy about the idea of going back into that dangerous world outside of this ranch quite yet. Lincoln will want me to turn myself in again, but I'm sure those men haven't given up. I'm not willing to walk back into another ambush. They could easily be watching his place again." He looked at Mason. "I think I know who I can call, though."

"Fine by me." Mason pulled his cell phone from his pocket. "Here you are. I take it this person you want to call is someone you can trust?" he asked.

"With my life," Dallas responded with intensity as he punched in Heather's number.

* * *

When her phone went off, Heather answered it on the first ring. She was at the airport, waiting for a flight to San Antonio. She'd spent the last several hours pacing her apartment, but she hadn't been able to find out any further information about Dallas's whereabouts. She'd finally decided that she could either go crazy waiting around in her apartment or do something about it. So she'd booked a last-minute flight to San Antonio, having no idea what she'd do when she got there. But just going there was doing something.

"Hello," she said breathlessly.

"Heather, it's me."

"Dallas!" she said in a loud whisper, her heart accelerating as she heard his voice, her shoulders slumping in relief. She quickly looked around to make sure no one had overheard her. "Are you okay? I heard what happened."

"I'm okay. I'm so glad I got ahold of you. I'm so sorry I haven't called before now." She heard him swallow, and she waited for him to continue. "Heather, it was awful. I shot a man. I didn't want to," he added in a rush. "You probably already heard about it . . . but I wanted to tell you myself. It all happened so fast, and he was shooting at Lincoln and me."

"I know," she said quietly. "You didn't have a choice, Dallas. And your attorney and some police officers are alive because of what you did," she said.

"How did you find out about all of this?" Dallas asked.

"Lincoln Graves. I called him."

"You did?" Dallas asked, sounding surprised. "Is he okay?"

"He'll be fine. He was wounded—hit in the shoulder—but if it wasn't for your quick action, he'd be in a lot worse shape.

He told me that he would probably have been killed if it hadn't been for you."

Dallas was silent for a moment. When he spoke, his voice was solemn. "I only did what I had to do, Heather. I can't talk long, but I was wondering if you would do something for me. Could you call Lincoln and give him a message from me? Just tell him that I'm safe but that I'm keeping my distance from him and the police until things calm down."

"Of course." Heather bit her lip. "Dallas, I'm so glad you're okay. I've been going crazy here not knowing what was happening. They thought the guys who ambushed you might have taken you."

Dallas didn't respond right away. "I caught a ride from someone else," he said vaguely. "I can't say who. And I can't say where I'm at right now. But I'm safe, at least for the moment."

"I'm glad." She paused, unsure whether to mention what Elliott had told her or not, but she knew she needed to get it out in the open before she saw him. "Dallas, Elliott told me something. I don't know if it's true or not . . . but I need to ask you about it. He told me that Rigo found a memo from Gordon in your truck—telling you not to write the story on Tito."

"What? Gordon was the one who assigned me that story," Dallas said, sounding confused. He was silent for a few seconds, then said, "Wait a second though . . . I grabbed some papers I hadn't looked at from my in-box the morning I left. It might have been in there . . . But that doesn't make sense either. I'm sure the box was empty when I left the night before."

A woman's voice came on the intercom at that moment, announcing that Heather's flight was about to board.

"What was that?" Dallas asked. "You're not at work, are you?"

"Well, the thing is . . . I'm at the airport," Heather told him hesitantly.

"The airport?" he asked in surprise. "Where are you flying . . . ? Heather, no," he said, and she could just picture him shaking his head emphatically. "Please, don't come. It's too dangerous—and you've been through enough already on my account."

"It's too dangerous everywhere," she countered. "Anyway, I'm a reporter. I go where the stories are. And there's a story in San Antonio," she finished stubbornly.

"Fine, but you and I both know that Elliott wouldn't want you coming here. What about your job? He and Gordon will fire you if you leave El Paso without their permission."

"They can do what they want. Dallas, I'm coming. I want to help you. I have to help—I'm going crazy here."

"Please, be careful," Dallas said softly, sounding resigned.

"I promise I will," she assured him. "If I need to, can I call you at this number?"

"Just a second."

A moment later Dallas came back on the line. "Only in an emergency," he said. "And if you do call, you'll have to ask for me."

"Okay," she said, gathering her things as she prepared to board. "And Dallas, you be careful too. When I didn't know what had happened to you . . . if those guys had gotten to you . . . I don't ever want to feel that way again."

"I'll be fine," he said softly. "I promise. Oh, when you call Lincoln, tell him about that memo from Gordon. He'll need to know about that."

"I'll call as soon as you hang up," she said.

"Thanks," Dallas said. "I knew I could count on you. And Heather, I need you to do one more thing for me."

"Whatever you need me to do, Dallas, I'll do it. So what do you need?"

"I need you to take care of you for me."

She smiled to herself. After the past few days, she knew that she'd do anything for him. She'd never had a better friend than Dallas Dixon.

* * *

News of the shooting in the outskirts of San Antonio spread fast. As the radio report ended, Nick changed the station with a disgusted snort. He was anxious to get out of the state as quickly as possible. They'd managed to get ahold of another vehicle and were driving north through Dallas now, but the miles were rolling by far too slowly for Nick's taste. He glanced over at Tito and rolled his eyes. *Kid still doesn't know what we're up against,* he thought as he watched the arrogant young man slouched in the seat with his feet resting on the dashboard. He looked like he didn't have a care in the world. Despite his short stint in jail, Tito stupidly still seemed to consider himself untouchable.

After another moment, Nick's frustration bubbled to the surface. "Listen, Tito, I think you and I should split up." He forced a softer edge to his tone of voice. "It'll be safer for both of us that way."

"Maybe for me," Tito said flippantly and shot an arrogant look in Nick's direction. "But you need me to watch your back. Anyway, I'm starting to think we're making a mistake trying to get out of Texas."

Nick shook his head. "Haven't you been listening to anything I've been telling you? It doesn't matter how we lost the load of coke. All that matters is that we lost it. I've been around a lot longer than you, kid. Luisa'll kill us."

"And I'm starting to think you're full of baloney," Tito said. "I'm going to call her. I'm her favorite. Yeah, she's gonna be mad, but she'll understand. She'd do anything to help out her favorite nephew."

Her only nephew, Nick thought to himself, but he didn't respond to Tito. It was time to get out. He'd go to Chicago, or better yet Miami, and start over. He gritted his teeth as Tito punched in Luisa's number.

"Luisa, it's Tito." He listened for a moment then said, "I know, I'm sorry. We ran into some trouble. That newspaper guy nearly killed us both when he stole the truck."

Tito was silent for another stretch. Then he glanced sideways at Nick and said, "I told Nick you'd be reasonable, since it wasn't our fault. I was right, wasn't I?"

He listened for a long minute then grinned broadly. "Okay, Luisa. You got it. Have Marco call me. Oh, and Dallas Dixon's gonna pay for what he did. You can bet on that."

He disconnected and turned with a smug look on his face. "See, Nick? All it takes is a little smooth talking. She was cool with it. Anyway, she needs our help with something. We're supposed to meet up with Marco in San Antonio. He's gonna call us and let us know where."

"Sounds good," Nick lied. "How about we get off the freeway and get some gas and food first," he suggested. "Then we'll head south."

"I'll get the food, you get the gas," Tito said and jumped out of the vehicle as Nick pulled up to the pumps. "I'll bring yours out with me. A double cheeseburger, fries, and a Coke okay?"

"Sounds great," Nick said to Tito's back as he got out of the car and toyed with the pump. There was plenty of gas in the car to get him another two hundred miles or so. Watching as Tito scrutinized the menu of the McDonald's inside the convenience store, Nick eased himself back into the driver's seat, shut the door, and hit the gas.

* * *

Tito picked up his order and started back toward the gas station entrance, wondering what was taking Nick so long. He was sure he hadn't come in to pay for the gas yet. He narrowed his eyes and craned his neck to look out through the windows but was unable to see the vehicle by the pump or in the parking spaces by the building. He shoved the door open and went out to look around.

There were only two vehicles in the small parking lot—a VW bug occupied by an elderly woman and a yellow convertible a couple of spaces beyond it. His anger and disbelief growing with every second, Tito began cursing under his breath.

He strode angrily inside again and plopped his food and drinks down on a table in the McDonald's. Then, pulling his phone from his pocket, he quickly dialed Luisa. "Nick up and left me here in Dallas," he complained, half whining, half growling. "He thinks you're mad at us because of what Dallas Dixon did."

"Where do you think he might be going?" Luisa asked. She sounded unruffled, and Tito replied, "Probably Chicago. At least that's what he's been saying. There or Miami."

"I see," Luisa said quietly. "I'm glad to hear that you're being smart. Now here's what I want you to do, Tito."

After the call had ended, Tito congratulated himself. Luisa had no idea what had happened to the semi. She was going to take care of him, and he could stop running. It was Nick's loss. He sat down and began to eat the lunch he'd ordered for Nick and himself.

* * *

Rigo turned a page in his notebook and studied the information he'd written down in the past fifteen minutes during a meeting with Sergeant Cullen and half a dozen local officers, including those who had been involved in the recent shoot-out. He tapped the page and then said, as much to himself as anyone else, "According to the ballistics report, Dallas Dixon is carrying a 9mm pistol with hollow-point rounds, most likely a SIG Sauer. The weapon profile is identical to the proposed description of Andy Norton's murder weapon. And the bullets are just like the ones found in Dallas Dixon's briefcase."

"I'm going to ask the obvious," Sergeant Daryl Everton broke in. "Are you going to make a simple comparison of the bullet removed from the gunman with the bullets taken from your victim?"

Rigo nodded his head. "As soon as I get back, I'll get them to our lab. It won't take long once we have the bullets there to compare. But I'll be surprised if there's a match."

"Why's that?" Will Cullen asked.

"He didn't have a thing on him when he was taken out of the semi over by Fort Stockton. I don't see any way he could have gone back to El Paso and got it from wherever he might have hid it after the killing."

There was a murmur of assent around the room, but when nobody commented, he continued. "We now know that the prints taken from the semi that Dallas allegedly wrecked belong to several people. At least three prints from the window area of the passenger door are Dallas's. However, none of his prints show up on the steering wheel, the console, the gearshift lever, and so on. Tito Maggio's prints appear in several places on the inside of the truck, but they likewise do not show up on the gearshift lever or the steering wheel. The prints we do have on the steering wheel are unidentified. The computer shows no matches," he summed up.

"What about Dallas's Silverado?" Will Cullen asked.

"Of course Dallas's prints are all over his pickup. We expected that. And we've already established that Tito Maggio was a passenger in the truck at some point in time. His prints are all over the passenger side, but again not on the steering wheel or gearshift. And once again we have the same mystery prints all over the driver's side. The logical conclusion is that Tito was with an accomplice who was driving the semi, wrecked it, and then tried to frame Dallas Dixon, who may have simply stopped to help them, just like he claims. Then, like he also said, they stole his truck after assaulting him and left him in the cab of the semi."

No one disagreed with the analysis so far. So Rigo continued. "If Dallas was fleeing the scene of a murder he committed in El Paso, why would he stop to help the driver of a wrecked truck? It doesn't seem like something a man on the run would do."

Again, he saw several heads nod. "Then, while attempting to turn himself in, Dallas is caught in an ambush, in which he saves the life of his attorney as well as some of you gentlemen," he said. "Dallas doesn't exactly fit the mold of prime suspect. I really think we should be focusing our attention elsewhere."

"Tito Maggio comes to mind, as well as whoever was in that truck with him," Will suggested.

"Exactly," Rigo agreed. "And I still can't help but think that his aunt is mixed up in all of this somehow."

Rigo's phone rang. He glanced at the screen and then stood to leave the room so he could answer. "I need to get this," he explained. "It's one of my detectives. I asked him to attend our victim's funeral."

Once outside the room, Rigo asked, "So, see anything interesting?"

"The funeral was huge," CC answered. "Apparently the paper actually shut down so everyone could attend. And all the employees were there—except for Heather Scott, since she's off on medical leave."

"Interesting," Rigo mused. "She seemed pretty intent on

not letting her injuries stop her. I'm surprised she didn't attend. What about the Maggios?"

"Andy's sister, Martha, was there. Frankie's still in custody of course, so he couldn't go if he'd wanted to. Tito was a no-show—big surprise. But Luisa was there. Stayed near the back the whole time. She was wearing black. I even saw her offer condolences to Gordon Townsend. Or maybe it was just the opposite. Andy and Luisa were in-laws."

"Strange, but go on," Rigo prompted.

"Elliott Painter and Gordon Townsend gave eulogies," CC said. "They both seemed pretty broken up. Other than that, there's not much to say about it, I guess. Sad affair."

"Thanks, CC," Rigo said. "I better get into the meeting again, but I should be back tonight."

"No sign of Dallas Dixon?" CC asked before he hung up.

"Nothing," Rigo said with a sigh. "I can't decide if I think he's gone into hiding again or if those guys have gotten to him. The more time that goes by, though, the more I worry that even if he is in hiding, he's going to be found—but not by us."

CHAPTER 18

"You want me to pick the brat up? I thought you wanted me to get rid of him," Marco said incredulously.

"What I said still stands. I'm just asking you to delay a little," Luisa said on the other line. "He's become a sneaky little rat," she said. "But until you're finished with Dallas Dixon, I think he might be useful to you."

Marco slowly released a sigh and ran a hand over his slick black hair. "What about Nick?" he muttered.

"He jumped ship," she replied. "When you're finished with your current assignments, we'll worry about finding him. Just find Dallas Dixon. And find him soon." She didn't mention that she'd already warned him after the botched attempt in Junction and the one in San Antonio. He didn't remind her. She already had him on edge. Luisa did that to people.

Marco hung up the phone and glanced up at the men lounging in the run-down motel room outside San Antonio. "Listen up, men. This is our last chance, and we'd better use it well. We know Dallas took off with some guy in a brown truck. We've got plenty of connections in the area. It's time to call in those connections to find them." His expression hardened. "Now, here's what I want you to do."

As Marco finished instructing his men, his cell phone began to vibrate. With a grunt of disgust he pulled it from his pocket and looked at the screen. When he saw that it was Luisa again, he tried to pack some cheer into his voice even as he felt ice forming in his veins. "Luisa? What's happening now?"

"I just learned that Dallas's girlfriend is on her way to San Antonio," she said sharply. "She's on a commercial flight. She'll be landing shortly. You know what she looks like, right?"

"I've seen her," Marco confirmed.

He heard a trace of laughter on the line as Luisa added, "Keep a sharp lookout. She probably doesn't look quite the same. Apparently Frankie did a number on her face."

"I'll know her when I see her," Marco responded evenly. "And I'll make sure my men do too."

"Good. Then get someone to the airport right now," Luisa barked. "Remember, Marco, three strikes and you're out." Before he could say anything more the line went dead. The ice in his veins did not begin to thaw.

* * *

Lincoln Graves's shoulder was throbbing, but he refused to go home and go to bed as urged by his secretary. He had a client to worry about, and he wanted to be available and reasonably alert in case Dallas tried to get in touch with him. He realized that Dallas might very well be unable to make contact—or he might even be dead—but he refused to give up. However, as the hours slowly passed, his worry intensified.

The time continued to tick by slowly, and when the phone finally rang, Lincoln was jolted out of his chair and answered on the first ring. He sighed with relief when the caller identified herself as Heather Scott.

"Do you have any guesses as to where he could be?" Lincoln asked when Heather had finished delivering Dallas's message.

"He won't tell me," she said with a sigh. "But he insists that he's safe for now."

"This is good news. Thank you for calling, and please keep me informed if you can," he said wearily.

"I will," she promised. "I'm sorry I wasn't able to get ahold of you right after talking to Dallas. I was just boarding the plane and had to wait until after I landed here in San Antonio."

"You're in San Antonio?" Lincoln asked with some alarm.

"I know, I know. It's dangerous. But it's dangerous everywhere," she replied.

"Miss Scott, please listen carefully to me," Lincoln said sternly. "The men who ambushed us might resort to . . . other means to try to get to Dallas. You could be a target now."

"They won't have any idea I'm here," Heather replied. "I know how to stay under the radar, and I'll be careful," she promised.

Being careful may not be enough, he thought grimly. After hanging up, Lincoln dialed a number he knew by heart. When he needed a good man on the streets either to watch over a client or to investigate for him, Lincoln always turned to the same man—Sam Reynolds. Sam was a former detective who ran a private investigation agency in San Antonio. Like Dallas, he had once been an Army Ranger, and he was smart, tough, and fearless. He had intended to call Sam after Dallas was safely in police custody, but the ambush had changed things. Now Heather's presence in San Antonio had changed things once again.

Sam's secretary put Lincoln's call right through.

"Lincoln?" Sam said in his distinctive, raspy voice. "Heard you had some trouble this morning."

"I'm fortunate to be alive," Lincoln told him and quickly filled Sam in on the details of the morning's events. Then Lincoln told Sam all about Dallas Dixon.

"Sounds like a tough guy for a reporter," Sam observed.

"He's former Army Ranger like you," Lincoln told him.

"So what can I do to help?" Sam asked. "I'm assuming you didn't call just to chat."

Lincoln chuckled. "You're right, my friend. Here's what I need." He gave the detective instructions and added, "I think this guy's the real deal, Sam—he's innocent. Let me know how everything goes."

"I'll be in touch," Sam promised.

* * *

Marco smiled as he hung up the phone. His man at the airport had Heather Scott in sight. If Luisa was right, soon he'd know where Dallas Dixon had gone after the shoot-out. This time he'd take more men, and this time they'd also be prepared for any possibility. He rubbed his casted wrist, knowing he'd particularly enjoy taking Dallas Dixon down.

* * *

Dallas fought the urge to tap his foot impatiently. As difficult as it had been being on the run, it was infinitely worse just waiting. He put down the novel he'd been skimming and stared out the mobile home's tiny window. He glanced down to see that he'd read fifty pages so far, but he couldn't for the life of him remember what the book was about. Mostly, his thoughts kept drifting to Heather. That young woman had really gotten to him. He worried more about her than he did about himself. He felt responsible for her safety yet helpless to do anything to keep her out of harm's way.

"How you doing, Dallas?" Mason asked. He'd been out skinning a hog for one of the Easterners hunting on the preserve.

"I'm okay," he replied with a nod.

"Dinner's almost ready at the bunkhouse," Mason said hopefully. "The bosses said it'd be fine for you to eat with us while you're here. It'll be good food. We have one of the best cooks in all of Texas."

"Have you told them who I am?" Dallas asked, suddenly a little nervous.

"I told them that you're my son," Mason said with a shrug. "I didn't mention your name, but I figured we'd use my last name instead of your mama's. Dallas Huggins. Has kind of a ring to it, don't you think?"

Dallas hesitated. "Well, okay," he said after a moment.

Mason grinned and stared down at his feet. But his face grew serious. "Maybe we shouldn't use Dallas. How about if I just call you Dee?"

"That'd be better," Dallas agreed. As he looked at his father, he was overcome with a sudden, inexplicable urge to give him a hug. All through his youth he'd thought of his absent parent with anger and disgust, but deep down he'd always wished he had someone to claim as his father.

"I guess it would make sense for me to call you Dad . . . if that's okay, anyway," Dallas said as he fought to keep his voice even.

He was surprised to see his father's eyes fill with tears. "I'd like that," he said. "I'd like that a lot."

* * *

After dinner, Dallas and his father returned to the mobile home where they passed the time attempting to get to know each other better. Despite Dallas's decision to call Mason Dad, he'd stumbled over the word each time he said it. After a few attempts, he'd avoided calling him anything. He hoped it would get easier after a while.

After visiting for a few minutes, both men grew silent. "I think I'll read for a little while," Mason said. "If you'd like to turn the TV on, help yourself."

Instead, Dallas picked up the novel he'd been reading earlier. As he did, his mind began to drift once more. His thoughts turned to the man he had killed that day, and he knew the nightmares would come with renewed intensity that night. The guilt he felt was overwhelming, and yet he knew he'd had little choice in what he'd done. He tried to tell himself that what he'd done wasn't so different from what he'd been required to do in Iraq, but it was of little comfort. This was America, not a war zone in the Middle East.

He glanced up at his father, who was reading a shiny brown leather book. A moment later, he did a double take. He knew that book. His heart began to pound as he looked closer to make sure his eyes weren't playing tricks on him. But there in gold lettering on the spine were the words "Book of Mormon."

"Where did you get that?" he asked softly.

Mason's face went red and he grinned the lopsided smile that Dallas was coming to expect and beginning to like. "Oh, a couple young pups gave it to me. They were nice kids, and I told them I would read it. I feel kinda obligated now. It's no big deal."

"It's a lot bigger deal than you think, Dad. That's the Book of Mormon," Dallas said. "I love that book."

Mason stared at his son. Then he narrowed his eyes. "You don't drink coffee," he stated.

"That's right."

"I'll bet you don't smoke, either."

"That's right."

"And you probably never have a beer with the boys."

"Absolutely not."

Surprise filled Mason's expression. "Are you one of them?"

"Mormons?" Dallas asked with a smile. "Yeah, I am. I joined when I was a teenager, and I did it with Grandpa and Grandma Dixon's blessing."

"Well, I'll be . . . Were you ever one of those, you know, kids in suits, like the ones who gave me this book?"

"I served a mission, yes. Best two years of my life."

"Really?"

"Yes, really. I loved it. I went to Germany."

"Wow," Mason mused. "So you speak German then?"

Dallas nodded.

"Well, I'll be darned," Mason said. "You are full of surprises." He looked thoughtful for a moment and then said, "Maybe you can answer some questions for me."

Dallas was more than happy to oblige, and for the next hour they talked about the Book of Mormon, the Bible, and the Church. The discussion soothed away some of the hurt of so many years, and Dallas found the word *Dad* slipping more easily from his mouth as the two men discussed the gospel.

As the flow of religious conversation slowed, Mason said, "You fought in Iraq, right?"

"You seem to know a lot about me," Dallas said in surprise.

"I was a deadbeat dad, but yes, I've tried to keep track of you. Can you tell me about the war?"

Dallas swallowed and looked down.

"I'm sorry, Dallas," Mason said gently. "Is it hard to talk about?"

"Some of it is," Dallas answered and tried to smile. "It's just that after what I did this morning, it all kind of came back to me in a rush. I hate what I did today."

"But you had no choice," his father said.

"Maybe I should have shot to wound. It all happened so fast . . . I was on autopilot. I shot to kill the way I did in the war."

"The way you were trained," Mason reminded him.

"Yes, the way I was trained. But this isn't Iraq. Dad, I feel awful about what happened today."

Mason shook his head emphatically. "Son, you did what had to be done. And I believe you're innocent before God."

"That's what I keep telling myself, but I keep thinking about the what-ifs, too."

"You did right, Dallas," Mason said firmly. "And someday you'll feel that."

"I hope so," Dallas said quietly.

"Maybe we could read some of the Book of Mormon together for a little while," his father suggested. "You could help me understand what I'm reading."

"That would be great," Dallas said, and for the next hour the two men read the book together.

That night as Dallas knelt beside the bed in his father's tiny spare bedroom, he thanked the Lord for helping him find his father. And he begged the Lord to forgive him for the life he had taken that day.

CHAPTER 19

HEATHER SLEPT FITFULLY IN THE hotel she had rented for the night in San Antonio. When she looked at the clock and saw that it was 6:00 AM, she finally stretched, pulled on a robe, and gave up trying to sleep. Later, when she thought Rigo might reasonably be awake and at work, she punched in his number.

Rigo sounded exhausted when he answered the call. "Good morning, Heather. How are you this morning?"

"I'm better," she said and glanced in the mirror. "I can open my eye a little bit now, anyway."

"I'm glad to hear that. Are you getting some rest? I assume you're taking some leave after what happened."

"Well, sort of . . ." she replied vaguely.

"Don't tell me you're working right now."

"No, actually . . . well, I'm in San Antonio," she admitted.

"San Antonio!" Rigo said. He sounded worried.

"I'm being careful," she added before he could say anything else. "I just called to see what's happening in the case."

"I wish you hadn't gone there," Rigo said. He sounded angry. "It really isn't safe. Anyway, I'm sorry, but I can't give you much information." He sighed heavily. "I can tell you, though, that we ran a ballistics test on the bullet Dallas shot the man with in San Antonio and compared it to the bullets that killed Andy

Norton. They're the same type of bullet, but they were fired from different guns."

"I could have told you that," Heather said.

"I honestly didn't expect them to match either. There's one other piece of information I can share with you. The DEA is involved in the investigation of the semi Dallas was found in. The evidence they've found leads them to believe Dallas wasn't involved in that case except as a victim. They believe the truck is linked to a criminal organization. They're working on that now."

"That's great news," Heather said, feeling more hopeful by the minute. "Hey, there's one more thing I'd like to know. Is Frankie Maggio still in custody?"

"He is, but I think he'll be out soon. I understand a bail bond agent has been talking to him at the jail."

"So I'm better off staying out of El Paso after all," she said carefully.

"I don't think he'll bother you again," Rigo told her. "But I'd personally worry less if I knew you were at home."

"I feel okay where I am," she said, forcing confidence she didn't feel into her voice.

"Heather," Rigo began again. "Have you received any further information about Dallas's current whereabouts?"

"I don't know where he is," she said honestly.

Rigo was silent for a moment. Finally, he said, "I assume, though, that you've gone to San Antonio hoping to find him."

"I'd like to know where he is," she said evasively. "And I want you to know I appreciate what you're doing. I know you want to get to the bottom of this as much as I do."

"You can say that again. So please, keep me informed. And if you hear from Dallas, tell him that it would be in his best interest to turn himself in."

Heather felt the heat rise in her cheeks. "He tried that, Rigo. And he nearly got killed. I don't think he's got a lot of confidence in anyone right now, and I don't blame him. Listen, I've got to run. I'll talk to you later." With that, she hung up the phone.

* * *

"Does she know where Dixon's at?" CC Cornwell asked as Rigo slowly closed the phone, shaking his head. CC had entered the room just before the conversation had ended.

"I believe her when she says she doesn't know where he's at," Rigo said. "But I'm also sure she's holding something back." He looked up and raised an eyebrow. "Oh, and get this—she's in San Antonio."

CC looked surprised but only nodded. "Rigo, I've got something to say. I know you think we've all but ruled out Dallas Dixon as a suspect, but I'm not sure we're there yet. I'm sure he wasn't the one who was driving that semi. And we know that the gun he was using in San Antonio isn't an exact match with the one that killed Andy Norton. But I still think there's a possibility he's connected to the murder."

"What did you find?" Rigo asked.

"Dallas Dixon has a permit to carry a concealed weapon," CC said, shaping his index finger and thumb into a gun as he spoke.

Rigo looked closely at CC, his interest piqued. "When did he get it?"

"Right after he got out of the Army. As far as I can tell it's still current."

"We didn't find evidence of a weapon when we searched his truck, though. And he couldn't have been carrying a weapon without the officers in Fort Stockton knowing it when he was in the hospital there."

"I know that," CC grumbled. "But he does have a permit. That's the important thing. If he has a weapon, it could be anywhere. And if it is linked to Andy Norton's murder, that's all the more reason for him to keep it well hidden or even get rid of it."

"That also isn't the only question we have left to answer, unfortunately. What about the gun he used in the ambush? Where did that come from?"

Detective Cornwell's face brightened. "Well, let's consider this. Yesterday was the second time he was supposedly ambushed, right? We don't know much about what happened the first time—just that he called you and told you he was scared, right?"

"More or less," Rigo agreed.

"Could he have taken the gun he has now from one of the men involved in the first ambush attempt?" CC asked. "I remember you saying that the officers in San Antonio believe that the man that got away had a cast on a wrist. What if Dallas . . ."

"You might be on to something," Rigo said thoughtfully. "But until we find Dallas, these questions are going to stay just that—questions."

* * *

The sky was cloudless, and only the slightest breeze stirred the sweltering air. It wasn't much better in Mason's mobile home, so Dallas stayed outside most of the time. He wiped his brow as he sat watching his father working beneath a small, open-sided building. Dallas tugged at the collar of the shirt he was wearing—his father's. His father's clothes weren't exactly his style—mostly a combination of long-sleeved western shirts and blue jeans—but they would work until he could get more clothing of his own.

His ears perked up as he heard his father's cell phone begin to ring. Mason answered, listened for a moment, then said, "He's right here, Miss Scott."

"Hi," he said, unable to keep the relief from his voice. "Are you okay?"

"Hey, Dallas. Yeah, besides being worried sick about you, I'm okay. I was wondering . . . is there any chance we could talk in person?" she finished in a rush.

Dallas was thoughtful for a moment. He'd worry less about her being in San Antonio if she wasn't on her own. And he'd love to see her, to just be with her for at least a little while. "If I send someone to get you, will you come here?" he asked cautiously, looking over at Mason, who nodded.

"Yes, of course I will," Heather said without hesitation. "But you don't have to send somebody. Just tell me how to get there. I rented a car at the airport."

"You want me to give you directions?" He glanced at Mason, who shook his head emphatically and gestured toward himself and then to his truck. "No, I don't think that's a good idea," he said slowly. "I think it'll be better if I have someone come and pick you up."

"But I can't just leave the rental car sitting at the hotel," she protested.

"Then take it back. I'll have someone meet you there."

"Okay," she said hesitantly. "I got it from the airport. Will that work?"

Dallas nodded. "That will be great. Just wait by the passenger pickup area outside the first terminal." He looked at his watch. "It's 9:45 right now. Someone will meet you there at eleven thirty." Mason nodded in agreement.

"How will I recognize him?" Heather asked.

"His name is Mason Huggins. He's about my size with graying brown hair and blue eyes. He's wearing a dark brown western shirt and blue jeans. He's about fifty years old. And he smiles a lot."

"Okay, so I just need to watch for someone who's smiling," she said lightly.

"That'll work," Dallas said. Heather was some kind of woman.

"What will he be driving?" she asked.

"He'll be driving a brown—" Dallas saw Mason shake his head and said, "Just a second, Heather." He put a hand over the phone and asked, "What's up?"

"I'm not sure I should take my truck," Mason said with a frown. "The guy that got away at your lawyer's office probably saw my old wreck. They might be looking for it," he said. "I want to help, not make things worse."

"Maybe this won't work after all," Dallas said doubtfully.

"Nah. I'm pretty sure I can borrow one of the other guy's trucks," Mason suggested. "I'd prefer my own truck because I know the power it has under the hood." He winked and grinned. "But Hal has an extended-cab Dodge and he's a good buddy. It's parked in front of the bunkhouse right now."

"Will he wonder why I'm not going with you?"

Mason shrugged. "Just stay in the house. I'll tell him you're not feeling too well. Hal won't ask any questions; he'll just go along with it."

Dallas nodded, then got back on the phone and relayed the details to Heather.

"Okay," Heather agreed when he finished. "And you're sure I can trust this guy?"

"I'm sure," Dallas said confidently.

"I'll leave right now, then. Once I meet Mason, will it take very long to get to where you're staying?"

"Only about an hour. It's outside San Antonio. It's a small place, but there's a spare bedroom you can sleep in, and a sofa for me."

As he ended the call, Dallas looked at his father with a tentative smile. "I hope that's really okay. I'm so worried about her being out there on her own . . ."

"It's fine," Mason said, smiling back. "My house isn't much to look at, but as long as you don't think she'll mind too much, she's welcome."

"Heather's not the type to judge. Besides, your house is amazingly clean for a bachelor."

Mason chuckled. "If you say so. Anyway, I'd love to meet this woman. You obviously think a lot of her." He winked and turned back to his work. "I'll hurry and finish up here so I can get on my way to the airport."

"Be careful, Dad," Dallas said as he turned to go back inside the house. "I don't want you running into trouble because of me."

"You're my son," Mason said, the customary grin fading from his face. "It's time I did something for you. And I will."

* * *

Heather jumped when her cell phone rang immediately upon hanging up with Dallas. She looked at the screen and groaned. *Elliott.*

She watched the phone ring several more times before finally sighing loudly and answering.

"Hi, Elliott. I can't talk right now."

"I'm glad I got ahold of you," he said, ignoring her statement. "I stopped by your place, but you didn't answer the door. Your car's there, but I'm guessing you're not."

"You're right, I'm not home," she said. "I'm on leave, Elliott. I need to go now."

"Where are you?" he asked peevishly.

"I'd rather not say," she told him.

"I just hope you're being careful is all. Did you know that Frankie was released from jail on bond today?" he asked

"No, but I expected it to happen," she said.

"Take care of yourself, Heather. I wish you'd tell me where you are."

"I'm fine. And for the last time, I need to go. Good-bye, Elliott." Without waiting for him to respond, she ended the call and closed the phone.

CHAPTER 20

"FOLLOW HER," MARCO'S VOICE BARKED over the phone. "I want to know exactly where she's going."

"You've got it, Mr. Santini," Bo Elwood, the man who had been assigned to tail Heather, replied as he scratched his sandy brown beard. Bo had been a part of Luisa's organization for several years now. He had an extensive criminal record but was currently off parole and had managed to avoid being arrested for a long stretch. He'd accepted this last assignment with gusto, eager to be back in Luisa's inner network.

Bo smiled as Heather's rental car pulled out and headed north. He followed, keeping a reasonable distance behind. A few minutes later, he called Marco back. "She's turning in at the airport," he said in confusion.

Marco grunted. "Keep me posted. If she's leaving town, we'll know where she's going soon enough."

A few minutes later, Bo called back. "She turned her car in. She's standing in the passenger pickup zone now, looking around like she's waiting for somebody." He eased his vehicle forward a few feet.

Excitement filled Marco's voice. "It could be Dixon. You know what he looks like. If it is him, do whatever it takes to keep on them. I can't wait to get my hands on the guy."

"Wait a second." Bo stiffened as he watched a blue Dodge

pickup pull up alongside Heather Scott. It definitely wasn't Dallas Dixon, but after a very short conversation, the man grabbed the lady's bags and loaded them into the truck. Bo kept a running dialogue of what was happening as he watched.

"I'm behind them," he assured Marco as he snapped his phone shut and eased into traffic a few cars behind the Dodge.

* * *

"We need to talk," Elliott said to Gordon as he caught him leaving his office.

"I've got a lot on my mind right now," Gordon said with a glance toward his open office door. "Can't it wait?"

"No, I don't think so."

Gordon sighed. "Fine, but make it short. I've got a hundred things that I need to do today." He led the way back to his office and sat down heavily in his chair. "So what's wrong?"

Elliott looked nervously toward the door. "I've been hearing a lot of chatter lately. I don't think the staff is too happy with us. They think we were too hard on Heather."

Gordon looked annoyed. "We have her best interest at heart—you know that, Elliott. And the only reason she's not here is that we want her to have time to heal."

"That's not the way a lot of our staff is thinking," Elliott warned.

"Then straighten them out, Elliott," Gordon muttered. "Can't you handle that?"

"I've been trying, but they aren't buying it. They think it was wrong of us to take her off the crime beat."

"Well, that's too bad, isn't it? They clearly don't understand some of the issues we've been dealing with. Her wild-goose chase to try to exonerate Dallas Dixon was getting way out of hand. Not only was it making us look bad, but it was putting her in danger as well." He shook his head. "I hope they find that idiot soon."

"I spoke with Rigo Garcia a little while ago," Elliott piped up. "They don't have any new leads."

"What about the truck wreck? Have they proven that Dallas was the driver?" Gordon asked.

"No," Elliott mumbled and picked up a pen from Gordon's desk, which he began flipping over with his fingers. "The word I'm getting is that the DEA agents think he was trying to help whoever was driving it after they crashed."

"Hmm," Gordon said. "That flies in the face of what the caller told me. He sounded like he knew what he was talking about." He sat thoughtfully for a moment, drumming his desk with his fingers. Then he asked, "What happened to Frankie Maggio? Is he still in jail?"

"No, he was released earlier this morning," Elliott reported.

"Call Heather and let her know," Gordon said decisively. "Or better yet, run down to her place and tell her. And let some of the staff know what you're doing. We don't need them thinking that we're not concerned about her," Gordon said.

"She knows. I already called. And anyway, she's not at home," Elliott said plaintively. "I talked to her on her cell phone."

Gordon looked up quickly. "She's not at home? Where is she?" His face was turning red. At Elliott's look of surprise he shook his head and sighed. "I don't want anything else happening to her. And I hope she's not attempting to dig up more information on Andy's murder. She's on leave, and she's not a crime reporter anymore."

"I don't know where she is. She wouldn't tell me," Elliott said.

"Call her again and press her until you find out where she's at and what she's up to," Gordon demanded. "I'm afraid I don't trust that woman like I used to. So get on it now, Elliott."

"I'll try, but she might not answer my calls."

Gordon grumbled and shook his head. "She's a foolish and stubborn girl," he muttered. "Anyway, try her house again. Maybe she's come back by now. And remember, let some of the staff know you're going to check on her. I don't want anybody thinking we don't care about our people."

* * *

As the Dodge pickup rolled smoothly down the highway, Heather glanced across the seat at Mason Huggins. She knew she'd never met him before, but something about him seemed familiar.

It was Mason who broke the silence a few moments later. "It sure is nice to make your acquaintance, young lady. I just hope you aren't too uncomfortable in my humble home," he said and smiled shyly.

"I'm sure it'll be great. So Dallas has been staying with you?" Heather asked.

"He sure has. Good kid, that one."

Heather nodded and watched the green landscape fly by outside the window. "I've been worried about him. How's he doing?"

"He's doing pretty well, considering. He's a tough one." Mason looked over at her. "He's worried about you, though. Doesn't want his problems causing anyone else grief." His smile faded a bit. "He sure is feeling bad about the way you got roughed up."

"I'll be fine," she replied with a shrug.

The grin returned. "You two are a lot alike, you know. Both tough guys. Anyway, tell me about yourself, why don't you? We've still got nearly an hour ahead of us before we get there."

"Dallas and I worked together at the paper. We realized

we had something in common when we found out we're both Mormon. We've become good friends since then."

"I see. Been hearing that *Mormon* word a lot lately. I've been reading the Book of Mormon myself," Mason said proudly. "Course, I've had to have Dallas explain some things to me. I like the book. You Mormons seem like pretty decent folks."

"Thanks," Heather said with a smile. They rode in silence for a few minutes and then Heather tentatively said, "I have to ask you, Mason. How did Dallas end up staying with you? I've been sitting here trying to figure out why you look so familiar to me, and something just hit me." She paused, and her eyes flicked up to his. "You look a lot like Dallas. Are you a relative of his?"

Mason cleared his throat. "I wasn't sure what Dallas would want me to tell you, but you may as well know. I'm Dallas's father."

Heather looked up abruptly, but she did her best to conceal her shock. "Wow . . . that's . . . I've never heard Dallas talk about his dad. I assumed he didn't have one anymore."

He grunted and shook his head, his smile gone. "He didn't. And he wouldn't have mentioned me. I walked out on Dallas's mom before Dallas was born. It's the worst thing I ever did in my life."

"Oh," Heather replied awkwardly, unsure how to respond. They rode in silence for several miles, and it was Mason who eventually broke the silence again.

"I suppose you're probably wondering how my son and I happened to get together for the first time in our lives," he offered.

"Yeah," Heather said, grateful that the silence had been broken. "I was just thinking about that. It seems like a pretty big coincidence."

"Well, if you don't mind listening, I'll tell you how it happened." She nodded and he began. "Even though I walked out on his mom, I kept track of her. And after she died, I kept track of Dallas the best I could." He went on for several minutes, only occasionally glancing over at her.

When he had finished, Heather shook her head, amazed. "That's quite the story. Sounds like it was anything but a coincidence that you two found each other."

"I'm beginning to think you're right," Mason said softly. "Hey, would it be all right with you if we stopped for a minute at the next rest stop? Nature's calling."

"Sure," Heather said with a smile. *This is all too crazy,* she mused as she once again turned to watch the countryside roll by.

* * *

Bo Elwood clenched the steering wheel tighter as the Dodge put on its blinker and took the next exit, stopping near a convenience store. He eased his black Ford sedan off the highway, careful to stay a safe distance behind, and pulled into the parking area, facing the Dodge. He put the car in park and waited.

As he watched the driver walk into the store, he dialed Marco. "Miss Scott is alone in the truck," he said after telling Marco what had just taken place.

"Grab her and run," Marco said decisively.

"Marco, I thought we were going to let her lead us to Dixon," Bo reminded him, scratching his beard in confusion.

"That was my plan, but I've changed my mind. Get her now. There's always the chance that she's not going to meet him somewhere. This way, we can make sure she takes us to him, and we'll get a hostage as a bonus to make sure he doesn't give us any trouble. Where exactly are you at?"

Bo didn't get a chance to answer Marco's question. His cell phone seemed to jump from his hand, and before he could even turn his head far enough to see his assailant, he was rendered unconscious.

CHAPTER 21

WANTING TO REMAIN UNSEEN, SAM Reynolds ducked down beside the black Ford, swiftly looking through the man's wallet before dropping it back in the vehicle along with a baggie of illegal drugs. *That should keep him out of circulation for a while,* he thought as he silently hurried back to his car. He smiled as he pulled off his gloves and punched in a number on Bo Elwood's own cell phone. Sam had recognized the man's name when he saw it on his driver's license. It was an unlucky day for Bo.

The officer who answered listened as Sam, who was holding a handkerchief over the cell phone to disguise his voice, said, "There is an ex-con sitting in a black Crown Victoria. He's got drugs in the car. Fixing to sell them." He gave the officer Bo's name and the address of the convenience store, and then he added, "He's illegally armed and up to no good. If you hurry, he'll be waiting here for you."

Sam closed the phone and watched as the driver of the Dodge pickup came out of the convenience store and climbed back in the truck. Sam pulled out and headed down the street. As he turned a corner, he saw a squad car approaching at a high rate of speed. "Perfect," he muttered, knowing Bo would be regaining consciousness before long. He pulled to a stop so he could see what was about to happen.

* * *

"I'm telling you, she's not home. I think she skipped town."

The voice on the other end of the line let out a disgusted sigh. "Fine. Just find her. And then eliminate her very discreetly. She's become quite the little nuisance, and I don't want her sticking her nose anywhere else. I assume you know me well enough that we don't have to discuss payment?"

He laughed. "I'm not worried. And I'll take care of her for you."

* * *

Heather's pulse sped up as she watched the speeding police car approach just seconds after Mason had reentered the truck. For all she knew, the cops could be looking for them. Mason's gaze was also riveted on the cruiser, and he seemed as worried as Heather was. She breathed a sigh of relief as the officers passed by them and then slid to a stop beside a black car parked not far behind them. The officers, with weapons drawn, ordered the driver out of the car. He didn't move.

They used their squad car for cover and waited as a second police cruiser drove past Heather and Mason. Sirens blasted the air in the distance, and the officers shouted orders to the driver of the black sedan. Heather saw a slight movement from within the vehicle, and the officers pounced. In a matter of seconds, the man was pulled from the car, thrown to the ground, and handcuffed.

One officer began patting down the man and quickly pulled a gun from inside his coat and handed it to another officer. A third officer pulled a baggie of something from the car and held it up for the others to see. He was grinning.

"What's that all about?" Heather asked, her heart rate still elevated, as Mason started the truck.

"I don't know," Mason answered, shaking his head. "I'm just glad we weren't involved. We'd better get moving, though."

* * *

Sam watched as the Dodge pickup passed by, then he once again pulled onto the highway and followed several hundred feet behind. He had two phone calls to make. The first was to Lincoln Graves.

When Sam reported what had happened, leaving out one little detail that Lincoln didn't need to know about and would never have approved of, the attorney said, "I appreciate what you're doing, Sam. Keep her safe. And if you can give me an idea of where Dallas is while you're doing that, I'd appreciate it."

The second call Sam made was to the man Bo Elwood had called Marco just before Sam took his phone away from him. Sam opened the phone and pressed redial. He was grinning. He enjoyed this kind of work.

"Do you have her?" the voice on the other end of the line asked. Sam assumed the man speaking was Marco.

"You're down a man, Marco," Sam said softly. "You're next if you don't back off."

He ended the call and shut the phone before Marco could reply.

* * *

Heather's phone rang. The screen identified the caller as Lincoln Graves, and she answered nervously, unsure why Lincoln would be calling now.

"You have got to be more careful," he admonished without even saying hello.

"What do you mean?"

"Did you just see a man get arrested?"

"Yes," she said as a chill ran up her spine. "How did you know that?"

"That's not important. What is important is that that man's name is Bo Elwood. He works for a man named Marco, who I have reason to believe planned the ambush on Dallas and me. Please, Heather. Let the police and me handle this matter. If you aren't more careful, you're going to become a victim."

Heather was stunned. "Back up a second. Are you saying you think that guy was after me?"

"Positive. And you're lucky he wasn't successful. You need to get out of Texas. Right now you aren't safe anywhere near here."

Heather didn't know what to say. "I'll be careful," she said weakly. Mason cast a worried glance in her direction

"Please follow my advice, Miss Scott. And call me if there's anything you need. If Dallas contacts you, I'd appreciate you letting me know."

"Okay," she said, still in a daze. The call ended and she looked over at Mason. "That was Dallas's lawyer. He said . . . he said that guy who was arrested back there was after me."

"How does he know that?" Mason asked, clearly alarmed.

She shook her head. "I don't know. He said the guy's name was Bo something and that he was working for a man named Marco." She hesitated. "He also said I should get out of the state." She sighed and then nodded firmly. "But I'm not going anywhere until I see Dallas. Then we'll decide together what to do."

Heather was more frightened than she cared to admit, but she was still determined to help Dallas in any way possible. Just the thought of getting to see him soon caused her heart to beat faster.

The phone interrupted her thoughts again. "Miss Scott, this is Lieutenant Garcia," she heard as she lifted the phone to her ear.

"Hi, Rigo," she said, trying to sound cheerful. "What's up?"

"I'm afraid I have some bad news, and I need you to be aware of it." Her stomach sank as he continued. "Frankie Maggio has disappeared."

"What? How do you know?" Her chill returned and she literally began to shiver.

"He was last seen leaving the jail in a cab. I was surprised he allowed himself to be bailed out at all—he told me he would be safer in jail. He's afraid of Luisa, his sister. But not only did he allow bail, he arranged it. One of the men at his shop worked with a bondsman at his request. I assumed he must have had a change of heart and was going home, but just a few minutes ago his wife called me. She said she hadn't seen him and was worried. None of his friends or employees have seen him, and she's afraid he's up to no good. She specifically asked me to call you and warn you."

"I'm glad you did," Heather said, having a hard time keeping her voice from quivering after all that had happened in the past few minutes. "And I can assure you that I'm being careful."

"Let me know if you need anything," Rigo said and then ended the call.

She explained to Mason what had happened and then hunched over in her seat, taking a few steadying breaths. "Okay, I'm getting really scared now," she admitted after a moment.

"I don't blame you," Mason said gently.

Heather nodded then closed her eyes and began a fervent prayer.

* * *

"After you, CC," Rigo muttered distractedly as he held open the office door behind him and the two men walked toward the parking lot. He'd just hung up the phone with Heather Scott, and already another call was coming through.

"Lieutenant Garcia," a muffled male voice said, "I don't want to get involved—let's get that straight right now. But there's something you should know."

"Okay," Rigo said cautiously. "Go on."

"I know the location of the gun that was used to kill Andy Norton."

Rigo came to attention, signaling CC. "Keep talking," he prodded.

"It's hidden above a piece of false ceiling in the spare bedroom closet in Dallas Dixon's vacated apartment."

"Can you tell me how you know this information?" Rigo asked, but the line was already dead.

"What was that about?" CC asked.

"The caller wouldn't tell me his name, but he claims he knows where the murder weapon is. Long story short? We need to get a search warrant for Dixon's old apartment, pronto."

* * *

"Is there anybody back there?" Heather asked, trying not to make it obvious she was studying the rearview mirror as Mason made a turn. "I've been watching, but I haven't seen anything. Is there any chance that we are being followed right now?"

"I suppose it's possible, but I haven't seen anything suspicious either," Mason replied. "But if we are being followed, I'll see what I can do to lose them." He chuckled mirthlessly. "One thing I can do is drive. I raced cars professionally for a few years when I was a bit younger."

Over the next few minutes, Mason cut down several dirt roads and rounded a few sharp corners. The speeds he drove were breathtaking, and the turns he made were like nothing Heather had ever experienced. She just braced herself against the dashboard and prayed. Eventually, Mason pulled up to a tall gate on a straight stretch of paved road with patches of dense trees and wide fields on both sides of the highway. "I'm going to be just a moment," he said as he opened his door. "When I get the gate open, you slip over and drive the truck through. Then, after I lock the gate, I'll get in the passenger side and you gun it up the road and out of sight of the highway. Keep your eyes open for anything suspicious."

Mason unlocked and swung the gate open in record time, and Heather gunned the truck through. When Mason got back to the truck, she hit the gas again, and soon the highway had vanished.

"I didn't see a single car while we were getting through the gate," she said, releasing a shaky breath.

"That's good," Mason said. "We'll be to the ranch headquarters in just a few minutes now."

* * *

Sam Reynolds slapped the dashboard in frustration. What had just happened to him didn't happen very often. Whoever was driving that blue Dodge pickup Heather was riding in was one whale of a driver. Sam had driven like he was possessed, but it wasn't good enough. The truck had lost him after what must have been five or six miles. He was both embarrassed and angry. And yet in a way, he was a little bit relieved. Whoever that young woman was with wasn't any slouch. Hopefully she'd be safe until he could find her again.

* * *

Dallas heard what he hoped was the Dodge coming toward the cluster of buildings. He stepped out of his father's trailer and into the shade of a green-and-white-striped awning, gazing

intently toward the bend in the road where the vehicle would be
appearing at any moment.

As the truck came around the bend and into view he was
surprised to see Heather driving the truck, her battered face
wrenching his heart. He swallowed hard as the vehicle drew
closer and he could see more clearly the extent to which Frankie
Maggio had hurt her. The bruising around her eye was a mottled
purple and yellow, and her mouth was swollen to double its
normal size, making it look like she was curling her lip up a bit.
Despite it all, though, she was beautiful. His heart began beating
faster, and a small smile crossed his lips.

Heather parked the truck in front of the bunkhouse, and
Mason got out of the passenger side. Heather shut it off, climbed
out, and threw the keys to Mason.

"Dallas!" Heather shouted as she finally spotted him, and she
began to run toward him. She stopped short as she reached the
place where he stood, looking slightly embarrassed.

He reached out a hand and ran it gently across her cheek.
"Look at what he did to you," he said tenderly, a catch in his
voice.

"I look awful, don't I?" she said, glancing up at him and then
away.

"You look beautiful," he said softly, and then pulled her into
a gentle hug. "And I can't tell you how glad I am to see you."

Mason shuffled his feet awkwardly next to them, and Dallas
stepped back from the embrace and smiled. "Let's go inside
where it's a little bit cooler," he suggested. "Then you can fill me
in on what's been happening."

"Sounds good," Heather said, tucking a strand of dark
hair behind her ear. "I just hope we're safe here. Someone was
following us earlier."

Dallas stopped in his tracks and spun toward her in alarm.
"Someone was following you? Did he see where you turned off?"

"No, the whole thing was crazy, Dallas. The police arrested him in a convenience store, then Lincoln called. Somehow he knew the guy had been following us." She shook her head in confusion. "We were really careful after that. We thought there might still be somebody else back there, but your father . . ." She glanced up at him quickly, and he nodded and shrugged, so she continued. "He drove around for a while, just to throw anyone else off our trail." She grinned then. "Did you know your father used to be professional race car driver?"

"I've ridden with him too," he said meaningfully. He took a deep breath and stared off in the direction of the highway. "I'm glad you're both okay. I don't know how Lincoln could have known what he knew, but I'm glad he did."

Heather nodded. "I'm glad you're okay too," she said softly.

He smiled at her. "So am I." He glanced at Mason. "And as for proper introductions, yes, this is my father, Mason Huggins."

She smiled. "He told me a little about how you two met, but I want to hear more later."

"Of course. Let's get inside now, though. And Dad, thanks for taking care of her for me. As you can see, she's wonderful."

Heather blushed, but she said nothing. She did, however, give Dallas a smile that warmed his heart. He couldn't believe how glad he was that she was here with him.

CHAPTER 22

Luck was on Rigo's side. Dallas Dixon's apartment had not been rented out again—in fact, the manager told him and CC that he had not even shown it to anyone since it had been searched earlier.

Rigo led the way directly to the guest bedroom and opened the closet door, unsure of what he was about to find. He had his suspicions about the anonymous phone call. A refusal to identify oneself always sent up red flags in Rigo's mind. But if there was a gun, there was a gun. He had to know.

"Ready?" he asked CC.

"Yep. Lets get started."

Rigo pulled on a pair of gloves and then began to poke at the ceiling. A panel moved, and his heart rate spiked.

"I'll need something to stand on before I can feel around in there," he told CC when he couldn't get his hand beyond the loose panel.

The detective disappeared and then returned a moment later with a kitchen chair. As Rigo stepped up and began feeling around, his gloved fingers brushed against something hard. He grasped it and pulled a 9mm SIG Sauer pistol with a silencer through the opening in the ceiling.

"All right, then," CC said in amazement. "I can't wait to hear Dallas Dixon explain this."

Rigo replaced the ceiling tile and then stepped off the chair, still holding the pistol in his left hand. "Let's not get ahead of ourselves. First we'll need to do a ballistics test on this gun—see if it's the real deal."

"We'll want to check it for fingerprints, too," CC said.

Rigo nodded and frowned. "It looks like we may have found the reason he had a permit to carry a concealed weapon."

* * *

That night Dallas, Mason, and Heather sat beneath the awning and enjoyed the slightly cooler air, the soothing sounds of the ranch, and one another's company. It was the first time Dallas had felt even slightly relaxed since he'd been fired on Monday. It was strange, but he felt like he'd known his father for years now. The two of them got along surprisingly well, and that gave Dallas a sense of satisfaction he'd never known. The shadows grew longer and night closed in as Dallas and Heather filled one another in on the events of the past week and Mason asked both of them more about themselves.

However, when Dallas watched Heather's face as she laughed at one of Mason's jokes, her eyes sparkling in the lamplight, he felt the tenseness and fear he'd lived with for the past week return. He wanted to get to know this woman a lot better, but he knew that this was only a temporary reprieve. There were dangerous people out there, people who wanted to hurt him, and, clearly, anyone close to him as well. And if that wasn't bad enough, he was wanted by the police for crimes he hadn't committed.

The sound of rifle shots nearby made Heather and Dallas jump. "It's just the hunters," Mason said quickly. "But don't worry, the guys here now aren't very good shots. They shoot a lot but don't get much game. I'm hoping it's the same tonight. If they kill something, it's my job to go out and bring it in, clean it, and skin it."

"How will you know if they do?" Heather asked.

"They'll call me," Mason answered.

"How do they hunt in the dark like this?"

"We only allow them to hunt hogs and varmints at night. The other game is off-limits after dark. They use hunting stands for their night hunting. We bait the ground around the stands with corn, and then they sit in the stands and wait. They have to use lights with red lenses to see the hogs. The red lights don't alarm the animals like white light does. But even then it's not very often that anyone gets any game at night." There was a single shot off to the east. "Probably another miss." He grinned.

She nodded but wrinkled her nose. "Is the hog meat any good?"

"Actually, it's excellent meat. And one big hog can feed a lot of people."

"That's good," Heather said weakly, and Dallas suppressed a smile. She looked a little queasy.

Mason shrugged and started to speak, but he was interrupted by his phone. He answered, listened for a minute, and then said, "What's your location?" He nodded. "Okay, I know where you are. I'll be right there."

He shook his head as he ended the call. "I spoke too soon. Looks like I have to work. Feel free to go to bed as soon as you want. Dallas, I left an extra blanket and pillow on the couch for you."

"Thanks, Mason," Heather said.

"Do you need any help?" Dallas asked.

"If you don't mind, you could ride out with me, Dallas." He turned to Heather. "I'd hate to leave you alone here, though. You can come if you like."

She shook her head. "Don't worry about it. I can call you on the cell phone if anything comes up, right? Will you be far?"

"Yes, you can, and no, we won't be too far." He looked at Dallas. "You'll need to ride one of the four-wheelers. Do you know how to drive one?"

"Sure do," Dallas said. "Are you sure you'll be okay, Heather?"

She nodded, brushing aside her disappointment that she wouldn't have a few moments to herself with Dallas.

As the men left, she looked at her watch. It was almost eleven thirty. She hadn't realized it was so late. She was tired, but her mind was still spinning from the day's events.

After Mason's truck pulled out of sight, she got out of the chair she'd been sitting in and walked toward the bunkhouse. Some of the hunters were scattered across the porch on chairs, many with a beer in hand, seeming not the least bit interested in hunting. They stopped talking when she strolled near. One of them called out for her to join them.

"No thanks," she said. "I'm just stretching my legs for a minute."

Not wanting to seem unfriendly, she stepped onto the long porch that extended all the way along the front of the main ranch house, the kitchen and dining area, and the bunkhouse.

"You all right?" one man asked, squinting at her through the darkness. "Looks like you ran into a tree."

"Oh, uh, I had an accident," she said, momentarily flustered. "I'm fine now. Are you all having a good time out here?"

They assured her that they were. She chatted with them for a moment longer, then continued on her way, walking on toward the hunters' parking area. It wasn't long before Dallas and Mason came roaring back on the four-wheelers.

Dallas waved and then jumped off his four-wheeler to help his father unload the large hog that had been killed. "I thought you'd be fast asleep by now," he commented.

"I'm tired, but I don't think I can sleep."

"Would you like to go for a walk?" he asked, shrugging a shoulder.

Her heart gave a happy little leap. "Sure," she said. "If it's safe, that is."

"The hunters are calling it a night. They're all heading back to the bunkhouse. We'll be able to walk out on the roads."

"What about the animals?"

"We'll be okay," Dallas assured her. "Anyway, I'd rather face them any day than those guys who are after me."

Fifteen minutes later, the last of the hunters had returned, and Heather and Dallas headed east toward the far side of the hunting preserve. Dallas had borrowed a flashlight from his father, but he only clicked it on occasionally, as the bright moon overhead provided plenty of light to guide their way.

As Heather stumbled over a dead branch in the path, Dallas quickly caught her hand. She smiled with contentment as it became clear that he didn't intend to let go.

The two walked companionably in silence for a few minutes, and Heather sighed, unsure how to feel. The way his hand felt in hers contrasted so sharply with the storm of violent and unpredictable events swirling around the two of them.

It was Dallas who finally broke the silence between them. "Thanks for coming here," he said. "I've missed you."

"You too; more than you know. You're a good man, Dallas Dixon," she said softly.

He shook his head, and there was sadness in his eyes. "I don't know about that, but I'm glad you think so." He looked up at the wide, dark sky and then back into her eyes. He moved slightly closer to her, and her breathing quickened.

The silence was broken as something moved in the brush near the road. Heather gasped and stepped closer to Dallas. He pushed her behind him and shined his light in the direction of the sound, breathing a sigh of relief as the light's beam rested on a large bull elk feeding in the tall grass near the trees. The animal looked up abruptly and then moved silently, majestically, into the trees and disappeared.

"That was beautiful," Heather said after the pounding of her heart slowed down.

"It was," Dallas agreed. "A lot of the larger animals around here aren't very wild. But it's still amazing to see them this close."

Dallas took Heather's hand once more, and the two continued on their walk. However, before they'd gone far, Heather stopped, looking at him with her brow furrowed. "Why did you say that earlier? When I told you you were a good man."

He shrugged and offered a weak smile. "I just don't feel like a very good person sometimes, after everything I've done. That ambush today . . . it brought a lot of things back to me."

"You know, you only did what you had to in that ambush," she said gently but firmly. "And it wasn't just your own life on the line—Lincoln and those police officers probably owe you their lives too."

"I know all that, but I still killed a man," he said, his eyes downcast. "It's not an easy thing to get over something like that. Not a day goes by that I don't think about the lives I took in Iraq."

Unsure how to respond, Heather squeezed his hand and said nothing. They walked on in silence for a couple of minutes. The sound of crickets trilling filled the night air, and in the distance an owl hooted. After they had walked a ways farther, Dallas spoke again. "I think what bothers me most about the ambush is that I pulled my gun and fired without even thinking about it. What does that say about me?"

"It says you didn't have time to do anything else," Heather said quietly.

"I shouldn't have even had the gun," he told her, shaking his head. "I took it from one of the men who came after me in the motel in Junction."

"You've got to let this go, Dallas. It's tearing you up inside. Can't you see it's not your fault?" she asked, pleading with him.

"Let me ask you something, Heather," he replied, turning her so she faced him. A cloud passed beneath the moon, throwing them into sultry darkness. "And please, be totally honest with me."

"Okay," she said hesitantly.

"What would you say if I told you that I'm guilty, that I did shoot Andy Norton for firing me?" he asked evenly. "I was awfully mad at him, you know."

Heather swallowed, shocked by the question, but she hesitated only briefly before whispering, "I wouldn't believe you. I would say you weren't being totally honest with me."

He looked at her for a moment, the shadows of his features made deeper by the moonlight as the cloud moved on. "Thank you," he said. "I didn't do it, but sometimes I worry . . . I worry about what I'm capable of. I killed those men in Iraq, and it all came back to me so easily when we were ambushed . . . I worry that it's who I am now."

"You're not a murderer, and you never will be, Dallas," she said firmly, looking into his eyes. "You've got to give yourself some time. Someday you'll have a different perspective on all of this."

"I hope you're right," he said, looking up at the night sky once more. Clouds continued to move across it, getting thicker. "Sometimes I still wake up with nightmares." He was silent for a moment. "Sometimes it's easier to not fall asleep."

"I'm sorry, Dallas," she said, squeezing his hand more tightly.

Dallas shook his head and offered a slim smile. "I should stop. I'm sorry I've burdened you with all this. But I appreciate you listening. Sometimes it helps just to talk."

Heather held tightly to Dallas's hand. "I know it probably sounds weird, but there's really nowhere else I'd rather be right now than here with you. You're a good friend. I'm glad you can open up to me about some of those things."

For a moment Dallas didn't say anything. Then, very softly, he whispered, "It's not fair."

"What's not fair?"

"That you're caught up in all of this," he said. Before she could open her mouth to respond, he went on. "That's one thing that's not fair. It's also not fair that all of this blew up right as I felt like maybe things were headed somewhere . . . with us. I thought I'd worked up the courage to ask you out again." He glanced at her quickly then looked away. "I know we only went on one date—and that was just lunch, not a real date—before I was fired, but it was the best date I've been on in a long time. I felt like I could talk to you, Heather . . . you made me feel comfortable right from the start."

Heather felt a blush rise in her cheeks, and she smiled. "I know what you mean."

Slowly, he lifted her hand to his lips and softly kissed it. Then, pulling her closer, he tilted her chin upward. As their lips met, she melted into him. Despite the nightmare they were both living, she'd never felt so good in her life.

For a while the two simply stood, caught in an embrace. Then Dallas stepped back, took her hand in his once more, and started leading her back to Mason's trailer. *Back to real life,* Heather thought with a shake of her head.

Twenty minutes later they again approached Mason's mobile home. Mason was just finishing up his work on the hog and was walking in their direction.

"All cleaned up?" Heather asked Mason with a smile.

"Oh, yeah," Mason answered and grinned back. He looked down and saw her hand entwined with Dallas's, and his smile widened. "I hope I'm not too much of a third wheel around here."

"You aren't anything of the sort," Dallas said, and Heather thought she could see a hint of color in his cheeks. He nodded toward the trailer. "Now let's get inside and get some sleep. Tomorrow's probably going to be a long day."

CHAPTER 23

HEATHER WAS AWAKENED BY AN earsplitting scream. She jumped from her bed and ran into the living room, where she flipped on the light and saw Dallas sitting up on the sofa, his head in his hands. His forehead was beaded with sweat, and his whole body was shaking. Heather ran to him, knelt beside him, and put her arms around him. "One of your nightmares?" she asked tenderly as she tried to keep from grimacing. She'd moved just wrong, and her ribs shot pain clear through her body. She shifted slightly, keeping her arms around him.

"It was the worst one yet," he managed after a moment. She took his hand and he leaned into her. She grimaced again but did not move. She just bore the pain.

"Do you want to talk about it?" she asked.

"Not really, but I will because I think it'll help. You were being shot at," he said, his voice shaking and his body trembling. "I pulled out my gun, but I couldn't shoot. They . . . they shot you . . . and that's when I woke up." She winced at the pain she saw in his eyes. "I'm sorry that I woke you guys."

Mason had entered the room and now stood quietly in the doorway. Dallas looked up at him and then back at Heather. He spoke with obvious strain in his voice. "I could never live with myself if I let anything happen to you. What can I do?"

Heather knew the question was rhetorical, but she gave him an answer anyway. "You can let me sit here and hold you."

Dallas didn't argue, and Mason disappeared silently into his room. For several minutes, Dallas and Heather sat on the sofa. "It'll be all right," she told him. "We're safe, and that's the way it's going to stay."

"I hope so," he said.

They held each other for a while longer, and then he said, "I'm so glad you're here. At least when you're with me I don't have to worry about what's happening to you out there."

"As long as you need me, I'll be here," she promised.

He nodded. "I think I'll be okay now. You should get some sleep."

Heather sat beside the sofa until he fell asleep. Then she kissed him gently on the forehead and went back to her tiny bedroom, where she tossed and turned, her ribs crying out at every turn. It was over an hour before she finally fell asleep again.

* * *

The ballistics test was complete. Rigo sat in his chair studying the report and shaking his head. The pistol taken from the ceiling of Dallas's apartment was indeed the weapon that had been used to murder Andy Norton. He now had no choice but to seek a warrant for Dallas's arrest. He knew he should be elated that this giant piece of the puzzle had been solved, but for some reason it didn't sit right with him.

He was waiting for CC to arrive before going to the prosecutor with this evidence. As he stood to wait for CC in the hallway, his phone rang and he stepped back to his desk and picked it up. "Rigo, this is Elliott Painter. Do you have any new information for me?" he asked abruptly.

Rigo couldn't believe the man's timing. But he could see no reason to keep the latest information private, so he explained what he'd learned. "We'll be seeking a warrant this morning for Dallas Dixon," he said. "And then we'll intensify our search for him."

"Who tipped you off to the location of the murder weapon?" Elliott asked.

"I have no idea, unfortunately."

Elliott paused a moment, then said, "That's strange. You'll let me know if you pick him up, right?"

"I'll let you know," Rigo promised as CC walked up beside him. The expression on his face told Rigo he wasn't any more excited about the news on the murder weapon than Rigo was. They had both come to suspect that the Maggio family was somehow responsible for this murder.

"What about fingerprints?" CC asked when Rigo had hung up the phone.

"Wiped clean," Rigo muttered. "I'm afraid we've got to find Dallas Dixon now."

* * *

Heather had just opened her eyes and stretched as her phone rang. She sleepily looked at the number and wondered if she should just ignore it. However, after a short debate within herself, she took the call. "I guess I still technically work there," she mumbled before she answered.

"Good morning, Elliott. How are things?"

"Things are fine," Elliott said. "When are you coming home?"

"I don't know," she said patiently. "I still have a lot of time left on the leave you and Gordon forced on me."

"I know that, Heather. I'm just worried about you," he said as if she were a young child.

She stepped out into the main living area of the trailer and found Dallas on the sofa, reading his father's Book of Mormon. "It's Elliott," she mouthed, rolling her eyes.

Elliott spoke again, and she dragged her attention back to the phone. "I'm afraid I have bad news."

Heather felt a chill run through her. She didn't need more bad news. "What's happened now?" she asked.

"I just got off the phone with Rigo Garcia. They found the gun that was used to kill Andy. It was in the ceiling of Dallas's apartment."

Heather felt as though someone had just smacked her on the back of her head, hard. She finally choked out, "How did that happen?"

"They got a call from an unknown informant. He told them where to find it."

"Anything else?" she managed.

"No, it was wiped clean of prints. But things don't look good for our pal Dallas. They found out he has a permit to carry a concealed weapon, and it looks like this pistol they found was why. They're issuing a warrant for his arrest as we speak. I'm sorry, Heather."

"I'll bet you are," she said, fighting the tears stinging in her eyes. "I need to go now. Thanks for letting me know."

"What was that all about?" Dallas asked as she hung up, his eyebrows raised in concern.

As she repeated back the conversation she'd just had with Elliott, Dallas's face took on an ashen tone. "That's impossible," he said quietly. "Someone planted it there."

"I know," she agreed. "And whoever did it made sure it was wiped clean of fingerprints when the cops found it."

"Who is doing this to me?" Dallas asked despondently.

"The only conclusion I can come to is that the real killer is behind all this. I think that's who's after you, too."

"But why would they do that? They need me alive to try me for murder."

"You've already been tried by the press," Heather said. "And if you turn up dead, it'll make it easier for the police to wrap up the case, since so much *evidence* points toward you."

"I guess so," Dallas said. "Did Elliott say anything else?"

"He said they've learned that you have a concealed weapons permit," she said slowly.

He shrugged. "I've had one ever since I was discharged from the Army. I haven't actually carried a pistol in a long time. The one I did have, I sold a few months ago. It was a .38 caliber revolver. But I doubt that will be of much interest to the police or the press."

"It makes a difference to this person of the press," Heather said with a smile.

Dallas managed a smile in return, but it didn't reach his eyes. "I wonder what other pieces of *evidence* they have against me," he said. "I'm sure that whoever's planting evidence against me wants to make sure that there's plenty to keep the police from continuing an investigation after I'm dead."

"You are not going to die," Heather said forcefully and buried her head against his chest.

* * *

Both Elliott and Gordon had come in to work at the *Chronicle* that Saturday. Shortly before noon, Gordon summoned his assistant into his office.

"I wanted to make sure you're keeping on top of developments in Andy's murder investigation," Gordon said, nodding for Elliott to sit down.

"I'm trying to," Elliott responded.

"Good," Gordon said dismissively. "Make sure we have an article on it every day."

"I'm doing that," Elliott said enthusiastically. "In fact, I just learned that Dallas has been officially charged with Andy's murder. The police are launching a nationwide manhunt for him," he said with a touch of pride.

"That's good news," Gordon said, nodding. His eyes hardened as he added, "He killed a good man. Dallas hurt every one of us when he committed that despicable act." He fiddled with the paper-clip holder on his desk and then said, "Andy should be sitting in this chair, not me. Don't get me wrong, Elliott. I was glad to serve when the board asked me to, but no one will ever quite fill Andy's shoes."

"He was a good boss," Elliott replied. "But you shouldn't be so hard on yourself."

"You're probably right," Gordon said with a shrug. "Anyway, I want the public to be informed as quickly as possible of every development on the case. I'm counting on you, Elliott."

"I'll keep right on top of it," Elliott promised. "Is there anything else?"

"Yes, actually. What have you heard from Heather Scott? You have been in touch with her, haven't you?"

Elliott looked down at his shoes. "I've talked to her on the phone. She still won't tell me where she's at, though."

Gordon nodded thoughtfully. "Fine. But I've been thinking . . . I'm not sure it's such a good idea to keep her at the paper after her leave's over. I worry her feelings for Dallas have dulled her instincts as a reporter, and this latest news will only add to the problem."

"She is a good reporter, though," Elliott argued.

"I know that. But so was Dallas Dixon. That doesn't stop them from being bad for business. Of course, Dallas has pretty well fixed himself. Now you and I need to make sure that Heather doesn't bring any more shame on the *Chronicle*. Damage control is the name of the game, Elliott. How does it look for one of our reporters to be sympathetic toward the man who killed Andy Norton?" he asked as he shook his head.

* * *

Lincoln Graves's shoulder throbbed as he reached for his phone. His wife had tried to convince him to stay home that Saturday morning and rest, but he'd insisted on going into the office just in case Dallas Dixon called him.

"Mr. Graves, this is Lieutenant Rodrigo Garcia," he heard the El Paso detective say when he answered the phone.

"Good afternoon, Lieutenant," Lincoln said as he shifted in his chair in an attempt to ease the discomfort in his shoulder. "What can I do for you today?"

"I'm sorry to bother you on a Saturday," Rigo said, "but I thought it would only be fair to let you know that we have brought official charges against your client and that the court has issued a warrant for his arrest."

"What exactly has he been charged with?" Lincoln asked.

"First-degree murder in the death of Andy Norton," Rigo told him.

"I see," Lincoln replied, keeping his voice steady. "And I'm supposing that you have new evidence on which to base the charge? The last time we spoke, you certainly didn't have anything except for what you folks think might be a motive."

"That's right," Rigo said. "We now have the murder weapon. And we found it in Dallas's apartment."

Lincoln waited a moment to respond, truly taken aback. "You searched his apartment on Tuesday. As I recall, you didn't mention having found it then."

"That's correct, sir," Rigo said. "We received a tip from an anonymous caller, and we found it right where he told us it would be."

"I see," Lincoln said, his senses on alert. "And did this informant tell you how he came to know about the location of the gun?" he asked. "This gun that you missed on your first search?"

"No," Rigo answered. "We're hoping to get answers to that question when we talk to Dallas Dixon. The district attorney was hoping, as I am, that this new evidence might move you to encourage your client to turn himself in."

"I think the chances of him doing so are highly unlikely, after what happened the last time he made that attempt."

"Will you at least ask him?" Rigo asked.

"If I hear from him, I'll certainly do that. Now, are you willing to tell me how certain you are that you have the murder weapon?"

"Completely certain. We did the normal ballistics testing. It's the one, all right."

"And I suppose you found Mr. Dixon's fingerprints on the weapon?" Lincoln prodded.

"No, it was wiped clean," Rigo said.

Lincoln breathed a sigh of relief then said curtly, "Well, I appreciate your call. You might let the assistant DA know that I will be filing a motion to suppress the weapon as evidence."

"But it was in the apartment," Rigo argued.

"That may be true, but we don't know who put it there, now do we? It's very unlikely that Dallas Dixon has been in that apartment since you last searched it. But thank you for calling. I'll let you know if Dallas decides to turn himself in. But I very much doubt that will be the case." With that, Lincoln hung up the phone.

Lincoln stroked his chin as he mulled over the information he'd just received. He had to admit he was surprised by the call. Usually he had to file for discovery to get anything from the prosecution. But in this case the prosecution had allowed an officer to volunteer information in an attempt to reach the accused. Lincoln wasn't buying it. Despite the supposed evidence that had been brought to light, his gut still told him that Dallas Dixon was telling the truth, which meant that the gun—the murder weapon—had been planted in the apartment. Which also meant that the real killer was working overtime in an ongoing effort to frame Dallas for the crime.

He began forming a plan of action. The first thing he would do Monday morning would be to prepare a motion for suppression. Since the informant was anonymous and the pistol hadn't been found on a previous search and Dixon clearly hadn't been there since, he knew he stood a good chance of succeeding. It was certainly worth the effort, anyway. Then if he could just talk to Dallas . . . He glanced at the phone, willing it to ring.

He decided another call to Sam Reynolds was in order. Sam had lost the man and woman he'd been tailing in the truck the night before—a rare occurrence for him. He'd been embarrassed when he made the report. But he'd also acknowledged that whoever had picked Heather up at the airport was a skilled driver. Lincoln knew that things like this happened from time to time. He tried not to stress over it. Sam had already proven his worth by preventing Heather Scott from being taken by Bo Elwood.

"Nothing new to report, Lincoln," Sam said when he came on the line.

"That's all right, Sam. I'm calling for a different purpose. I have reason to believe that the Maggio family may be trying to both frame and kill Dallas Dixon. However, new so-called evidence has come to light that I think will make the police pull some of their attention away from the Maggios and back to Dallas," Lincoln said.

He went on to explain about the murder weapon that was found in Dallas's apartment, then asked, "Will you go to El Paso and see what you can learn about the Maggios?"

"I'm glad you asked," Sam said, and Lincoln thought he could hear the smile in his voice. "I'll get right on it."

* * *

Mason looked around carefully before getting back in his truck. The hunters had left the preserve that afternoon and more were not due in for a couple of days, so he had taken the opportunity to drive into San Antonio to buy some groceries. He wasn't used to feeding more than himself, and he'd been shocked to look in the cupboard and see only a lonely can of beans inside.

After he'd picked up the groceries he needed, he had located a gunsmith who was open on Saturday. Mason didn't hunt much, but he liked to have his old lever action rifle in working order in case he needed it. The firing pin on his gun had recently broken, and he knew he'd feel safer with a weapon around, given the current circumstances. However, the process of getting it fixed had taken several hours, and he was getting worried. He didn't want to leave Dallas and Heather alone at the ranch for too long. It added to his nerves that since the hunters had left, all of the other ranch employees had been given a couple of days off and left the premises too. So they really were alone there.

He was relieved when he finally got the rifle and was able to hurry back to the ranch. Heather and Dallas helped him put the groceries away when he arrived, and then Heather volunteered to fix them some dinner. After they had eaten, Mason stayed in the trailer when the pair decided to go for another walk. He shook his head as he watched them leave, praying that his son's problems would soon be over and that he could get back to his life—hopefully one that would include Heather Scott.

CHAPTER 24

As Heather and Dallas walked away from the little mobile home, he took her hand in his in an easy gesture that had become familiar to both of them. However, his expression was serious when he turned to her.

"Heather, I'm worried it might not be safe here anymore. I'm positive that they've filed that warrant for my arrest by now, and I'm sure it's only a matter of time until the guys that work here see or hear something on TV or in the paper. I'm sure they'll recognize me." He sighed and kicked at a rock in their path. "Where do I go now?"

"Where do *we* go?" Heather said. "I'm not letting you get out of my sight."

To her delight, Dallas didn't argue but instead gripped her hand more tightly as they walked on in a companionable silence. After a few minutes, they veered back toward ranch headquarters.

When Dallas shared his worries with Mason, concern and a flicker of sadness crossed his features. However, there wasn't much room for argument when Dallas told him that he and Heather needed to leave the ranch.

After a moment of mulling things over, Mason said, "Let's wait until late tonight, then I'll take you back to the airport and you can get a flight out of state."

Dallas and Heather looked at one another and nodded. The farther they were from both El Paso and San Antonio, the better.

* * *

Waiting for the hours to pass was difficult for everyone in the little mobile home. They talked, played games, and talked some more as the hours inched by. Finally, an hour after dark, Heather and Dallas began making preparations to leave.

As Dallas lifted a backpack he had borrowed from his father into the truck, he turned to Heather and smiled. "You know, when all this is over—"

However, before he could finish his thought, Mason burst from the trailer, carrying his cell phone. His face was white, and he slowed down as he approached Heather and Dallas, breathing heavily.

"What's the matter, Dad?" Dallas asked, furrowing his brow.

"They . . . they know where you are," Mason wheezed.

"The police?" Heather asked.

"No, the guys from the ambush. They know you're here on this ranch."

"What? How do you know that?" Dallas asked in alarm.

"Leon just called me," Mason said urgently. "He and Brody were hanging out in a bar tonight. Some guy came in showing a picture around and saying he was looking for a murderer on the run. Brody was drunk, like he always is on his days off. When he saw the picture, before Leon could stop him, he said, 'Hey, Leon, ain't that the guy that's staying out at the ranch?' Leon tried to convince him otherwise, but that only made Brody surer."

Heather's face had gone pale in the darkness. "We've got to get out of here," she whispered.

Dallas gave a slight nod and placed an arm protectively around Heather's shoulders.

"Leon finally got Brody to shut up," Mason continued, shaking his head, "but not before the damage was done. That's why Leon called . . . said he didn't know what was going on, but he figured he owed me at least a heads-up."

"Did Leon say anything about the guys who were showing my picture?" Dallas asked.

"Yeah. Said that one of them was just a kid, probably too young to be in a bar, and the other one was older, in his thirties maybe. Both of them looked kind of Italian, and the older one had a cast on one wrist."

"That's the guy whose wrist I broke," Dallas said. "The younger one might be Tito Maggio."

Heather shuddered and leaned closer to Dallas when the name Maggio was mentioned.

"The bar is forty miles away, so even if they are planning on coming here, they'll be awhile yet," Mason said, obviously trying to infuse some hope into the situation.

"Even so, we'd better leave right now," Dallas said.

Just then a shot sounded in the direction of the main gate.

"Oh no, I was wrong. I think we just lost the lock on the front gate," Mason said and gestured urgently to his left. "Jump on one of those four-wheelers and get into the woods. You can hide there. I'll hold down the fort out here."

"No, you come too, Dad," Dallas said urgently. "It's too dangerous."

But Mason refused to be persuaded, and Dallas and Heather, after grabbing a couple of flashlights, headed to the farthest point of the ranch. "We'll find somewhere with a good lookout, so we can see them coming if they come looking for us in the woods," Dallas said as they raced away from the ranch head-quarters. He glanced back, worry for his father forming a hard lump in his stomach.

* * *

Marco resented having to call Luisa every time he made a move, but he didn't dare cross her. So as he and Tito pulled onto the freeway a couple of hours after dark that night, he drew in a breath and dialed.

"Good news?" Luisa said with just a touch of annoyance in her voice.

For a change, Marco had just that. "Tito and I are on our way to the place where Dallas is hiding," he revealed. "I have two men who are closer than us. They're almost to his location. They'll have him before we can get there."

"I'm very glad to hear that," Luisa said. "I was beginning to worry that our relationship might be drawing to an unfortunate end."

"He's a sitting duck," Marco said gruffly. "Nothing to worry about." He paused and then added, "Oh, and you'll be pleased to know that Heather Scott is with him."

* * *

Dallas and Heather drove for two or three minutes before Dallas stopped the four-wheeler. "I can't leave him alone back there," he told Heather. "I'm going back."

"Then I'm going with you," Heather said, holding tightly to his jacket.

"No!" Dallas barked. "I couldn't live with myself if something happened to you. Please, stay." He quickly looked around, and his eyes lit up as he saw one of the tall hunting stands used by the hunters at night. "There," Dallas directed her, pointing to the stand. They hurried over to it. He pointed to the ladder. "Climb up there and then stay down and out of sight. And here," he said, pulling out his gun. "Keep this. It's loaded and ready to fire."

"Dallas, I can't," she protested.

He ignored that. "Do you know how to shoot a pistol like this?" he asked.

"I don't know," she said.

"Here, let me show you. It's loaded and the safety is on. This is the safety," he said. Just move it like this and then all you have to do is pull the trigger. It will do the rest. Do you understand?"

"Yeah, I've got it, but I'd rather you take it."

"No. You keep it, Heather, and use it if you have to."

"Dallas, you might need it."

"I can handle myself without it, Heather. Now please, get up there. I've got to make sure my Dad's okay."

"If you insist," Heather said reluctantly. "But please be careful, Dallas." She gave him a quick kiss and then reluctantly accepted the pistol and climbed the ladder.

When she was safely out of sight, Dallas again started the four-wheeler and headed toward the trailer with the lights off. But a half mile or so before he had reached it, he drove the four-wheeler deep into a thicket and continued on foot at a fast jog. He knew it would cost him in terms of time, but he couldn't afford to announce his approach on the loud machine.

The moon had been quite bright just minutes before, but it was suddenly much darker. He looked up. Thick clouds had moved in and blocked the light from the moon. He was glad. What he needed now was darkness.

He'd only gone a couple of hundred yards when he heard a single shot come from the direction he was heading. His heart jumped into his throat and a prayer formed on his lips as he began to run as fast as he could.

* * *

Heather clenched her hands tightly as the sound of a shot

echoed through the preserve. It had come from the direction of ranch headquarters.

She stayed where she was a moment longer, then she took a deep breath and began to climb back down the ladder. *He'd do the same for me,* she told herself as her feet hit the ground. *I can't just sit and wonder what's happening.*

She murmured a prayer as she made her way to the rough, narrow road Dallas had taken on the four-wheeler a few minutes earlier. Clouds had darkened the night, but she didn't dare use the light much for fear of being seen, and so she made her way as fast as she could by what little light penetrated the heavy clouds overhead.

* * *

Dallas slowed to a walk, breathing heavily, as he neared the cluster of buildings that made up the ranch headquarters. He stepped off the road and into the brush, straining his ears to catch any sound that might come from the buildings. However, all he could hear were the usual sounds of the night—bird calls, crickets, the movement of the branches and leaves in the wind, and cicadas chirping.

He pressed forward again, listening carefully all the while. He had gone several yards when he heard a voice. He couldn't tell what was being said, nor could he identify the speaker, but he was certain from the tone that it wasn't his father. He was now close enough to see the lights of the bunkhouse lighting the yard. He moved closer and then stopped behind a tree to survey the area as he listened for more voices.

A black sedan was parked in front of the bunkhouse, partially hidden in the shadows. As he kept his eyes trained on the vehicle, a male voice clearly said, "We'll burn you out if we have to. Just send Dixon and the girl to us and we'll leave. No one else needs to get hurt."

His throat tightened as he heard his father's voice. "For the last time, I don't know who you're talking about, and I'd suggest you get yourselves out of here. My patience is wearing thin," Mason said from somewhere in the area of his trailer and the surrounding sheds and other mobile homes. Dallas couldn't tell exactly where his voice was coming from.

As he continued to watch and listen, his heart beating painfully in his chest, he saw a shadowy figure slip from behind a corner of the bunkhouse and run to the sedan. There the man hunched down behind the car.

When he didn't see more movement or hear more voices, Dallas slipped from behind his tree and worked his way silently through the brush and trees that bordered the road north of the cluster of buildings. He stopped and dropped to his knees when he was directly across the road and a short way from the rear of the black sedan. The man he'd seen move there was still hunched down behind the car. There was just enough light that Dallas could see the gleam of a pistol in his hand.

Dallas slipped silently from the protection of the foliage and headed straight for the man behind the car, knowing it was unlikely he'd get a better opportunity for surprise than this without a weapon. As he drew closer, moving with the stealth of a cat, the man's voice called out again, revealing his approximate location as well.

"I'm running out of patience too. Send them out or believe me, you'll regret it," After a few moments of silence, the man added, "I've got more men coming. They'll be here any minute. When they get here, we'll shoot this place up and then burn it to the ground. We won't leave any witnesses."

Dallas was now crouched directly behind the man near the sedan. Adrenaline coursed through his veins, and his ranger training and experience in Baghdad took over. He slipped his arm rapidly around the man's neck and squeezed tightly. The man struggled briefly and silently before losing consciousness.

Dallas lowered him to the ground and quickly tied the man's hands and feet together behind his back with his own belt. He also stuffed the man's own handkerchief in his mouth to keep him quiet just in case he woke up, although that wasn't likely to happen for a while. Then he picked up the gun, thought about keeping it for a minute, but then changed his mind. He threw it across the road and into the brush he'd just come from. It landed with a thud.

"Joe, that you?" the voice beside the bunkhouse called out.

"Yeah," Dallas grunted, doing his best to keep his voice muffled.

"Marco and Tito will be here soon. Hold your position until they get here, then we'll shoot 'er up."

Dallas waited several minutes, then he silently crossed the road again and hid himself in the bushes where he could watch the bunkhouse area without being visible.

The man beside the bunkhouse called out to Joe again, and Dallas gritted his teeth. When the man got no answer, he peered around the west corner of the bunkhouse. When Dallas studied the man's face, he saw a mixture of confusion and nerves. Dallas decided to move again. He couldn't be sure, but he suspected that this man was the only other one there at the moment. He hoped to put him out of commission before Marco and Tito arrived.

* * *

Heather stared at the barely visible fork in the road, unsure of which way to go. Her instincts told her that she should veer to the right, but she wasn't sure how much she could rely on her instincts in this dark and unfamiliar territory. She stood in the middle of the road and clicked on the light for a quick look.

Her heart leaped in her chest as the beam of light landed directly on a snake slithering from the brush onto the road. Its head turned toward her and she saw two calculating, amber-colored eyes staring at her, the animal's tongue flicking in and out in the flashlight's beam. A twig snapped under her foot as she stepped slowly backward, and the animal coiled its long, copper-colored body. It stared for a moment longer as Heather backed out of its range. Heather tripped over a rock, but she quickly regained her feet, ignoring the burning pain in her ribs. She shined her light again, and she could see the deadly copperhead slithering off. A moment later it had disappeared into the tall grass beside the road. She swallowed and prepared to continue toward the headquarters.

As she clicked off the flashlight, the snake's deadly gaze still emblazoned in her mind, a sudden memory jolted her like an electric shock. She almost screamed, unable to believe she hadn't realized it until now. *Of course . . .* she thought, more sure with every passing second. Once more she began walking as fast as she could in the darkness, praying that she was headed in the right direction. There was no time to lose. If she could get to Dallas and get out of this current situation, they just might be able to set things right. All she needed now was proof. Heather was reasonably sure that she knew who killed Andy Norton.

* * *

Dallas had moved as silently as he could as he approached the second man. But he must be getting rusty, he decided. He feared that the man had heard him. Dallas was within about three feet of him when the man turned. Dallas dove for his feet as the man's pistol fired, narrowly missing him. Dallas struck into him with his full weight, and the man fell with a thud. From the corner of his eye, Dallas saw the pistol fly from his hand.

Dallas twisted around, keeping hold of the man's legs as he rose to his feet, and causing the man's face to strike the gravel. But his opponent twisted free of Dallas's grip and leaped to his feet in a single bound. Dallas quickly readjusted and whipped around to find himself facing a man with a knife.

"You must be Dallas Dixon," the man said menacingly, a slight grin pulling at his features. "Now, we can do this the easy way, or we can do this the hard way. You can lie down on that gravel there and put your hands behind your back, or I can stick you with this knife. It's your choice."

Dallas reacted as the man finished speaking, spinning around, his right foot striking out like a copperhead. His shoe struck the man's arm, and the knife joined the pistol somewhere on the ground. Dallas didn't look to see where. Letting his momentum carry him forward, he struck the man's face with his right fist then again chopped him across the face with his left hand.

But Dallas's enemy never hit the ground. He spun as he fell, but just as quickly he was back on his feet, crouching, facing Dallas. By then they had both moved well into the light in front of the bunkhouse, and Dallas could see murder in his opponent's eyes. The man lunged, striking hard at Dallas with his right fist, but Dallas caught it with both hands, then twisted and literally threw the man over his shoulder, slamming him to the ground. He followed with a powerful chop to the man's throat, ending the fight—just short of ending the man's life.

"You handle yourself pretty well, Dallas."

Dallas looked up sharply to see his father standing over him, a rifle in his hand. Breathing heavily as he got to his feet, Dallas said, "I didn't know you had a rifle."

"It wasn't working. I got it fixed today," Mason said. "I only fired one shot, but it kept those two crazies at bay." He glanced out into the darkness. "I thought you were going to stay out there where you were safe."

"I couldn't leave you here alone," Dallas said with a shrug.

A slight smile pulled at the corner of Mason's cheeks. "I wasn't alone. I had my trusty .30-30 here. Where's Heather?"

"I'm right here," Heather said as she ran from the darkness of the trees.

"Am I seeing things, or are you holding a pistol?" Mason asked, squinting his eyes as Heather drew closer.

"It's Dallas's. He made me keep it," she said.

Mason shook his head and frowned. "Dallas, I know now just how good you are in hand-to-hand combat, but you might have needed that pistol."

"I don't want to use it," Dallas said and looked away. "I don't want to kill anyone else—not ever again."

Mason nodded with understanding, and Heather took hold of Dallas's hand and squeezed it. Then she said, "Take it, Dallas, just in case."

"I don't want to use it again," he repeated stubbornly.

"What if my life were in danger?" she asked, narrowing her eyes.

Dallas gave her a long look. "In that event I'd use it," he said with a sigh of resignation and tucked it back in his pants. "Let's get these guys secured. They might regain consciousness before too long. And we'd better be ready for Marco and Tito. They'll be here anytime now."

"So will the cops," Mason said.

"What?" Dallas asked.

"Yes, cops. I called them. But before they get here, you two need to be gone. You can take my truck. I'll say you forced my hand," Mason said.

"No, I'll stay and turn myself in—if they get here before Marco and Tito," Dallas said.

"No, Dallas," Heather said urgently as sirens sounded in the distance. "There's something you need to know first. I . . . there's not time to explain now, but I think I know who killed Andy. It's going to take some work to prove it, though. And I can't do it if you're in jail. I need your help."

Dallas didn't respond at first, his brows raised in surprise, but then he nodded decisively and turned to Mason. "We'll take that sedan over there. If you have to, you can tell the police I left, that you tried to stop me, but I got away anyway."

Mason hurried to grab their things, and Dallas ran to the car. When he saw that the keys were in it, he turned to Heather and said, "Let's go! Dad will be out soon."

A moment later, Mason tossed several things in the vehicle. "Call me as soon as you're able," he said, concern and love evident in his eyes.

"Dad, I really don't want you to have to lie for me," Dallas said quickly. "You know that at some point they're going to figure out that we were here. They'll figure it out even if you don't tell them."

"They might figure out that you were here, but not Heather. Not unless Leon and Brody say something. And I don't know where you're going, so I can't tell them that. With a little luck, I think I can hedge long enough for you guys to get away. Now get going," Mason said.

CHAPTER 25

THE SIRENS' WAILS GREW LOUDER as Heather and Dallas approached the ranch entrance, so Dallas backed the sedan onto a narrow, rough side road near the fence. Then he shut off the lights and waited, praying that the police would simply continue on to the ranch headquarters.

There were three police cars. All of them raced past the little road where the black sedan was hidden, and Dallas breathed easier as they drove out of sight. As the sirens grew more distant, Dallas started the engine and drove out of the hiding spot. He didn't turn his lights on until he was on the highway and heading north.

As they drove farther into the night with no sign that anyone was following them, Dallas allowed himself to relax a bit. Then he turned to Heather, a question in his eyes. "Who?" he asked quietly.

"Like I said, I don't have any proof. It's just a feeling . . . But it makes sense." She swallowed, looking over at him for a long moment. Then she told him.

His gut churned. He didn't argue with her. There was a very good possibility that she had stumbled onto the truth.

* * *

Mason met the police and frantically pointed to the two men lying tied up on the ground. "There's more on the way," he said urgently. "And they're bound to be here soon. And I know at least one of them was involved in the ambush in San Antonio."

That was all it took to divert their attention from Dallas and the missing black sedan. The officers backed their vehicles out of sight, fully aware that they might well be involved in another shoot-out shortly. They only had to wait a few minutes before another vehicle could be heard leaving the highway and pulling onto the ranch.

A black Cadillac Escalade entered the compound. It sped up to the bunkhouse, and the driver hit the brakes, sliding to a stop and sending clouds of dust into the darkness. After a moment's pause, it began to back up rapidly. However, one of the patrol cars that had been hidden in the trees a short distance from the highway pulled out and blocked its retreat. An officer jumped out and leaned over the hood of the cruiser with a shotgun.

The Escalade slid to a stop, and the officer yelled a command for the driver to exit the vehicle. But the driver of the Cadillac shoved it into drive and peeled forward. Another police vehicle pulled into his path. The Escalade again slid to a stop. From the darkness next to one of the clustered buildings, another officer spoke through the loudspeaker of his patrol car, ordering the occupants of the car to step out with their hands up.

The Escalade started up once more, but the third police cruiser blocked any hope of escape short of driving into the bushes and trees. All was silent for a few short moments, and then a gunshot exploded from the passenger side of the vehicle, the bullet striking one of the police cars, as the Escalade accelerated. A barrage of police gunfire followed.

The Escalade left the roadway and rammed violently into a large oak tree. Steam began to pour out from under the hood.

The shooting stopped. For a moment, it was silent except for the escaping steam.

Then the officer, using his loudspeaker again, ordered the occupants to exit the vehicle. When nothing happened, the officers began to slowly close in on the vehicle, their firearms ready. A spotlight from one of the patrol cars lit the area surrounding the Escalade. A second spotlight made it even brighter.

Mason continued to watch from his position beside the bunkhouse as the passenger door opened and two hands appeared, raised high in the air. The officers barked out orders for the suspect to slide out slowly while keeping his hands high and in sight, and then to lie on the ground. A young man with a dark complexion and black hair emerged from the car. Mason craned his neck to see inside the vehicle. He couldn't be sure, but from his angle it looked like the driver was slumped over the steering wheel.

As soon as the young man was handcuffed on the ground, the officers opened the driver's-side door. After a moment's struggle, they pulled a limp, bloodied body from the vehicle.

More officers arrived about the same time as the ambulance pulled in to pick up the two injured men from the sedan. The driver of the Escalade had run out of luck. Mason pulled his eyes away from the gurney with the sheet covering a still body as the ranking officer at the scene approached.

"We've been so busy I haven't introduced myself. I'm Sergeant Bradley Marks. Are you Mr. Huggins?"

"Yes, sir, I'm Mason Huggins," Mason said.

"You called this situation in?"

"I sure did."

"Did you overpower those two men by yourself?" the sergeant asked, his eyebrows raised. "If you did, I won't ever try to tangle with you."

"I could never have done it myself. I had a little help. You see . . . Dallas Dixon was here," Mason said slowly. "He's the one these guys were after."

The officer was clearly doing his best to take this information in stride. "Where is Dixon now?" he asked, his eyes locked on Mason's.

"He took off after he'd taken care of the two men who were threatening to kill me."

"Do you know where he's headed?" Bradley asked.

Mason shrugged. "He didn't say."

"How did he get away?"

"He took the car those guys came in," Mason said. "It's a black sedan. I'm sorry, but I didn't get the license number or make. It was a little crazy here."

"If you don't mind, I'd like to sit down with you to get a few more details on this story," the officer said.

"I'd be glad to," Mason replied and led the way to his trailer.

* * *

"Are you sure that's who it was?" Dallas asked again, trying to take in what Heather had suggested.

Heather shook her head. "I know it sounds crazy, but hear me out. Think about it, Dallas." She then laid her reasoning out for him. And it made a lot of sense to Dallas.

Heather tucked a strand of hair behind an ear and looked into the rearview mirror as she'd done every mile or so while they'd been in the car. Seeing nothing, she turned back around and asked, "Does what I've told you make sense?"

Dallas nodded. "I think you might be on to something. One thing's for sure, we've got to get back to El Paso before we can even begin to find out if your theory is right," he mused. "How do we get back without running into more of the kind of men we left behind on the ranch? The fastest way to get there would be to fly."

"I don't think we can take a plane," Heather said with a shake of her head. "These guys—however they're connected to this mess—aren't amateurs. I'm sure they'll be watching for you."

"The other problem is the gun," Dallas said. "We'd have to leave the pistol behind. There's no way to take it on a plane."

"I don't think that's an option at this point. We need to be able to defend ourselves. Didn't you say you had a concealed weapons permit?" Heather asked.

"Yes, but I still can't take it on a plane."

Heather thought a moment. "Here's an idea. What if we chartered a private plane?

Dallas considered this option then said, "Maybe. It'd still be risky, but there's not much that wouldn't be at this point."

"Let's try it," Heather said. "I can make the arrangements. I have my press credentials with me. That should expedite things."

"Wait a second. How are we going to pay for this? I'm a little short on cash right now," Dallas said with a thin smile.

"I happen to have a *Chronicle* credit card," she said with a grin, waving the card in her hand after pulling it from her purse. "After all, who knows? Maybe I'll end up getting a story out of all this. Then it would be money well spent by the paper."

They got lucky. The city of Gonzales was coming up, and it had a decent airport. Dallas waited near the car while Heather entered a building. When she returned ten minutes later, she was grinning broadly. "We've got us a plane," she said. "We leave in about thirty minutes. It's small, a single-engine Cessna. But it can have us to El Paso in a few hours."

"Good work," Dallas said wearily. "Now we've got to figure out what to do about this car. We don't want it being found here when the police figure out what we're driving."

"Come on, I have an idea," Heather said as she got back in the car.

* * *

They left the vehicle on the opposite side of town in the parking lot of a twenty-four-hour supermarket. Then Heather phoned for a cab. "See? Nothing to it," she said with a smile as they got in the cab and sped back to the airport.

Shortly after their plane had taken off, Mason called Heather's cell phone to give them a quick report of what had taken place at the ranch.

"The guy with the broken arm is dead," he told her. "The young guy—the one Dallas mentioned in the article that started this whole mess, Tito Maggio, is ready to talk to the cops about your boss's murder. I heard him saying that he knew who did it and that he wanted to talk about it."

After the short call, Dallas and Heather looked at each other. "I'd give anything to be a fly on the wall during that interview," Dallas said and put his arm around Heather, drawing her close as they flew toward El Paso.

* * *

Rigo groaned when the phone started to ring. He badly needed a good night's sleep, but that seemed unlikely now. His wife stirred in their bed, but she made no attempt to get the phone. They both knew it would be for him.

He picked up the receiver and stepped out of the bedroom before he answered. "Hello, this is Rodrigo Garcia," he said.

"Lieutenant Garcia?" a male voice asked.

"Yes, that's right," he answered.

"This is Sergeant Bradley Marks," the voice on the other end of the line said. "Does the name Tito Maggio mean anything to you?"

That brought Rigo wide awake. "It certainly does—why?" he asked.

"I have him in custody," the sergeant said. "I think you might want to talk to him. He claims to know something about the murder of Andy Norton. I'm pretty sure he wants to trade information for light treatment here. He's in a heap of trouble."

"I would definitely like to talk to him," Rigo said. "How is it that you have him in custody?"

"He and a man by the name of Marco Santini came onto a hunting preserve out here thinking that Dallas Dixon was there. They were backing up two more men who had already been overpowered by Mr. Dixon—he left them unconscious and tied up in front of the buildings."

"Is Dixon in custody as well?" Rigo asked hopefully.

"I'm afraid not. He took off before we got here, and there's no sign of him so far. The last person to see him was a man by the name of Mason Huggins, an employee of the ranch. He claims to have saved Dixon's life the day of the San Antonio ambush. He hauled him out of there while the gun battle was still going on."

"So Huggins called you but let Dixon leave?" Rigo asked.

"Not exactly. When I asked him why he didn't keep him there until we came, he told me that Dixon didn't want another gun battle," Bradley said. "So he just took the car the two men had come in and left."

"Was he aware that we have a warrant for Dallas Dixon's arrest?" Rigo asked.

"He said he wasn't surprised but asked me how he was supposed to know. He claims he was trying to help Dallas stay alive after the ambush in San Antonio, but he wouldn't say much more than that. He seems like a decent guy, though. Might open up more if you talk to him."

"This case only gets more interesting," Rigo mumbled then

asked, "Did he tell you where Dixon was going by any chance?" Rigo asked.

"Said he didn't know."

Rigo sighed. "It's never that easy, I guess." He thought for a moment and then said, "You say Dallas Dixon overpowered two men. Did he shoot them?"

"Nope. From what Mr. Huggins says, Dixon is a genius in hand-to-hand combat," Sergeant Marks said.

"But he has a gun," Rigo said, shaking his head in confusion. "Why would he take a chance like that when he was armed? The men he overpowered were armed, weren't they?"

"Oh yes, they were armed. And they were threatening to kill Mr. Huggins. But Huggins claims that Dallas didn't have a gun on him when he went after the attackers. He says the only gun either of them had was his old .30-30 rifle—which Huggins used to fire one warning shot to keep the men at bay while Dixon apparently sneaked up on them one at a time and took them out."

Rigo shook his head, trying to make sense of it all. One thing was for sure—someone wanted Dallas Dixon dead, whatever it took. *But why? Could it all be over the wrecked semi and lost cocaine?* he asked himself.

Sergeant Marks spoke again. "If you can make it over here to San Antonio soon, I think this Maggio kid will spill his guts to you. The other two men I'm not so sure about. They seem to think they're pretty tough despite what Dixon did to them."

"I'll be over your way as soon as I can get there," Rigo said. "By the way, what is Dixon driving?"

"Like I said, Huggins claims he took the car the first pair of thugs came in. All we know is that it's a black sedan. We don't have a make or license number."

"I see. Well, thanks for the call, and I'll see you as soon as I can get there," Rigo said and ended the conversation. He looked back at his bedroom door longingly then sighed heavily and went to call his pilot, Sergeant Will Cullen.

* * *

As one Cessna flew toward El Paso, another was on its way east. Somewhere they passed each other, the occupants of each unaware of the other.

When Dallas and Heather landed in El Paso in the early morning hours, they rented a car in Heather's name and paid for it the same way they'd paid for the chartered plane—with an El Paso *Chronicle* Visa card.

They quickly found a downtown hotel and had booked two adjoining rooms there by the time the sun had risen. They had both slept a little on the plane ride, and even though they were still tired, there was no time to waste—they needed to find evidence to support Heather's theory.

The first thing they did was make a list of people to call. However, since it was too early to do anything about the list, and since they were both hungry, they called room service and ordered breakfast.

"I wish we could go to church," Heather said wistfully. "It is Sunday, isn't it?"

"I think so," Dallas agreed. "But it seems like a month since last Sunday."

"Oh!" Heather suddenly exclaimed. "I'm supposed to teach Sunday School today. Oops. I need to call the Sunday School president." She grinned. "Think getting shot at and then aiding and abetting a fugitive is a good enough excuse to get out of my lesson?"

Dallas grinned back and tossed a roll in her direction. "Watch who you're calling a fugitive. But, yeah, make that call first," he suggested. "Just make sure he doesn't know where you're at."

* * *

Luisa had slept very little during the night. Something was wrong. The last contact she'd had with Marco was just before he and Tito had turned into the ranch where Dallas Dixon and Heather Scott had been hiding out. It should have been a very simple operation. She had expected a call back from Marco within twenty or thirty minutes. It had now been four hours, and every attempt to call Marco had failed. She'd had the same result with Tito's phone. She glanced at the clock on the wall one more time, then she let out a slow breath before throwing her glass of orange juice into the sink with a resounding crash.

CHAPTER 26

RIGO RUBBED THE SLEEP FROM his eyes and got his bearings before answering the cell phone. Remembering he was no longer in his home but on a plane headed for the San Antonio area, he yawned and answered.

"Lieutenant Garcia, this is Special Agent James Mahoney of the Drug Enforcement Administration. I have some information I thought you'd want to be aware of."

"What's going on?" Rigo asked.

"We have obtained a federal warrant to arrest Luisa Maggio this morning."

"What have you charged her with?"

"Several things, but all of them are tied to the wreck of the semi on I-10. It took a lot of work, but we've finally been able to confirm the semi's tie to Luisa Maggio's trucking company."

"Wish I could be there for that," Rigo said. "I'm flying out of El Paso right now. Luisa's nephew is in custody outside of San Antonio. I'm told he has critical information for me on the murder case I'm working on."

"I'm glad to hear that. I believe he has some information for us as well," Special Agent Mahoney said, "since we're certain he was in that truck when it wrecked."

"You want me to do a little digging for you while I'm with him?" Rigo asked.

"If he's in the mood to talk, sure. I'd appreciate it. In the meantime, do you have anyone who can go with us to serve the arrest warrant on Luisa?"

"Sure do. I'll call Detective Cornwell. He's been working closely with me on this murder case. Where would you like him to meet you?"

After the arrangements had been made, Rigo closed his phone and sat back in his seat. "Will," he said to the pilot. "Next time I say this case can't get any crazier, tell me to stuff a sock in it."

* * *

Lincoln sat in a chair in his study, looking out the window and thinking things over as he often did on Sunday mornings. He'd just returned from attending Sunday services with his wife, but he had to admit he hadn't absorbed much of the sermon. His mind had been too preoccupied with thoughts of Dallas Dixon.

He stood, intending to go downstairs, when the phone rang. Usually he let the machine get it on Sundays, reserving his day of rest, but today he picked it up.

"Lincoln? This is Heather Scott," she began tentatively. "I hope it's all right I'm calling you at home."

Lincoln smiled. "I hope you're calling to tell me you've heard from Dallas Dixon."

She hesitated, and there was silence on the line for a moment. Then she said, "Lincoln, I think I know who killed Andy Norton."

"I'm listening," he said carefully. "Why don't you tell me your theory?"

Heather explained, and Lincoln considered a moment. "You just might be on to something," he said. "Where are you?"

"I'm in El Paso," she said.

"El Paso? I wish you'd see reason and get clear out of Texas," Lincoln said firmly. "Dallas is not the only one in danger. I wish you could see that."

"Believe me, I can see that, and I am being careful, Lincoln. But I need to follow this lead."

"Well, I'm glad to hear from you, and I'm interested in this theory of yours. But it would be better if you let Lieutenant Garcia do the investigating, or even let me do it."

"I'm sorry, but this is something I've got to do. And I won't be talked out of it," she said stubbornly.

"Okay, but I think you're making a mistake. Now I just wish I'd hear from Dallas. He might not be all right, you know."

After a brief pause, Heather said, "Just a minute."

He was sure she'd just put her hand over the phone. As he waited, he thought about Sam Reynolds. He'd sent Sam to El Paso to dig into the affairs of the Maggio family. Maybe he should have Sam get in touch with Heather instead, to provide protection and help her prove her theory. Yes, that's what he'd do, he decided firmly.

Suddenly, to his surprise, he was hearing Dallas Dixon's voice on Heather's phone. "Hello Lincoln," Dallas began. "First off, I'm sorry I had you worried. Things have been a little crazy, to say the least. I am okay, though." He cleared his throat. "Heather has been with me for a little while now. But we didn't feel like we could tell anyone but my father."

"Your father?" Lincoln asked in surprise.

"Yes, let me explain," Dallas began.

"I'd appreciate that very much," Lincoln said. "But before you do, I need to send you some help, some protection. If you tell me exactly where you are, I'll send a man by the name of Sam Reynolds over. Sam's the man who saved Heather at the convenience store outside San Antonio. And he's an outstanding investigator to boot. If Heather's theory's correct, Sam will help you prove it."

"All right," Dallas said hesitantly. "But send him as soon as you can. It makes me nervous having anyone knowing where we are. Call me back at this number after you talk to Sam. I'll explain everything."

Lincoln called Sam and sent him to the address Dallas had given them for their hotel on the double. Then he called Dallas back. For the next fifteen minutes, he listened to Dallas's story. By the time he hung up, he was shaking his head. *Got more than I bargained for with this one,* he murmured to himself as he headed back downstairs.

* * *

Before they made any more phone calls, Dallas and Heather went over everything they knew with Sam Reynolds. Dallas was impressed with him. Sam seemed both smart and capable. And on top of that, like Dallas, Sam was a former Army Ranger. That clinched the deal for Dallas. He was glad for the help.

Sam made some suggestions and then said, "Let's see if Heather can lure Mr. Painter over here. If she can, you and I will wait through there," he said to Dallas while pointing at the door to the adjoining room. "Everything he says will be recorded." He produced a small recording device. "It picks up sound very well." He showed Heather how to operate it and then placed it on the nightstand behind the telephone book. "When Elliott arrives, turn it on before you answer the door." He cocked his head to the side and smiled. "And then we'll see what happens."

* * *

Heather took a deep breath and dialed Elliott's number. He

sounded pleased when he answered. "Well, hey there. Didn't expect to hear from you this morning."

"Hi, Elliott. How are you?"

"Better, now that you called. When will you be back in El Paso?"

"I already am," she told him, glancing at Dallas.

"You're at your duplex?" he asked quickly. "What about Frankie Maggio?"

"That's actually why I'm calling." Heather forced a tremor into her voice. "I'm scared, Elliott. I don't know who else I can turn to."

"I'll come over and pick you up," he said immediately. "Don't let anyone in but me. I'll hurry."

"Wait, I'm not at my apartment," Heather said quickly. She lowered her voice. "Please, you've got to help me."

"Tell me where you are and I'll be right there," he promised eagerly.

"Okay, but don't let anyone follow you," she said, her voice pleading.

"I won't," he said. "I promise."

She gave him the location and added, "Thank you, Elliott. You don't know how much this means to me."

Heather hung up the phone and looked at the two men. "I actually feel kind of bad," she said with a shrug. "It was almost too easy."

"We just need to make sure he comes alone," Sam warned. "It's too early to say it was easy."

* * *

Detective CC Cornwell hurried to the office. He was to meet Agent James Mahoney there. He was looking forward to being in on the arrest of Luisa Maggio. She'd been on his radar for a long time but he had nothing to show for it. It was high time.

The federal agents were waiting for him when he arrived. After some quick introductions, Agent Mahoney rattled off a few instructions and then said, "Let's go."

* * *

When the knock came on the door, Heather looked through the peephole, nerves getting the better of her for a moment. Despite the fact that Sam and Dallas were waiting just through the door in the adjoining room, she felt a shiver of anxiety work its way down her back.

When she opened the door, Elliott smiled broadly. "It's good to see you. Your face looks lots better. How are you feeling?"

"Except for my broken ribs, much better, thanks. Come on in, Elliott," she said, forcing a smile and trying to appear at ease. "I really appreciate you coming."

"My pleasure," Elliott said. "Let's get you out of here. You'll be safe at my place. Frankie would never think to look for you there."

"Um, that sounds like a possibility. Sit down, Elliott. There are some things I want to ask you first," Heather said, trying to sound friendly but not about to let Elliott get her out of the room.

"Sure, whatever. But we should get going soon," he said as he sat on the sofa she'd indicated.

Heather perched on the edge of the bed and debated how to start. Finally she simply said, "Elliott, you know I don't think Dallas killed Andy. But I've been thinking a lot lately. What if I'm wrong?" She took a deep breath and continued. "I know the police must have evidence. I wondered if you could tell me what you've learned from them . . . help me analyze it."

"I'm glad to hear you say that," he said with a smile. "I've been keeping in close contact with Rigo, so pretty much if there's anything to know, I know it," Elliott said with a touch of pride.

"Okay, let's start with Dallas's motive," Heather said. "I know you don't like him, but put that aside for a second. Do you honestly think Dallas is the type to kill someone for firing him?"

Elliott didn't respond right away, which gave Heather some hope. When he spoke, she was relieved to hear that his tone of voice was serious. "I know it seems sort of far-fetched, but under the right certain circumstances, you never know how anyone will react. And he *did* run right after the murder."

Heather nodded. "Maybe. Or maybe he'd just lost his job, so he wanted to start over somewhere?"

Elliott narrowed his eyes. "I guess that's possible."

"He was found in a semi," Heather went on. "And not just any semi, but one hauling an unbelievably large load of cocaine. Do you really think that he'd be that dumb to get mixed up in something like that so quickly? And even if he was, how could he have arranged it all in such a short time?"

"Okay, okay," Elliott said. "You're right. They know Dallas wasn't the one driving that truck. And they know Tito Maggio was somehow involved."

"But Dallas did have something to do with the truck. The most likely explanation is that he stopped to help whoever did wreck it," Heather said flatly.

"Sure, maybe." Elliott glanced toward the door. "Can't we talk about all this on the way to my place?"

Heather shook her head firmly. "I think we should stay here a little longer . . . I don't feel safe leaving yet." She paused and then asked, "Does stopping to help out people in a wreck seem like something a killer who is on the run would do, Elliott?"

Elliott was very thoughtful before he answered. "I guess not," he finally said. "It would be strange behavior, wouldn't it?"

"Very strange," Heather said. "Now let's talk about the memo in Dallas's briefcase. Dallas claims that Gordon told him to write the Tito Maggio story. But, according to what you told me, Rigo found a memo from Gordon to Dallas in Dallas's briefcase when the pickup was recovered, telling him not to write it."

"That's simple; Dallas lied," Elliott said with a shrug. "That's a strong piece of evidence against Dallas."

"Or did Gordon have second thoughts and slip that memo in there after the fact?" Heather asked. "Isn't it possible that Gordon realized he might have caused a problem for Andy and wrote that memo and planted it in the briefcase in order to make it look like Dallas was lying?"

Elliott shook his head firmly. "Gordon's a good person. He loved Andy like a brother."

"Which could explain why he'd do that, don't you agree?" Heather asked. "He was trying to help Andy after making a big mistake."

Elliott thought for close to a minute before he said, "Okay, I suppose that's possible. I could ask Gordon about that."

"I'm not suggesting you do that," she said. "I'm just trying, with your help, to analyze the evidence against Dallas. Let's move on. Two bullets were found in Dallas's briefcase when it was recovered. They were both 9mm, the same caliber that was used to kill Andy."

Elliott spoke up quickly this time. "And the gun that was used—a 9mm with a silencer—was found in Dallas's apartment. That's the most important piece of evidence in the entire case."

"Is it, Elliott?" Heather asked. "Think about this. The gun was not found when the first search warrant was served by the police. But days later, when an anonymous person calls and says exactly where to look, it's found."

"It could easily have been missed the first time. After all, it was in a strange place, above the ceiling in a closet," Elliott said.

"True, but there were no fingerprints on it," Heather pointed out. "Now tell me, Elliott, why would Dallas wipe it clean if he thought it was in a good hiding place? And while you're thinking about that, think about this. How could someone other than Dallas have known it was there, in such a strange place as you just said—a place even the cops missed on the first search? Surely you can't think that Dallas would tell anyone."

Elliott began to shake his head. He rubbed his eyes. Finally, he said, "Heather, you should have been a defense attorney instead of a reporter."

"Those are the very arguments that Lincoln Graves will use to defend Dallas with—unless someone finds the real killer first. Face it, Elliott," Heather said sternly. "There's no way the evidence against Dallas will ever hold up, now is there?"

"Heather, I don't hate Dallas Dixon," Elliott suddenly said. "I don't want to see him wrongly convicted. I'm being sincere about this."

"Do you think he's innocent, Elliott?"

He spoke softly with his head bowed. "Dallas didn't kill Andy."

"Then who did?" Heather fired back at him.

"I don't know, but I'm guessing that it was Frankie Maggio or Tito. They're both capable of it."

"What about Luisa Maggio?" she asked.

"Could be," he said. "She's a bitter woman."

"Someone is determined to kill Dallas," Heather said. "Why would anyone want him dead if so much effort has been made to frame him for murder?"

"A backup plan? If the evidence is good and he dies, it's likely that the cops would simply close the case and quit looking," Elliott reasoned.

"That's what I think too," Heather told him. "Now tell me,

if you can, why someone would be after me? I haven't done anything wrong."

"Because people might think you are trying to help Dallas, and they don't want him helped," he said softly.

CHAPTER 27

"Hello."

"It's me."

"Do you have something to report?"

"Heather's back in El Paso."

"Is she at her duplex?"

"No, she's staying in a hotel."

"Do you know which one?"

"Yes."

"Is she alone?"

"I don't know. I just barely figured out that she's here."

"Are you ready to fulfill your contract?"

"I'm outside her hotel right now."

"Call me when it's done."

* * *

Elliott seemed humble and sorry for the stand he'd taken against Dallas. For the past few minutes they'd talked about the paper and the impact that all this had had on the staff.

"Even Gordon is struggling," Elliott revealed. "I didn't realize how much he admired Andy. He told me that he feels inadequate filling his shoes. And now that I'm an editor, I feel a little in over my head. I think we all wish things could go back to being like they were."

"Especially Dallas," Heather said softly, a touch of emotion in her voice.

"You care for Dallas, don't you?" Elliott said.

She nodded.

"Do I have a chance with you?" Elliott asked.

Heather shook her head.

He took a deep breath, got up, and looked out the window for a moment. When he turned back toward her, his eyes were somber. "I'm truly sorry about that," he said. "But I respect you, Heather. I've been acting out of jealousy, and now I feel like a fool. I won't interfere in your life anymore."

"Thank you, Elliott."

"There is just one thing," he said. "I would like for us to be friends and be able to work together if we both stay at the paper."

"I'd like that too," she said. "You're a good reporter. I can learn a lot from you."

"Thank you. So, now what do we do?"

"Are you saying that you're willing to help me?" Heather asked Elliott.

He nodded. "I don't want to see an innocent man convicted, even if he's not my favorite person. Yes, I'll help if I can. What do you want me to do?"

"There won't be just the two of us involved," Heather said.

"Who else is going to help? There aren't many people you can trust," Elliott responded.

"I know that. I also knew I was taking a chance asking you for help," Heather said with a smile.

"Thanks," Elliott said. "I hope I don't disappoint. Who else do you have in mind?"

"Dallas Dixon is one of them. Can you live with that?"

"I'll have to, I guess. But how do you know where he's at?"

"He's with the other man who will be helping us. His name is Sam Reynolds. He's from San Antonio. He's actually working for Lincoln Graves, Dallas's attorney. He's a private investigator, a former cop and, like Dallas, a former Army Ranger. He's one tough man and a smart one. I'll get them now," Heather said.

"Don't leave the hotel alone," Elliott said protectively, rising to his feet.

"I won't have to do that," she said with a grin as she stepped to the adjoining door. "They're right through here."

"Why am I not surprised?" he said. "I truly underestimated you."

Heather opened the door and said, "Why don't you fellows join us?"

Dallas entered the room first, followed by Sam. He looked at Elliott warily. "Elliott has agreed to help us," Heather said.

Elliott stepped past Heather and held out his hand. "I've been a fool, Dallas. I'm sorry."

"Thanks," Dallas said.

Sam's eyes darted to where the recorder was hidden and he stepped over to it. He glanced at Elliott, who was still facing Dallas. He reached in, grabbed the recorder, and slipped it into his pocket. Heather nodded her approval.

Sam was suddenly all business. "We need to make some plans," he said.

The other three agreed. "But before we do, there's something else you need to know, Mr. Painter," Sam said.

"Elliott," Elliott said. "Let me hear it."

"Do you have any idea who Andy's killer is?"

"Heather already asked me that question. I have ideas, but I don't honestly know."

"We're pretty sure we do," Sam said. He turned to Heather. "Would you like to tell him?"

"How well do you really know Gordon?" she asked.

"Pretty well, I think," he said, looking puzzled.

"He moved up the paper pretty fast, don't you agree?" she asked.

He nodded.

"Didn't it seem a little fast to you?"

"Well, yes, but he's a capable man."

"Who was the only person that stood between him and the top job?"

"Why, Andy, of course." He hesitated, and then he said, "Don't tell me you think it's Gordon," as the color drained from his face.

"I do, and let me tell you why," she said. She proceeded to do just that.

There was very little color left in Elliott's face by the time she'd finished.

* * *

Special Agent James Mahoney gave the signal, and his men moved into position around Luisa Maggio's large house. Two men covered each of the four doors. CC Cornwell stood next to Mahoney at the front door, and two more officers—one from CC's department and one from the DEA—stood behind them. He keyed a small radio that he held in his hand. "I'll knock," Agent Mahoney said softly. "We'll give it two minutes from right now. If either CC or I haven't called you back by then, go in with guns drawn."

He touched the doorbell, and then handed the radio to CC, who put it in his pocket. Then they waited. One minute passed. CC glanced at his watch. Forty-five seconds left. Five left. Then the door opened. Though he'd never seen her before, CC knew it was Luisa Maggio the moment he saw her standing there, her face drawn in an angry scowl. Agent Mahoney presented his ID and said, "I'm with the Federal Drug Enforcement Administration. I have a warrant for your arrest."

Luisa's scowl deepened, but she said nothing. Mahoney stepped inside and said, "Put your hands behind your back, ma'am."

She complied, seeming resigned as the other officers surrounded her and CC keyed the radio.

"What is this about?" Luisa finally hissed. "I want to call my attorney."

"You'll be able to call him soon enough," Agent Mahoney said. He held out a copy of the arrest warrant and quickly advised her of the numerous charges that had been filed against her and finished by reading her rights. Then he said, "Let's go."

It was over so quickly that CC almost felt let down. But he knew that this show was just getting started. When Luisa was brought into an interview room for questioning was when the real fun would begin. He knew from what Agent Mahoney had told him on the way over that they already had an excellent case against Luisa and an as-yet-unidentified partner. If they played their cards right with Luisa, they'd have a second name before the day was over.

* * *

Rigo pulled off his headset and answered his phone, pressing it tight to his ear to cut out the noise from the Skyhawk's engine.

"We got her," CC said into his ear. "And she's one angry lady."

"Thanks, CC. That's great news. Hopefully our luck holds out for questioning her and Tito," Rigo said. "Stick with Mahoney. Let me know if Luisa gives up any information."

A few minutes later he received another call. "Yeah?" he answered, expecting it to be CC again.

"Rigo, it's Elliott Painter," he heard and groaned inwardly.

"What's happening, Elliot?" he asked.

"That's what I was about to ask you. What's new on the Dixon matter; anything?"

"Not much," Rigo responded. "I'm working on something right now, but I'd rather not discuss it until I wrap it up. Then maybe I'll have something for you."

"Now you've got me curious," Elliott said. "Come on, loosen up."

"Have you called my headquarters?" Rigo asked.

"No, should I?"

"It might be interesting to you."

"Won't they just refer me to you when I call?" Elliott asked.

"That's not likely—I'm out of town."

"Now you've really got me curious," Elliott said. "Wait a minute; I know what you're up to. You're going to have a little visit with Tito Maggio, aren't you?"

"What makes you think that?" Rigo asked, wondering how Elliott knew about the arrest.

"He's in custody—I know that. And it sounds like you're in a plane. Do you think he can add something to what you already know about Dixon?" Elliott asked.

"Okay, Elliott, I don't know how you learned about Tito so quickly, but yes, I do hope to learn something more from him," Rigo responded. "In the meantime, please don't print anything about what I'm doing."

"Agreed, if I get the story when you have it ready," Elliott said.

"You've got it."

Rigo was thoughtful for a moment and watched the ground through the window beside him. The fact that Elliott had learned about Tito being in custody gave new urgency to getting that interview done as soon as possible.

He looked at his watch and then put his headset back on. "Will, how much longer before we get there?"

"We have a decent tailwind," Will told him. "We'll be landing in just a few minutes."

"Good. I can't wait to talk to the kid," Rigo said. "I figured when I got the call about Tito that he simply would try to tell me something more that would finger Dallas Dixon. But now I wonder. I'd better call CC back and warn him that Elliott Painter will be calling, if he hasn't already."

Will gave him a puzzled look but said nothing.

* * *

CC answered the phone without a hello. "Mr. Painter," he began, "what has you calling on a Sunday morning?"

"I realized we don't have a satisfactory update on the Norton case for the next edition," Elliott responded. "Anyway, what are you doing in the office on a Sunday morning?"

"I've been busy," CC said. "And I'm still busy. So I'll give you the basics real quick-like. I'm with Special Agent James Mahoney of the DEA."

"What are you doing with a DEA agent?" Elliott broke in.

"Agents, actually. I'm assisting them. We just made an arrest related to the wrecked semi that Dallas Dixon was found unconscious in."

"That sounds newsworthy," Elliott said.

"You bet it is," CC agreed. "We have Luisa Maggio in custody on a host of federal charges."

"Any chance I could get in on this?" Elliott asked.

"Sure. We're preparing a press statement right now. Ms. Maggio has asked for her attorney, so we're waiting to talk to her. But we expected that. We'll give you what details we can, though," CC promised.

"Excellent, I'm on my way," Elliott replied and disconnected.

"They've arrested Luisa Maggio on federal charges," Elliott said to Heather, Dallas, and Sam. "I'll head over there and call you all in a few minutes."

"Do you mind if I come with you?" Sam Reynolds asked.

"That would be fine," Elliott said, "as long as Dallas and Heather promise to stay right here with the door locked."

Sam smiled. "I think Dallas has shown us that he can take care of himself when the going gets tough. But I don't think there should be a problem," he said. He turned to Dallas. "I'll be back shortly."

Elliott was out the door first, and Sam turned and whispered to Heather, who was standing the closest to him, "I think he's being straight with us, but I can't be sure. I've learned over the years to be careful where I place my trust."

Heather nodded in understanding and Sam followed after Elliott.

"Sam doesn't trust Elliott," Heather explained after closing the hotel room door.

"He's not alone. If Sam hadn't volunteered to go, I was going to suggest that he do so," Dallas said. "We can't be too careful at this point."

CHAPTER 28

THE INTERROGATION ROOM WAS A small, dingy place. It was also far too warm. Rigo wondered if they kept it that way intentionally. Maybe they thought it would make suspects confess more readily. If that was the case, he was all for it. He wiped his brow.

He was waiting in the room along with Will Cullen for a jail officer to bring Tito in. He had a small recording device in front of him. He wanted any waiver of rights that Tito made to be recorded. And, of course, he wanted to preserve every word the punk had to say.

When Tito entered in a jumpsuit and handcuffs a minute later, he seemed subdued. Rigo had expected him to be cocky, but not even a hint of a smirk crossed his dark features.

Rigo stood and asked Tito to sit down on the chair across the small table from him. "I'm Lieutenant Rodrigo Garcia," he began by way of introduction. "I'm the commander of the Crimes Against Persons section of the El Paso Police Department—and I'm in charge of the investigation of the murder of Andy Norton." He touched the little recorder and said, "Our conversation will be recorded."

Tito nodded in understanding, though Rigo thought he saw Tito's jaw tighten.

"This is Sergeant Will Cullen of the El Paso Police Department." Tito glanced toward Will and then back at Rigo.

Rigo then gave Maggio his Miranda rights, which Tito waived. Encouraged, Rigo jumped right in with the first question. "Tito, do you know anything about the murder of Andy Norton?"

Tito looked straight up at him and said, "My aunt was going to have Marco kill me, too, just like she had him kill my uncle Andy."

"Luisa Maggio?" Rigo asked, careful to conceal his shock.

"That's right. She's a double-crossing liar," Tito said angrily, rattling his handcuffs.

"Are you telling us that Luisa Maggio paid someone to kill Andy Norton?" Rigo asked in clarification. "A man named Marco?"

Tito nodded.

"The tape recorder can't hear you nod your head, Tito. Please respond verbally to my questions," Rigo instructed.

"Yes," Tito said loudly. "Luisa paid Marco Santini to shoot my uncle, Andy Norton."

"Can you tell me how you know this, Tito?"

"It's obvious," Tito said, a sneer on his face. "Marco was Luisa's hit man. And Andy was causing problems. So she took him out. Tried to take out that guy Dixon, too, but apparently he ain't as much of an idiot as we thought."

"Why did she want Dallas Dixon dead?" Rigo asked.

"Because the police—you guys—think Dixon did it. And if he's dead, then he can't defend himself, now can he? She figured you'd close the case and she'd get away with it."

"But Marco didn't succeed in killing Dallas?"

"He almost did—twice."

"He tried twice?"

"That's what I just told you," Tito said, the ugly sneer now fully developed on his face. "Marco was her favorite go-to guy, but after he messed up that third time, it's lucky for him that he's dead."

"What else did Marco do for your aunt?" Rigo asked.

"All kinds of stuff," Tito responded vaguely.

"Can you give me some examples?"

"Sure. He'd work the evidence, make sure she didn't get nailed for anything. Sometimes fix it so someone else took the heat. He'd beat people up for her—or else have someone else do it. Lots of people worked for Marco when he needed them."

"I see. And did Marco himself shoot your uncle Andy, or did he have someone else do it?"

"He did it himself. He always did the big jobs himself."

Rigo nodded slowly, finding it hard to believe how easily the questioning was going. "Do you know where the gun that Marco killed Andy with is now?" he asked.

"Of course I do. You have it," Tito said.

"Do you know where it was found?"

"Yeah, in Dallas Dixon's place." He rolled his eyes. "Don't you get it? Dixon didn't have anything to do with it. Marco had someone put that gun in Dixon's ceiling." He made a disgusted sound. "Never thought I'd be sticking up for that guy, but if it means sticking it to Luisa, then fine."

Rigo nodded. "Do you know all this information for a fact?"

"Sort of," Tito said, shrugging.

"What do you mean by sort of?"

"Well, when me and Marco were riding around together looking for Dallas Dixon and that woman reporter, Heather something or other, so we could waste them like Aunt Luisa told us to do, we heard about you finding the gun. Marco laughed and said, 'That was simple. And they won't find no fingerprints on it. It's been wiped clean.'"

"It was clean," Rigo agreed. Then he asked, "I thought you and your Aunt Luisa were pretty tight. Why are you giving me this information so easily? You said earlier she wanted to kill you."

Tito's expression darkened. "I thought we were tight. Now that I think back on it, she was just using me. But when she got tired of me, she told Marco to waste me, just like he did Uncle Andy."

"How did you find out?"

"Marco told me—just before he died. After the cops shot him on the ranch. He was gurgling blood, and he says, 'I'm dying, Tito. You should know what Luisa wanted me to do. I was supposed to kill you after we got Dixon and that woman.'"

Rigo suddenly changed the focus of his questions, hoping to catch Tito off guard. "Were you driving the semi that wrecked with the load of cocaine?"

Tito looked at him, and then his lips twisted in a sort of grin. "No, but I was riding shotgun."

"Who was driving?"

"Nick Abrams. He drove for Aunt Luisa. Wouldn't mind if he went down with her," Tito said angrily.

"So the truck was your aunt's?" Rigo asked.

"Yeah, that's what I'm saying. She hired me to go with Nick. We were supposed to deliver the cars and drugs to Chicago. We were going to get paid when we got there," Tito said. "But now I don't think she ever figured on paying us. Was probably planning on having us taken out when we got there so she wouldn't have to."

Rigo looked at Tito for a moment, studying his face. Finally he asked, "How did Dallas Dixon end up in the truck?"

For the first time in the interview, Tito began to look happy. "That was my idea. When Dixon wrote that stuff about me in the paper it made my dad real mad. It was those lies he wrote about me that got Dixon fired. It was good luck when we happened to knock him out, take his wallet and his truck, not even realizing it until after we'd gone through his wallet."

"What did you do with Dallas's pickup?" Rigo asked.

"We dumped it. But you already know that," Tito said. He smiled again. "We even called that new editor, my aunt's friend, and told him that it was Dixon who was driving the truck."

Rigo tried to hide his surprise and asked, "Are you talking about Gordon Townsend?"

"Yeah, that's him."

"He's Luisa's friend?"

"I guess so. I saw him with her a few times."

"At her business?" Rigo asked.

"No, not there—at her house."

"I see. Did you ever overhear any of their conversations?"

"I heard them talking a few times, but I can't remember what it was about." Tito shrugged.

"Maybe he was talking to her about a story?" Rigo suggested.

"Sure, that could be. But they were on a first-name basis," Tito said. Then he suddenly blurted, "Look, I've given you enough stuff to finish off Luisa. But I won't say none of it in court unless you help me get off from them bogus auto theft charges and whatever else you guys are planning to try to stick me with," he said.

"I don't remember promising you anything," Rigo said. "And everything you said has been recorded. It's a little late to start changing your tune now."

"I know a lot more, but you ain't getting none of it unless you promise to help me." His cockiness was back, and he was sitting up straight now, glaring at Rigo.

"We might be able to work something out," Rigo said hesitantly. "But I'll have to talk to the DA about that."

"Do it," Tito said. "I've given you plenty already, so you know I'm good for it. And there's lots more where that came from. Anyway, until I get a deal I want my lawyer."

"Okay, if that's the way you want it," Rigo said.

"That's the way I want it. And I want to go back to my cell now."

Rigo signaled for a jailer, and a moment later he and Will were alone in the little interview room. Rigo shut the recorder off and said, "Guess he decided he said too much." Then he smiled. "Time to go back and do some more digging."

"Do you think he was telling you the truth?" Will asked.

"He sounded pretty sincere to me—and pretty bitter. Anyway, you can bet I'm going to do everything possible to find out whether he's right about Luisa Maggio. I think she's definitely our prime suspect after what we've just heard."

Will nodded and said, "Tito sure didn't hurt the federal case against Luisa on the drug trafficking charges, did he?"

Rigo chuckled. "Special Agent Mahoney will be happy to hear what our friend Tito Maggio had to say, that's for sure."

* * *

Even on a Sunday, the *El Paso Chronicle* still hummed with life, getting the next day's paper ready to print. The lines had been particularly busy this day, and now the phone rang yet again.

"*El Paso Chronicle,* how may I help you?" the receptionist, a petite redhead named Summer, answered.

"Can you put me through to Heather Scott?"

"I'm sorry, but Ms. Scott is on leave for a few days. I can put you through to her voice mail if you'd like."

"No, it can't wait. Is there any way I can reach her?"

"Well . . . I can't give out personal information, but if you'd like, I can call Ms. Scott and give her your phone number and a message to call you."

"Yeah, do that. Just tell her it's extremely urgent."

* * *

Heather wrote down the number Summer gave her and turned to Dallas. "I guess I call?" When he nodded, she picked up her cell phone and punched in the number.

Her call was answered on the first ring. The man's hello sounded vaguely familiar, and Heather felt a prickle of fear slip down her spine.

"I was told to call this number," Heather said tentatively. "This is Heather Scott."

The line was silent for a few seconds before the man said, "Yeah, that's right. Just don't hang up when you hear who it is, okay? I've got some information you'll want to hear."

"I'm listening," she said, and so was Dallas, whose head was next to hers.

"This is Frankie Maggio."

It was all Heather could do to keep from dropping the phone. She felt Dallas's hand as he gripped her arm in support. "What do you want?" she asked, trying to keep the fear she felt out of her voice.

"Look, I've got mine coming for what I did to you. And believe it or not, I even feel sort of guilty. But now you need to listen up," Frankie said.

"Like I said, I'm listening, Frankie. So talk."

"Here's the deal. The police ain't gonna listen to me. And if they don't, both you and me are gonna be dead pretty quick here. So I need you to make 'em listen. You're a reporter. You've got clout."

"What information do you have?" she asked as Dallas tightened his grip on her arm.

"I know who killed my wife's brother," Frankie blurted out. "And if someone would just hear me out, I can prove it."

Dallas and Heather looked at each other for a moment, stunned. Dallas nodded at Heather, and she again spoke into the phone. "All right, tell me."

"Not over the phone," he said firmly. "We need to meet somewhere. And it needs to be quick. My hours are probably numbered as it is."

It's too dangerous, Dallas mouthed, but Heather turned back to the phone. "Where would you like to meet?"

"There's a little park off of Elm and Boulder. I'll be waiting there. Hurry."

With that, Frankie ended the call, and Heather slowly closed her phone.

"Heather, what are you doing?" Dallas asked, fear and concern shining in his eyes. "You know what this man is capable of."

"Yes, I definitely do," she said as she reached up to touch her eye, which was still dark with bruises. "But we've got to prove what we think we know, and this could be the break we've been hoping for."

"Or it could be a trap," Dallas warned and sighed heavily.

"Will you come with me?" she asked.

"I won't let you go alone," he said, taking her hand in his. "But I think we should wait for Sam to get back."

"There isn't time," Heather said. "You heard Frankie. We've got to go now."

"Okay, but I'll need to stay back a ways—back and out of sight." When she nodded, he added, "Let's call a cab. When it gets here, you can leave the hotel first. I'll keep a lookout and then join you in the cab."

"Then let's go," she said, her tone masking the fear tingling through her nerves.

* * *

Frankie slipped from the basement door and into Luisa's back-yard. He looked around to make sure he wasn't being watched and then strode to a tall privacy fence that bordered her property. He quickly opened the gate, slipped into the alley behind Luisa's house, and walked rapidly away.

CHAPTER 29

IT WAS SHORTLY AFTER TWELVE when Heather and Dallas watched the cab pull up outside the hotel. Heather glanced at Dallas, who gave her hand a reassuring squeeze, and then she stepped through the main entrance doors. Dallas waited until she was almost to the cab, then he followed, every sense on full alert.

As Dallas stepped outside, his eyes were drawn to a man who was partially secluded behind a tall cement pillar that supported the open entrance of the hotel. He was only about thirty feet from Heather and fifty from Dallas when he stepped from behind the pillar and leveled a gun at Heather.

Dallas hesitated only a fraction of a second as the promise he'd made to Heather flashed through his mind. He pulled his gun and fired in one swift, smooth movement just as the man spoke Heather's name. She screamed as the gun flew from the man's grip and he began howling in pain. He knelt on the ground as blood spurted from his hand.

Dallas rushed toward Heather. "Get in the cab!" he ordered. "He might not be alone."

The man began to scramble back behind the cement pillar, but not before Dallas caught him. A quick blow knocked him unconscious before he could even get his uninjured hand up to defend himself.

Dallas raced back to the taxi and jumped inside. The cab peeled away as the driver cursed under his breath. Dallas looked back to see someone in uniform running up to the man on the ground. A crowd was already gathering. Dallas turned back and looked at Heather. "Are you all right?" he asked in a low voice.

"He tried to kill me," she whispered and began to cry. He put an arm around her, and she buried her face in his shoulder. "Is he dead?"

"No, but most of his right hand's gone. I overpowered my instincts and training. I shot to disarm him, that's all."

"Who was it?" she asked.

"No idea, but he had the same look that the guys from the ambush and the ranch did," Dallas said.

"Dallas, what do we do now? Did Frankie set me up?" Heather asked fearfully.

"That's a definite possibility," he said, furrowing his brow.

"I think we should find out," Heather said, more determined than ever. "We'll go to the meeting place. If he isn't there, he probably expected me not to make it," she reasoned.

Dallas looked at her for a long moment, then gave a small nod. "Fine, but we have to keep our guard up. He might have a backup plan."

The cab soon pulled up to the small park Frankie had directed them to.

Dallas's expression was serious as he took her in his arms and said, "Don't leave my sight."

Heather nodded, and they both stepped out of the cab. The driver shook his head and quickly pulled away.

The park was filled with trees and packed with people. Children laughed and played as parents watched. Young couples strolled hand in hand. Dogs strained at their leashes. Dallas slipped from tree to tree, trying to keep out of sight of the large brick restroom that loomed ahead. If Frankie showed up, Dallas could hide himself behind a large water fountain a few feet away.

As Heather approached the restroom, Dallas peered around a nearby tree. There was no one near the fountain but a young boy. He took a quick drink then ran off again. Moments later, from the other side of the restroom, Frankie Maggio walked into view. Dallas gripped the gun so tightly his fingers began to turn white. Heather stood very still, watching Frankie approach.

Frankie stopped when he was nearly to her and began to speak, glancing around every few seconds. Dallas could hear his voice but was unable to make out the words. Heather listened intently. She spoke several times, and then Frankie offered his hand. Dallas held his breath as Heather first hesitated then accepted the offer. Frankie then strode quickly away. Heather didn't move until he was out of the park.

"Did he have any real information?" Dallas asked as soon as the two of them were back together.

Heather nodded. "You'd better believe it. Let's get out of here," she said.

* * *

Rigo felt the vibration of his cell phone, so he took off the headset and answered. "Lieutenant Garcia," he said.

"This is Frankie Maggio," he heard. "Can you hear me?" he added loudly. "You sound like you got the vacuum cleaner going."

"I'm in a plane," Rigo replied. "Where are you, Frankie? No one's seen you since you left the jail. I was starting to think something had happened to you."

"Not yet. I got lucky. I'm okay right now, but I need to talk to you," Frankie said.

"Then talk," Rigo encouraged. He wondered what other surprises might come his way from the Maggio family.

"Nuh-uh," he said. "Too risky. Meet me."

"I won't be back in El Paso for at least two hours, maybe a little more," Rigo said. "You'll either have to tell me whatever you have to say now or wait until I get back."

Frankie let out an exasperated sigh. "Heather Scott told me to talk to you now. It can't wait. But I ain't sayin' anything more over the phone."

"When did you talk to Heather Scott?" Rigo asked in surprise. He wondered if there was a way to find out Frankie's location and send CC and a couple of other officers to pick him up.

"She just left," Frankie responded. "What I got to say is important, you know."

"I'm sorry, but if you can't talk to me over the phone, it'll have to wait. Or I could send another officer to meet you."

"I don't want to talk to another officer. I want to talk to you. Can't you hurry it up some? My life is on the line here."

It seemed that several lives were in danger, and Rigo wished he was back in El Paso. He was anxious to hear what Frankie had to say, considering what Tito had told him and the fact that Luisa was in custody.

"Hide out somewhere," Rigo told him. "I'll call this number as soon as I'm almost to El Paso."

"Fine, but hurry," Frankie muttered and then terminated the call.

Rigo put his headphones back on. "You sure we can't make this thing fly any faster?"

Will looked at him and grinned. "That tailwind we had going east is now a headwind. I'm doing the best I can. What was that call about?"

Rigo began to tell him when his phone vibrated again.

"Rigo, this is CC. There's been another shooting. The victim is alive, but he lost most of his right hand."

"Slow down, CC. Tell me where it happened and who's been shot," Rigo said evenly.

"Another Italian mafia-type guy was shot outside a hotel downtown," CC said. "The shooter and a woman left in a taxi. According to several witnesses, the victim tried to ambush the woman. When he pulled a gun on her, the shooter took his hand pretty much off."

"Did you get a description of either of the two who got away?" Rigo asked.

"Yeah, and the woman's description matches up with Heather Scott, right down to the black eye."

"And I suppose the guy matches a description of Dallas Dixon?" Rigo asked.

"You got it."

"Why would Dallas come back to El Paso?" Rigo mused. "I thought he was on the run."

"You tell me," CC said. "The guy he shot is in the hospital, and we've got the hotel under surveillance. And here's something else interesting. Elliott Painter met me at the PD. But later, he was seen entering the hotel, the same one where the shooting took place. He was with some bald, athletic-looking guy. They weren't there for long. When they left, they were carrying a couple of traveling bags."

"Interesting," Rigo said. "I just got off the phone with Frankie Maggio—who claims he met with Heather Scott a few minutes ago. He also claims that his life is in danger and says he wants to meet me as soon as I get back."

"More fun and games with the Maggios . . ." CC murmured. "Anyway, I'll let you go. I'll call if there's anything new to report before you get here."

Rigo ended the call and turned back to Will Cullen, "Are you positive there isn't a way you can speed this old crate up?"

* * *

"Elliott, talk to me," Gordon Townsend said on the phone. "You're supposed to be keeping me up to date, but I'm in the dark here."

"Sorry, Gordon," Elliott said apologetically. "Things have been a little crazy here. We're shorthanded, and there's a lot of news to cover."

"What's going on?" Gordon demanded.

"I'm sorry, but I really can't talk right now. I'll get back with you," he said and hung up the phone.

* * *

CC looked down at the phone in his hand, seeing that another call from Rigo was coming through. As Rigo spoke, the creases in his forehead deepened, and a slight frown crossed his face.

When Rigo had finished, he asked, "Are you serious?"

"Very," Rigo said. "Now get on it."

* * *

After Sam Reynolds had gotten Heather and Dallas situated in a new hotel—and extracted a promise from them that they would stay out of sight this time—he once again left to continue his investigation.

The first place he went was Dallas's old apartment complex. He began knocking on doors and speaking to former neighbors. It wasn't long before he hit pay dirt. An elderly woman who lived directly across the street from the apartment complex reluctantly let him in when he told her what he was after. As she led him to her tiny living room, she said, "I'm awake at night a lot of the time. I've had a hard time sleeping ever since Eddie died, so instead of tossing and turning, I watch TV—or what's going on outside, if there's something to see."

She offered Sam a cold glass of milk, and he sat down on the sofa. "Ma'am, did you happen to see anything interesting going on at the apartments across the street any night from Tuesday through Thursday?"

The woman slowly nodded her head. "Seemed a little suspicious to me, but then again, anything going on at two in the morning can look a little suspicious. I thought maybe it was trouble with a new renter or something."

"Could you tell me a little about what happened?"

"Well, it was dark, but there was a man with dark hair, dark features. It was Thursday morning, and he went into the stairwell to the building. I couldn't see him anymore, but a few minutes later the faintest little light came on in one of the apartments. Then it wasn't long before the lights went out and the guy left."

Sam nodded for her to continue, and she took a breath. "Well, the next morning when the police were swarming all around there, I got to thinking about that man, wondering if he had anything to do with the cops being there. When I realized it was Dallas Dixon's apartment, I *really* wondered." She looked embarrassed and added, "I probably should have told the police what I saw. I just kept talking myself out of it . . . Who's going to listen to a little old lady who spies out her window? Anyway, like I said, I thought maybe there must be a new renter and that he was giving the management trouble."

Sam nodded, making mental note of all of it. Then he asked, "By chance did you notice if the man was wearing gloves?"

She thought a moment then nodded, a surprised look on her face. "Now that you mention it, yes. He was."

Sam just smiled. "Thank you, ma'am. You've been very helpful. I'll be going now. An officer from the El Paso Police Department will be contacting you shortly."

When Sam called Lincoln a few minutes later, Lincoln was impressed. "Now all you have to do is get the man with the wounded hand to admit he was after Heather and Dallas and to tell you who hired him," Lincoln said with a chuckle.

Sam understood the chuckle. Getting the man to admit to something would be anything but easy. But Sam wasn't an officer of the law, and he routinely operated outside the boundaries that restricted men like Rigo Garcia and CC Cornwell.

Sam quickly learned which hospital the would-be killer had been taken to. He bypassed the front desk with ease and located the man's room quickly enough. However, he was disappointed to learn that the man was still in surgery. Apparently an attempt was being made to put what little was left of the riddled hand back together again.

He placed a call to Heather after leaving the hospital. When he told her he'd found a witness who could place a man entering Dallas's old apartment early Thursday morning, she nearly cried with happiness. She quickly relayed the news to Dallas, then said, "You've got to tell Rigo."

"I will," Sam said. "But there's something else I'd like to do first."

* * *

As Rigo finished jotting down the final notes of his interview with Frankie Maggio, he clicked the recorder off and looked up at the man sitting in front of him. He believed what Frankie had told him. The worry lines etched in Frankie's face told him that he was honestly frightened.

"So can you put me back in jail?" Frankie asked for the second time.

"Like I told you, you're out on bond," Rigo replied. "You haven't done anything that would give me reason to ask that your bond be revoked."

"Then arrest me for burglary," Frankie insisted.

"Is there a reason I should pick that particular charge?" Rigo asked.

"Yeah. I broke into Luisa's house. That's where I heard most of what I just told you. I'll confess to that. Just put me in jail," he begged.

Rigo shook his head but complied with his wishes. He'd planned to make the jail his next stop anyway. He had some questions for Frankie's sister. He knew she'd want her lawyer present, but he wanted to speak with her as soon as possible.

He was on the way to the jail with Frankie in the car when a call came in from an unavailable number. He listened with growing interest as the man, who identified himself as Sam Reynolds, a private investigator who was working for Lincoln Graves, told him that there was a witness who could place a man entering Dallas's former apartment at about two in the morning on Thursday.

"Can I confirm this?" Rigo asked. He was careful not to let Frankie hear what the man was saying.

"I recorded our interview. I also told her that someone from the police department would be coming over to talk to her."

"I'll have someone over there as soon as I can shake a detective free. We have our hands full at the moment, but we'll get on this," Rigo said.

After arriving at the jail, Rigo asked the staff to inform Luisa he had arrived and to have her call her attorney. He knew this would take some time, so while he waited he called his office and asked one of his detectives to meet Sam, then go with him and take a statement from his witness.

* * *

Detective CC Cornwell was more than a little surprised to find himself back in the same neighborhood where Luisa Maggio had been arrested earlier. The man he'd been tailing had led him straight there. He slowed his vehicle down, taking care to keep enough distance between them that the man didn't suspect he was being followed. At first he'd thought Rigo was taking a shot in the dark with this assignment, but now he had to admit that his interest was more than piqued. His senses went on full alert as he watched the man slip into Luisa's backyard and disappear. Something very strange was going on—something ominous.

CHAPTER 30

THE LAWYER SITTING NEXT TO Luisa in the interrogation room was well known to Rigo. Grady Shade was well into his seventies, wrinkled as a prune, and couldn't weigh more than 125 pounds. His dark green eyes flitted from his client back to Rigo, and a slight frown crossed his face. His thick head of gray hair was unkempt, contrasting with a perfectly trimmed beard of the same color. Officers that had come into contact with him over the years preferred to switch his name around; behind his back he was known as Shady Grady.

Grady narrowed his eyes as Rigo sat down. "If I instruct my client not to answer any of your questions, I expect you to cooperate."

"I understand," Rigo acknowledged with a shrug. He hoped Grady wouldn't be this hard-nosed with every question. It would put a stop to the interrogation rather quickly.

Rigo had already advised Luisa that she had the right to remain silent and that she was a suspect in the murder of Andy Norton. Her perfectly formed dark features had grown even darker at the mention of murder.

It was with this in mind that he asked his first question. "What was your relationship with a man by the name of Marco Santini?" he asked.

Grady said nothing. Luisa hesitated but finally answered. "He did a little work for me from time to time."

"What kind of work?" Rigo asked.

Luisa glanced at Grady, who simply nodded. "He ran errands for me," she said.

"What kind of errands?"

"Nothing special."

Grady spoke up then. "Why do you want to know this about him?"

"I have reason to believe that he confessed to a murder for hire just before he died yesterday," Rigo said, watching closely for Luisa's reaction. Her eyes opened wider, but she didn't seem alarmed.

"Murder for hire?" her attorney asked. "And who did he allegedly murder?"

"Andy Norton," Rigo said smoothly.

Luisa shifted in her seat and snorted. "Impossible!"

"Is that so?" Rigo asked, giving her a hard look. "I happen to have a witness who is prepared to testify to Marco's dying declaration." He left it at that, omitting the detail that the dying declaration actually had to do with Luisa ordering Marco to murder her nephew, Tito.

"We have no further need to speak to you, Lieutenant Garcia," Grady said as he folded up his notebook.

"That's fine," Rigo said. "But you can count on me bringing charges against your client in the next day or two." He paused for effect, watching Luisa closely. Her lip was twitching, and her face had colored a deep shade of red. "Something you'd like to say?" Rigo goaded.

"I have a question," she said.

"Shut up, Luisa," Grady hissed. "We have nothing further to discuss with Lieutenant Garcia."

But Luisa continued as if she hadn't heard him. "Who did Marco say hired him?" she asked.

Rigo smiled and said, "Someone who hated Andy. Someone who had been blackmailing him for years."

Luisa actually began to look pale. "No more, Luisa," Grady Shade said sternly. "It's time for you to get back to your cell. And I'll be working on getting your bail reduced."

"I had nothing to do with Andy's death!" Luisa suddenly screeched. "He was lying!"

"I didn't say you had anything to do with it," Rigo said smoothly. "It's other people who have been leaking those tidbits of information. I have more work to do on the murder case."

"Dallas Dixon killed Andy!" she shouted again, her face purple with rage. "Everybody knows that."

Grady was still trying to shut her up, but she turned to him with venom in her voice. "You keep out of this, you worm. I'm being accused of something I didn't do."

"Actually, the only thing I'm accusing you of right now, and take careful note of this, Mr. Shade," Rigo said, turning briefly to the attorney, "is orchestrating the attempted murder of Dallas Dixon." He thought a moment, then added, "Well, actually, there is more. I'm also accusing you of ordering the murder of your own nephew, Tito Maggio."

"You're blowing smoke, Lieutenant," Grady said hotly. "You have no proof. I'm willing to bet on that."

"Actually, I do," Rigo said as he watched Luisa swallow. "Luisa's own brother is willing to testify that he believes she had Andy killed. Her nephew is ready to take the stand about what he knows—and it's quite a bit. I said that I'm not accusing Luisa of Andy's murder. What I should have said was that I was not accusing her *yet*."

Luisa banged her fist on the table. "Lies!" she seethed. Then she did what Rigo had hoped she would do. He held his breath as she said, "I can tell you who had Andy killed."

"I'm all ears," Rigo said, watching her.

"Luisa, you're talking way too much. Listen to me," Grady practically shouted at her. "If you have anything to tell this man, at least make a deal before you talk."

"Okay, I'll make a deal," she said and folded her arms across her chest. Twenty minutes later, with the DA on a speaker phone, a deal was made. Shortly after that Luisa Maggio spilled her guts to Rigo.

As Rigo walked to his car an hour later, he called the DA. Before he ended the call, the DA had agreed to contact the judge at home to dismiss the charges. He also instructed Rigo to immediately withdraw the warrant. New charges would be filed as soon as the evidence was in place.

* * *

Heather looked at the caller ID on her cell phone with surprise and then answered. "Lieutenant Garcia, what can I do for you?" she asked.

"I'm pleased to tell you I have good news for Dallas Dixon," he said.

"And what's that?" she asked as her heart began to beat faster.

"I'd rather tell Dallas himself. Why don't you hand him your phone," Rigo said.

"But he's—" she began.

Rigo cut her off. "Heather, I've always taken you for an honest woman. Don't lie to me now. I know very well that he's with you, and I have reason to believe that he has been for some time."

Dallas, who could hear the conversation, shook his head, mouthing that he was sure Rigo was bluffing. Heather faltered, then said, "Why don't you call Dallas's attorney? He'll be able to relay the message to Dallas. I'm sorry, but that's the best I can do for right now."

Rigo argued briefly, but Heather held firm. With an exasperated sigh, Rigo finally agreed and hung up.

"Let me talk to Dallas," Lincoln said when he called a few minutes later.

Heather did as she was instructed this time and offered the cell phone to Dallas. "Lincoln," he began, "I know I've been difficult—"

"You've done what you needed to do," Lincoln interrupted. "But I have good news now. The charges against you are being dropped. The warrant has already been recalled." Then his voice took on a more serious tone. "However, I think you still need to be very careful. Please call Lieutenant Garcia and arrange to meet with him. I made it very clear to him that I expect you to be protected until this situation is completely resolved."

"I'll do whatever you say, Lincoln. And I appreciate everything you've done for me," Dallas said. "I'll call you later and we'll settle up."

"I'll keep it reasonable," Lincoln said. "I'm still alive, thanks to you, and that's priceless. You should call your friend Michael, though. You owe him the fifteen hundred dollar retainer he paid for you."

After finishing his conversation with Lincoln, Dallas called Rigo.

"Can we stop playing musical phones now?" Rigo asked tiredly when he came on the line.

Dallas smiled. "I think so. We'd like to talk to you, but I still don't feel safe leaving the place we're at," he said.

Rigo didn't argue with that. "Give me an address and I'll be there as quickly as I can."

* * *

Detective Cornwell sounded sheepish when Rigo answered the phone. "He was right there in Luisa Maggio's house," he said in disbelief. "He stayed for a few minutes, came back out, then went through her backyard and out the gate to the alley. I saw where he'd parked his car, and I drove by it after a few minutes.

But he didn't come back," he said. "He left his car there. I don't know where he went. What do you want me to do?"

Rigo groaned. He was almost to the hotel where Dallas and Heather were waiting for him. The last thing he'd needed right now was a disappearing act. "Keep an eye on his car. Maybe he'll be back in a little while," Rigo told CC. It was all he could think of to have him do.

* * *

"I still can't believe the charges have been dropped," Heather said with a smile.

"Me either . . . I guess the nightmare is finally ending," Dallas said hopefully. Then a shadow crossed his face. "But even though the charges against me have been dropped, the real killer is still out there."

Heather nodded, her smile fading. She heard her cell phone, which was lying on the hotel dresser, and went to answer it. When she saw who the caller was, she breathed in sharply. "Gordon! It's Gordon," she called out and quickly motioned to Dallas. She took a deep breath and answered the phone.

"Heather, I'm shorthanded," he said without even a hello. "If you feel well enough, I'd appreciate you coming back to work."

Someone knocked on the door, and Heather signaled for Dallas to answer it. She watched as he peeked through the peephole and then let Rigo in. "Yeah, I want to come back," she said. "Would tomorrow be okay?"

"I need you today," Gordon said quickly. "I was hoping you'd be up to covering a story on the crime beat."

She watched as Dallas whispered something to Rigo, then the two of them stepped beside her. She tipped the phone so they could hear as she said, "Where do you need me?" she asked.

"Can you drive yet?" he asked.

"I can."

"Excellent. They've arrested Luisa Maggio. I need you to go to Fort Stockton this afternoon and dig around," he said. "I want to have the story in time for tomorrow's paper. I have quite a long list of things I'd like you to find out. I'll be going down to Luisa's company headquarters to do some digging of my own. Let me give you the address. You could just meet me on the street out front," he suggested.

Worry flickered in Dallas's eyes, but Rigo was nodding his head vigorously. "All right," she agreed. "But you'll need to give me a few minutes. I just got back into town, so I'll need to go by my duplex and get some fresh clothes. It won't take me long," she said. "See you soon."

Heather breathed a sigh of relief and collapsed on the bed as she hung up the phone. "Was that okay?" she asked. "Am I really going to meet him there?"

"Go pack your bag, just like you said. Then go to Luisa's headquarters. In the meantime, I'll be busy," Lieutenant Garcia said. "I've got you covered. You and Gordon aren't the only ones who'll be at Luisa's trucking headquarters." With a nod in Dallas's direction, he hurried from the hotel.

"I'm going with you, Heather," Dallas said firmly, and Heather didn't argue.

"I wonder what Elliott's been up to," he added a few minutes later as they prepared to leave. "I'd have thought we'd have heard from him again by now."

Elliott answered that question himself when Heather's phone rang a moment later.

"I just got some interesting information," he told Heather excitedly when she picked up the phone. "Are you still in your room?"

"We're just leaving," she replied.

"Where are you going?"

She explained what was happening. When she was finished, Elliott made a strange sound in his throat, then said, "I need to see you. Could we meet at your house?"

"I guess that would be okay," she said tentatively, looking at Dallas, who shrugged.

"Good, then I'll see you there."

Dallas called for a cab.

* * *

Sam was almost back to the hospital for his second attempt at getting in to see the man who had tried to attack Dallas and Heather when he got a call from Lincoln Graves.

"The charges against Dallas Dixon have been dropped," Lincoln told him. "So I guess I no longer have a client."

"Does that mean I'm off the case as well?" Sam asked.

"We've done our job," Lincoln told him. "As usual, you've been a great help to me, but you can head for home now. I appreciate all you've done."

Sam felt a twinge of disappointment. He was glad Dallas was no longer a suspect, but he always liked to see a case to its end. However, Sam wasn't the police. He worked only when clients wanted him to. He turned, heading away from the hospital, then called Heather to let her know he was leaving.

When she told him what was happening, the familiar surge of adrenaline began pumping through him. Something was up. He might be off the case, but Sam wasn't ready to leave El Paso quite yet.

* * *

Dallas and Heather pulled up in front of her duplex in the cab. For a moment they stayed put, surveying the area. Heather's elderly neighbor's car was gone, but hers was parked right where she'd left it before she had departed for San Antonio. Finally, seeing nothing out of the ordinary, Dallas grasped Heather's hand and squeezed it tight. They got out of the car, handed the cabbie some cash, and watched him drive away.

"Elliott's not here yet. Let's go in the back door," Heather suggested. "The same key fits both doors. I just want to make sure everything's okay inside. Elliott will probably just knock."

Nothing seemed amiss, so Heather opened the door. Dallas stepped in front of her, instinctively shielding her. The place was quiet, and finally they both moved into the small living room.

A noise from the hallway caused them both to whirl around. Slowly, the bedroom door opened, and Elliott emerged. He had a strange look on his face, and his voice cracked when he said, "Hi, Heather. Hi, Dallas."

"Elliott, what are you doing in here?" Heather asked angrily. "Did you break into my apartment?"

"We did it together, although Elliott wasn't a lot of help," Gordon Townsend said as he appeared behind Elliott. He was holding a pistol pointed at Elliott's back. "It's good to finally see you two again." His expression hardened, and he shoved the pistol against Elliott. "Don't do anything stupid, or Elliott here gets it. Then both of you do."

Heather's heart felt like it was going to burst, and her hands were shaking. "You were going to meet me at Luisa's trucking company," was the only thing she could think to say.

"Now that would have been stupid, wouldn't it?" he said with a smile. "I'm quite certain Lieutenant Garcia and his little crew are down there now, waiting for me to arrive. But they'll be disappointed. And you, you meddling little wench, won't be going to Fort Stockton."

Dallas spoke up in a clear attempt to buy them some time. "Why did you do it?" he asked.

"You mean why did I have Andy killed or why did I frame you?" Gordon asked, cocking his head to the side.

"Both," Dallas said.

"I'm sorry, Heather. I tried to warn you on the phone," Elliott said weakly. His knees were shaking, and he looked like he was about to vomit.

"Shut up, you idiot," Gordon said. "I never would have allowed the board to make you my number two if I'd known how smitten you were with Miss Scott here." He shrugged. "Now all three of you have to go."

"You don't seriously think you'll get away with this, do you?" Dallas asked, his hand inching toward the gun stuffed inside his belt. "Rigo already has most of the pieces put together."

"Oh, I'll get away with it. You can be sure of that. I just wish you three hadn't messed up the job I worked so hard to get. But at least I'll get the satisfaction of seeing you pay with your lives," Gordon said with a sneer.

Dallas's hand continued to move ever so slowly toward his weapon. Suddenly Gordon barked, "Put your hands in the air, all of you, or he dies right now."

They complied, and then Gordon said, "Heather, you move over this way." She swallowed but held her head high as she moved to her right.

Gordon pointed the gun at her. "Dallas, take your gun out with two fingers and drop it on the floor. If you don't do like I say, pop goes the weasel."

Dallas grimaced but slowly pulled the gun out and allowed the 9mm to fall to the floor. Gordon made him kick it toward him, then kicked it behind him. "You thought I didn't know you still had a gun on you? You never were very smart, Dixon. And neither was Andy. He could have just moved aside and let me have the job."

"He wasn't old enough to retire," Dallas said.

"He could have quit. I'm the better man. That job should have been mine. And then it was mine. And you three messed it all up for me."

"It's only going to get worse if you don't put down that gun," Dallas said calmly. "You have to know it's over, Gordon."

"Just shut up and let me think."

"There's nothing to think about. You just need to put down that gun and give up. You'll never get away with this."

Heather couldn't believe how calm Dallas was as he spoke. She felt like she was going to faint. "Dallas, move over here by your lady friend," Gordon ordered.

Dallas did as he was told, but added, "It might not be so bad. Maybe you can get off with an insanity defense." Heather was sure that Dallas was still buying time, hoping that at some point Gordon would let down his guard so that he could make his move.

"I'm not insane," Gordon said, his cheeks reddening. "I just wanted to be the managing editor, but Andy didn't act like he was planning to leave anytime soon. When Andy fired you, it made it possible for me to get rid of him and frame you. It couldn't have worked out better."

"But it didn't work out," Dallas said in a low voice. "As you can see."

Gordon scowled. "It should have," he snapped.

"But I still don't understand why," Dallas pressed on. "Andy couldn't have been making much more than you."

"It wasn't about money," Gordon said. "I have plenty of that. Luisa and I were making good money with our little side business. And lucky for me, most of it's in offshore banks. I'm going to need it, thanks to the three of you." He looked at them for a few seconds then said, "Get down on the floor, Elliott, before you fall down. You're shaking like a leaf. I'm going to have Dallas tie you up. Take off your belt and hand it to Dallas."

Elliott did as he was instructed, the whole time staring with terrified eyes at the gun in Gordon's hand, which was shaking badly. It looked like the gun could go off at any moment. *Apparently he's not used to doing his own dirty work,* Dallas realized. He'd paid others to do it for him. As Dallas began to tie Elliott's wrists behind his back, Heather spoke. "I knew it was you, Gordon," she said.

"How did you know? I covered my trail well. I put that memo and those two bullets in Dallas's briefcase when he was in Andy's office getting fired."

"That was stupid," Heather said. She too was buying time, praying that Dallas would get a chance to do something.

"No, what was stupid was the way you kept trying to interfere in the case the police were building against Dallas," Gordon said with an ugly frown. "Now you have to die, and it's your fault."

"You can't get all of us," Heather said fiercely. "One of us will get to you first."

"Shut up, Heather." Gordon waved the gun in her direction. "And you, Dallas, tie that tight on Elliott or I'll shoot her right here in front of you."

Dallas did as he was told, all the while keeping an eye on Gordon. His breaths came slow and steady as he bided his time. All he needed was for Gordon to give him a moment.

When he'd finished tying Elliott's hands, Gordon said, "Okay, now you, Dallas. Get down next to Elliott. And you, Heather, tie him up."

"And if I don't?" she asked.

"Just do it, Heather," Dallas said. "Don't give him an excuse to shoot one of us."

"That's right, Heather. Do you want me to shoot you?" Gordon asked.

"You aren't as smart as the guy you hired to kill Andy,"

Heather said. "He used a silencer. You don't have one. Someone will hear you, and then the cops will come."

"Down," Gordon said, pointing to the floor.

"You know, Heather's right. Someone will hear," Dallas echoed.

"Hmm, then I guess I'll burn the place down instead," Gordon said as if the idea had just occurred to him. "I'll be long gone by the time anyone shows up." He grinned. "And so will you. Get down, Dallas. Don't push me."

Just then, the sound of a gunshot exploded in the room, making their ears ring. Heather gasped. Gordon's eyes grew wide as a red spot spread on his chest. The gun dropped from his hand, and Dallas dove to scoop it up. Gordon fell as the air whistled out of him.

"Looks like I made it just in time," Sam Reynolds said soberly.

* * *

As Gordon was hauled off on a stretcher a few minutes later, his pained, hate-filled eyes caught Heather's. "How did you know it was me?" he croaked out.

"A snake told me," she said, meeting his gaze. "With his eyes."

EPILOGUE

"Are we still on for dinner?" Dallas asked with a smile as he approached Heather's desk.

Heather's heart rate accelerated as it always did when she saw him. It had now been six months since their world had turned topsy-turvy, and things were finally starting to feel normal again. But Heather knew Dallas would always make her heart beat faster, no matter how much time passed.

"We're still on," she said, standing to give him a quick kiss. A slight blush rose in his cheeks, because Elliott Painter had chosen that moment to appear around the corner.

Elliott rolled his eyes but made no comment. Heather stifled a laugh as he walked away. Things had improved dramatically since Elliott's brush with death, and in many ways he was a changed man.

"I still can't believe they promoted him to managing editor," she whispered to Dallas. "And even more surprising is the fact that he's actually not half bad at it. He's been almost tolerable for the past six months."

Dallas shrugged. "It's true. I never thought I'd be working for Elliott, let alone on the crime beat with you as my partner." He smiled, and his eyes shone as he looked at her. "I can't think of anyone I'd want on my team more."

Heather squeezed his hand then said, "Speaking of which, we'd better get back to this story. It's going to be a big one with

Luisa and Tito finally being sentenced." She glanced at her computer, where a partially finished story was waiting for her. Although Gordon Townsend hadn't lived to stand trial, Luisa Maggio and the man they now referred to as *the one-armed man*, Gordon's hired trigger man, had. Luisa had just been given a life sentence by both state and federal courts. Her nephew, Tito, would be going to prison as well, but on a lesser sentence. It was still surreal to Heather that she had actually lived this story. That Gordon was dead. That he'd actually done all those awful things. That Dallas had nearly taken the fall.

She shuddered involuntarily and brought her focus back to the present—back to the man standing in front of her. Tonight they would be going out to dinner with Mason, who had moved closer to be near his son and now worked at a local taxidermy shop. Dallas and his father were slowly building a relationship, made all the more complete by the fact that Mason had just finished the missionary discussions—and had asked Dallas to baptize him.

Heather hoped that one day soon Dallas would propose, but she wasn't rushing things. She knew he wouldn't ask her to marry him as long as he still struggled with his past. And she was okay with that. He'd told her that the nightmares were getting less frequent and were not as bad. The time would come. For now, just having him nearby, working with him, talking for hours at a time, and enjoying frequent formal dates was okay. It was great just having him in her life—especially after she'd almost lost him for good.

"Heather?" Dallas asked gently, bringing her back from her thoughts. "I'd better let you go so you can get back to work. I'll catch you later."

She nodded and watched him walk away, happy in the ordinariness of their lives after all they'd been through. "Don't you dare let me go, Dallas Dixon," she whispered with a smile and turned back to her typing.

ABOUT THE AUTHOR

 CLAIR M. POULSON RETIRED AFTER twenty years in law enforcement. During his career he served in the U.S. Military Police Corps, the Utah Highway Patrol, and the Duchesne County Sheriff's Department, where he was first a deputy and then the county sheriff. He currently serves as a justice court judge for Duchesne County, a position he has held for nineteen years. His nearly forty-year career working in the criminal justice system has provided a wealth of material from which he draws in writing his books.

Clair has served on numerous boards and committees over the years. Among them are the Utah Judicial Council, an FBI advisory board, the Peace Officer Standards and Training Council, the Utah Justice Court Board of Directors, and the Utah Commission on Criminal and Juvenile Justice.

Other interests include activity in the LDS Church, assisting his oldest son in operating their grocery store, ranching with his oldest son and other family members, and raising registered Missouri Fox Trotter horses.

With this latest book, Clair has published seventeen novels, many of them bestsellers.

Clair and his wife, Ruth, live in Duchesne and are the parents of five married children. They have twenty-one grandchildren.